Renys

est inster

KCy

15. 11. 07

ESCAPE TO PARADISE
A ROMANTIC NOVEL

Escape to Paradise
A Romantic Novel

KEITH MINTON

2006

Library and Archives Canada Cataloguing in Publication

Minton, Keith
    Escape to paradise / Keith Minton.

    ISBN 1-55246-698-1   ISBN 978-1-55246-698-8

    I. Title.

PR6113.I62E82 2006   823'.92   C2006-902836-2

Printed on acid free paper in Canada
First Printing, September 2, 2006

George A. Vanderburgh, *Publisher*
THE BATTERED SILICON DISPATCH BOX™
e-Mail: gav@bmts.com * *Fax:* (519) 925-3482
Website: batteredbox.com

P. O. Box 204   P. O. Box 122
Shelburne, Ontario   Sauk City, Wisconsin
CANADA L0N 1S0   U.S.A. 53583-0122

ESCAPE TO PARADISE

TO MY PARENTS

Prologue

'So this is where they filmed *Lawrence of Arabia*. Can't say it's changed much. It still looks like a bloody lunar landscape.'

The year was 1990, the place Miramar on the Costa de Almería, the speaker Don Spencer, retired accountant, aged 65 but still lithe and fit. He and Margarita his Spanish wife, ten years younger and more ample than in her sylph-like youth, had just got out of their Land-Rover to see what they were letting themselves in for.

The empty rocky terrain spread around them into infinity, devoid of any vegetation except cacti and stunted prickly pears.

'You could yell for ever and no one would hear you,' said Don. 'And is this where we are planning to settle – we must be stark raving bonkers...'

He pointed upwards to a bare ridge with nothing to recommend it but rocks, stones, and the occasional scorpion for good measure.

'This is just a desert,' Don went on. 'There's nothing here at all. Let's go back and tell José. If he paid us to take this, it still wouldn't be worth it. It's rubbish!'

They got back into the Land Rover. A silence. Then Margarita spoke: 'But you're sick of Almería..'

'Only at night!' Don exclaimed irritably. 'Almería in the day is great, no problem. It's at night when all hell is let loose. Those confounded people in the street yelling at the top of their voices, the cinema blasting away until two in the morning, I can't take another summer of it; it's not what we came here for...'

'And is this why we came?' Margarita made a wide gesture around.

'It could be, I'm not sure.' Don was calmer now, taking in the spectacular beauty of the landscape. It had an awesome power that couldn't fail to impress. In the far distance they glimpsed the snowy peaks of the Sierra Nevada, shining in the May sunshine, and closer rose grey, flat-topped mountains looking like extinct volcanoes.

'It's harsh, it's cruel, it's magnificent!' muttered Don.

'Then...?' Margarita put a hand on his arm and smiled.

'But how can we survive here? It's dry, there's nothing, no water...'

'But there is, José said there is. Under the rock in springs from the Sierra Nevada...'

'How does he know?'

'There are wells already – a few in the village. Can't you remember, he told us?'

Don nodded doubtful agreement. But the little Spaniard had been rattling away like a spitfire and he only just managed to catch the drift.

'Come on, let's go and look,' Margarita urged.

'All right,' said Don starting up the van. 'We'll see the village...'

They advanced very slowly for the track, unmade and primitive, now twisting violently into curves with on the right a sheer precipice falling away to the valley far below.

'One hiccup and we meet our Maker,' grunted Don, Margarita said nothing but her face was very pale.

But at last they were on the other side of the mountain, looking down on Miramar. An incredible sight. A necklace of white houses, not more than twenty, hugged the curve of a marvellous conch-like bay. The contrast of the dazzling white of the houses with the iridescent blue of the sea was breathtaking. Tears came to Don's eyes.

'We'll risk it!' he muttered. 'This is our place!'

'The water?'

'To hell with the water! We'll find the water! The water doesn't matter...'

They returned to Almería prepared to make an offer for the plot. But once the bay, the white houses, the panoramic landscape were only memories, Don had second thoughts.

'Water or no water, we must be mad, thinking seriously of going to that no man's land.'

'But the village ...'

'... is beautiful; but don't forget that bloody precipice, and us having to risk our necks day after day... And Miramar is remote, it has just one shop, no phone, what happens if something goes wrong?'

A silence, the silence of decision. And in the silence, almost imperceptible at first, came the familiar noise from the street. It was dusk, a Sunday evening, and after their siesta, the youth of Almería were going out to play.

Both Don and Margarita thought desperately of last summer. The sleepless nights with the cinema roaring away, the shouting and laughing that couldn't be blotted out. It was the moment of truth. In a flash Don decided.

'To hell with it!' he said pouring out two coñacs for good luck. 'Anything's better than this. We're going ahead.'

Escape

Chapter One

.

Tobacco smoke hung like a pall above the glass-topped committee table – in spite of Passworth Bororough Council's no smoking policy.

'Are you willing to accept the post, Mr Makepeace?' asked the Chairman of the Governors with a smile.

'Yes, sir, thank you very much,' Andrew replied.

'Congratulations! You will be very happy here. Next term begins on Tuesday September 3, with a staff meeting on the Monday morning at 10 o'clock. We will be in touch before then and offering you a formal contract. Thank you and good afternoon.'

Andrew bowed to the interview panel and went out, closing the door behind him.

'Well that's that!' said the Chairman cheerfully. 'I think he was the better of the two."

The stout little man got up with some difficulty and lit another cigarette.

'I'm not sure,' said Jones the headmaster, remaining seated. 'I'd rather have had the local woman.' His thin bearded face looked uneasy.

'That, if I may say, is typical of you,' the Chairman snapped. 'You had every opportunity to veto him...'

'Did I?' said Jones. 'I could see you liked him, and he has definitely the better qualifications.'

'Second class Oxminster degree in French, and the woman only had a Passworth B.Ed. There was no comparison! In addition Makepeace is a nice fellow.'

'He seemed pleasant enough,' Jones admitted. 'Though in my experience, they're all pleasant at interviews. But it's how he'll shape up with his colleagues and the kids that'll matter, not a nice interview manner. I'm not too keen on that sort of fellow anyway; blue eyes, fair hair, slim, and a la di dah accent. Wet!' he ended contemptuously.

'I think you underestimate him, Jones,' said the Chairman angrily. 'It takes some guts for a chap with his background and qualifications to come to a ropy place such as this... And I say again, why didn't you oppose him? It's your option in the end as headmaster.'

'You know as well as I do we need well qualified staff; there's hardly a graduate in the place at present. This chap'll look impressive in our prospectus.'

'Yes, we must please the Town Hall,' said an elderly lady in pince nez. 'One of the criticisms we had last year in the OFSTED report was we couldn't attract the staff we wanted; Mr Makepeace will be evidence to the contrary.'

'He may be all right,' said the Chairman. 'How can one tell? He passed his teaching practice.'

'In a boys' public school,' Jones reminded him.

'Okay, it wasn't like this place, a Manchester inner-city comprehensive full of slum clearance kids, but we've no evidence he won't fit in...'

'What puzzles me is why he applied,' remarked another of the Board, a young Labour councillor. 'I mean he could have got a good job in some independent school; why here?'

'He said something about being anxious to repay a debt,' said Jones.

'He lost me there,' said the lady. 'I couldn't understand what he was saying.'

'I know,' Jones grinned. 'He did get a mite philosophical. What I think he meant was this: he'd had a privileged background, Surrey, Oxminster and all that; now he's anxious to help kids less fortunate than himself. Sort of missionary approach.'

'Very laudable!' said the Chairman emphatically. 'That's another reason I backed him; he wasn't the selfish bastard most of those silver spoon gentlemen turn out to be. He had a conscience.'

'Fair enough, he had a conscience,' Jones admitted. 'Let's see where that gets him with 4H. Oh well, it doesn't really matter anyhow; we've got his name for the prospectus, and even if he comes a cropper, by that time we'll have some other likely candidate to take over. That's the big advantage of beginners, you can kick 'em out without too much hassle.'

'And what if he does succeed?' asked the lady.

'If he does,' said Jones rising to his feet. 'It's kudos for the school. Either way we can't lose.'

'Is that why you didn't oppose him?' asked the Chairman with a cynical grin.

'It is, but that doesn't stop me having a conscience – of sorts.'

Six hours later back home Andrew was struggling to push his yale into the lock of the new front door. It was one of those new security locks where you have to turn the key both ways a certain number of times, and tired after an eighteen hour day, Andrew had forgotten the number. At last he gave up and rang the doorbell. Deborah his sixteen year old sister answered.

'Haven't you got your key?' she said letting him in.

'I can't get the hang of the new lock.'

'You turn the key four times backwards, once forwards, silly!'

'That explains it – I was turning it the other way round.'

'Typical!' said Deborah. 'Are you hungry? We've eaten, you know. Where've you been?'

'Manchester.'

'Manchester? What on earth were you doing in Manchester?'

'Seeing a man about a dog,' said Andrew evasively. He went into the kitchen with Deborah following.

'It must have been a very large dog to go all the way to Manchester!' she said. 'I think there's some food in the fridge; Mummy said you'd be late.'

'Oh, so you knew I'd gone somewhere...'

'Yes, but not why. You haven't told me that yet...'

'And I'm not going to, nosey!"

Andrew put a plate of salad on the table and cut some bread. Deborah put the kettle on.

'You'll want some tea, I suppose?'

'Yes, thanks.'

While he ate Andrew was thinking – and not very cheerfully. He'd said nothing to his family about the school or the interview. But now that he'd been offered – and accepted – the job, the die was indeed cast; he had to come clean and confess. They would have to know some time, and all he had to decide was the least painful method of breaking the news. Only one thing Andrew was quite determined about; Deborah would *not* be the first to know. That was one victory his attractive, fairhaired, intelligent, and supremely inquisitive sister would not be allowed.

'You're very quiet,' she said as Andrew continued to eat without a word. 'Did the dog bite you?'

'I'm tired,' Andrew replied. 'And I wish you were.'

'I can take a hint; you want me to go.'

'Right in one!'

'Hullo, Andrew, you're back,' said Catherine, his mother, elegant, sophisticated, and still beautiful, whisking into the kitchen. 'Did you get on all right? I see you found the salad.'

'I'm fine, thanks, Mother,' Andrew answered, hoping desperately she wouldn't ask any questions with Deborah present. Fortunately Catherine got the message, and turning to her daughter, she said:

'You'd better go to bed, Deborah, you've got school tomorrow.'

'School, school, I hate school!' the girl chanted, but she did leave the kitchen. Catherine turned to Andrew at once.'

'Anything to tell me?' she asked.

'Yes, but not now,' Andrew muttered. 'Tomorrow.'

'All right, darling, tomorrow,' his mother smiled. 'Sleep well, won't you, you must be tired.'

Much to Andrew's relief she departed, leaving him to his thoughts; they were no happier than before supper. He slept very badly visualising a hundred ways his family might react to his new job – and not one was sympathetic.

The truth was revealed at breakfast; Andrew had his father to thank for that. At least, he consoled himself, Deborah wasn't the first to know.

'Did you get the job?' Peter asked and took a sip of coffee.

'Yes,' Andrew replied, not even wondering how his father knew that much.

'Good. In Manchester, isn't it? The Grammar School?'

'No.'

'Well, don't keep us guessing. What's it called?'

'Passworth.'

'Passworth? Never heard of it. Where is it?' For the first time Peter's nonchalance was disturbed.

'North East of Manchester.'

'So it's not Didsbury. I hope it's an independent school.'

'It isn't.'

'It isn't?' That really had some effect. Peter had to put down his cup, his moustache quivering. 'A state school?'   ·

'Yes.'

'What's it called?'

'Passworth Community College.'

At that you could have heard a pin drop. Andrew's family stared at him as if he had just committed an act of gross indecency in public. Horror and consternation were writ large on every countenance.

At last Peter asked: 'Good God! And what on earth is a "Community College"?' and stumblingly, nervously Andrew tried to describe the school that had offered him this job, and his family this bombshell.

'Andrew!' Deborah exclaimed when he'd finished. 'What have you done?'

His mother didn't say a word at that moment; she didn't need to for her face was still saying it all. Peter looked at his watch and stood up. 'I've got to go,' he said, sounding very glad about that. 'When do you go back to Oxminster?'

'This afternoon.'

'Goodbye then, you'll have left by the time I get back.' He paused and went on. 'I'm sorry not to be more enthusiastic, Andrew, but honestly, I'm convinced you're making a big mistake. They'll eat you alive at a school like that.'

'I'm sorry too,' Andrew replied. 'I knew this would be your attitude, that's why I said nothing before.'

'Oh well, you don't start till September, do you? You've six months to come to your senses.' Peter went out leaving a silent trio round the table.

'Andrew, dear brother,' said Deborah at last. 'You've done some crazy things in your time, but this takes the biscuit, a whole tin of them in fact..' It was just as well she left the room at this point, or Andrew might have said something he regretted.

And the crisis was far from over after she'd gone, for he and his mother were left sitting there in uncomfortable silence.

'All right, say it!' Andrew had to exclaim at last when the silence grew unbearable.

'Say what, darling?' Catherine asked as though surprised.

'Say I'm wrong, say I'm a bloody fool, if that's what you think...'

'I don't think you're wrong, not exactly,' she said after an appreciable pause for thought. 'I just can't understand what drove you to do this. Can you please explain?'

So Andrew did his best to put into words the conflicting emotions that had raged within him the past year. What they came to was this: he felt he owed a debt for his many advantages, and teaching at Passworth Community College was his way of settling it.

'But, darling, far be it from me to criticise your intentions,' his mother said. 'They are quite admirable. But do you know what you are going to be faced with?'

'I think so.'

'How can you? You don't know these children. They are quite different from the ones you have met and grown up with.'

'But that's what I want to put right!' Andrew exclaimed. 'I've always been protected. Father a stockbroker, a public school education, Oxminster, I've never been in contact with ordinary people; now I'm going to do something about it.'

His mother stared at him, feeling a mixture of respect and pity.

'I had an aunt who was a missionary in Africa,' she sighed. 'You must have inherited her altruism.'

'Perhaps,' said Andrew with a half smile.

'She was misguided though; she was killed by one of her converts. And that could happen to you...'

'I won't be killed, Mother, that's nonsense.'

'Maybe not killed, although teachers are attacked, you know. Children can be fiends if they have a grudge or think you're different from them.'

'I'll chance that,' said Andrew.

Catherine sighed and shook her head. "Rose was obstinate too. All right, darling. go ahead, and the very best of luck in this job. But remember we love you and you can always come back here if things go wrong.'

'I'm sure they won't but thanks anyway,' Andrew smiled. 'Now I suppose I'd better start packing.'

'You can give your mother a kiss first,' Catherine said.

Andrew obstinately went ahead and come September, the worst forebodings of his family – and Arthur Jones, headteacher of Passworth Community College, were duly fulfilled. Andrew's teaching career was a disaster from the start, 4H being his main assailants. They didn't take to him from the first day. His neat appearance and careful English didn't go down well with multi-racial kids in jeans and tee-shirts. Neither could he follow their heavy patois, and he was having to say "Sorry?" too often for their liking...

The kids were unhappy anyhow, many having been forced to move to Passworth from Manchester through slum-clearance, and Andrew wasn't the only teacher with problems; even so his were the worst.

Neither was Jones any help. He took a cynical satisfaction in being proved right, and soon began writing reports about Andrew, which he kept ready to send to the Town Hall. Andrew knew nothing about these, but Jones was preparing a dossier on him so that when the time was ripe and he wished to pounce, he would have his ammunition ready.

To help him in his labour of destruction, Jones enlisted the Machiavellian assistance of Terry Parsons, one of the school's half dozen deputy heads. Parsons would be posted near Andrew's classroom, out of sight, and he meticulously wrote down everything that went on, making sure any statements made by Andrew which could be called 'unprofessional' were clearly presented.

Andrew meantime was careful. He knew there were certain acts he wasn't permitted to do, without bringing down on his hapless head the wrath of the hierarchy. To touch a pupil was tantamount to a crime; neither could he verbally abuse a child; language had also to be carefully controlled and to allow to slip out words that could be regarded as in any way *improper* would be immediately pounced on and used as evidence against him.

So in fact, although the behaviour of Andrew's classes left a great deal to be desired, obscenities a-plenty issuing from them, amidst a level of noise that could be heard a quarter of a mile away, Andrew managed to keep himself in check. Parsons was disappointed about that, but he made doubly sure he reported fully Andrew's class behaviour at least.

The most dreadful day was Friday. For some reason 4H had French last lesson on Friday, and though only two thirds ever came to school then, they more than made up for their absent comrades by serving up their very worst behaviour.

Noise was perhaps the least of Andrew's problems. In addition, he was subjected to an unceasing fusillade of missiles, and after he'd given up turning his back on the class because a pebble hit him on the head, this didn't stop the bolder elements from continuing to throw chalk, paper darts, and anything else to hand, even when he was facing them.

It wasn't that he'd not tried retaliation. He'd given lines galore for the first fortnight – but abandoned that ploy when the lines were never done. He tried detention – but just received letters from parents explaining their child couldn't possibly stay in for reasons as varied as they were ingenious. He even kept a group back after the group 4H back after the bell one Friday without notice – but had to let them go because Parsons popped up from nowhere to tell him he was infringing school regulations. Classes had to be given at least 24 hours notice. And meantime Jones was busy compiling his "Get Makepeace Out" dossier.

'Should we send this to the Town Hall?' he asked, fingering the thick file one Friday after a particularly horrendous time had been endured by Andrew involving desk moving and a fight between two girls.

'I'm not sure,' Parsons replied, stroking his lip with a stubby finger. 'He's only been here a few weeks. I think they'd say it's too early to judge him. And unfortunately *he* hasn't done anything serious to complain about. I think we'd better wait till then.'

'Fair enough, he's bound to break shortly. The moment he lays a finger on anyone, let me know at once.'

'I will.'

It was fortunate Andrew knew nothing of this scheming or his wretchedness would have been compounded. Neither were his colleagues any help. Frank Stephens his head of department, was politely distant, and the others were mostly unconcerned about his problems, they often found them amusing. Forster, head of geography, built like an ox and with not much more intelligence, never lost an opportunity to poke fun at Andrew.

"Been workin' you, have they, the little darlins'?" he chortled. "Why not invite a couple into yer back cupboard? That's what I did me first week, never had a peep from any of 'em since.'

A titter rippled across the staff room; only Miss Seymour didn't join in. 'Don't mind them, Andrew, and I mean the kids not the staff,' she said with a smile. 'They're little bs but you'll get the better of them, I know...' 'I wish *I* did!' Andrew sighed, touched by her sympathy.

Diane Seymour was amazing. She taught history, and was one of the few teachers at Passworth who seemed to have no problems at all. She went effortlessly around, invariably charming, always with a smile. She was young and attractive too, with long fair hair tied in a different style every day, and so many outfits she looked like an advert in *Vogue*. Today she was wearing a dark green mohair skirt with matching jacket, and made everyone else look like tramps. Andrew wished he had the nerve to ask her out, but in spite of his loneliness he didn't think he'd ever dare to. He couldn't bear the thought she might turn him down.

'She's probably got at least one boy friend,' he thought bitterly.

He was now quite certain his noble act of coming to this God awful school had been a complete blunder. His family had been right, and it took all his determination on Fridays not to catch the next train to London and return to the nest. He knew none of his family would criticise; even Deborah would be kind.

But something deep within him caused him to hang on. He wouldn't be beaten by these little fiends, he just wouldn't! There must be a way of getting through to them. And once he had recovered a little by Saturday morning from the rigours of 4H, he was again determined to stick it out at least to the end of term, and if possible the end of the year. It was just as well he knew nothing of Jones's Machiavellian plots.

But in spite of Andrew's great determination, there were still moments, irrespective of the school, when he nearly threw in the towel. Passworth town was a far cry from leafy, prosperous Camberford. In Passworth, the residential area was just two square miles, while the rest of the town was dominated by vast council estates, snaking over the hills, the roads looking from the distance like black strips of liquorice with crimson borders. The whole panorama on grey, rainy days, and there were many, was unbearably depressing, although Andrew could see that before these houses were thrown up in the 'twenties, the area must have been beautiful indeed. Rolling hills, covered with woodland and in the valleys shining streams, this fringe of the Pennines could have competed with any national park.

Passworth Community College was in the town centre. It had been purpose-built in the 'eighties to provide for the disadvantaged of the area and no money had been spared on equipment and facilities. It had a sports hall second to none, a language lab, computer rooms, and well equipped science laboratories.

But since it was built with so many aspirations it had deteriorated. Vandalism was soon rife, truancy was endemic, the kids did not benefit from the equipment, in fact they tended to destroy it, and many of the large areas of glass of which the school consisted, were smashed. There was a constant police presence to ensure that at least the front and more visible parts of the school were protected. The school was at this stage when Andrew arrived.

Near the school had been a shopping centre but this was replaced about five years ago by a vast commercial complex which attracted people from all over the country. In order to construct the complex the existing shopping centre and many domestic houses had to be demolished, the only survivors of this carnage were the school and Passworth Electrical Engineering Works. This vast factory was Passworth's only claim to success and employed most of the working population in some form or other. It even had a computer department attracting specialists from all over the UK and abroad.

Andrew lived about a mile from the school on the edge of a large council estate. His two rooms were in one of these council houses, and were cheap as he had no teaching allowance and the limited accommodation in the residential area was very expensive. His niggardly teacher's salary could not run to one of the smart flats. The other teachers often shared and so could afford a flat but so far Andrew had been unable to find anyone willing to share accommodation with him. The staff at Passworth were both insular and cliquish, all of them drawn from the area and in fact jealous of Andrew's posh background and manner. He often wondered how Diane Seymour seemed to be accepted; she was as posh as he was, posher, but noone seemed to envy her and she was treated like royalty both by the staff and the kids. It was a bit of a mystery.

Andrew's living room consisted of a solid single bed, an armchair, and a seat and table, plus a hideous functional wardrobe, whose only redeeming feature was its size. All Andrew's food had to be prepared on the tiny electric cooker in the corner, and the adjacent bathroom served its purpose – and nothing more. His washing had to be taken to the laundrette, fortunately nearby.

But the biggest problem for Andrew in his dismal accommodation was Mrs Reynolds, the landlady. She lived downstairs and was constantly in, so whenever Andrew entered the house he had to pass her room. She would always stick her head round the door as he went past as she had heard him open the front door, and invariably there was some instruction or other.

The first day Andrew arrived Mrs Reynolds handed him, with a smile, her list of 'house rules' designed for 'everyone's benefit'. One was that Andrew should retire to bed or at least make no further noise with radio or television after 10.30. Another was that he was to entertain no visitors, certainly no females... Andrew resolved at that to leave as soon as possible, and bitterly regretted the fact he had paid two months in advance. On their first meeting, Mrs Reynolds, vast and smiling, had seemed acceptable, and the school *had* recommended her as reliable and cheap.

'She's cheap,' thought Andrew bitterly. 'But it's a high price to pay for the rest.' He resolved to leave as soon as the two months were up.

The two months seemed to last forever. But when Andrew was on the very edge of despair, ready to leave Passworth, go back home, even kill himself, hope shone in the shape of a friend. They met in the laundrette, which for Andrew was the only place to hand with a resemblance to a social venue. The lad was about Andrew's age and, miracle, he started talking to him at once. His name was Steve, he had red curly hair and a cheerful grin, and he worked in Town Planning. He lived in a council house a bit further away, and his situation was much the same as Andrew's though he took it more cheerfully.

The two began going out in the evenings which gave a terrific boost to Andrew's morale. School remained awful but at least he was less depressed by it – much to Jones' annoyance for he'd been hoping to catch the lad out before now and he still seemed to be surviving – if only by the skin of his teeth.

One of the haunts he and Steve began to frequent was the Green

Parrot, a hostelry fairly close to their rooms. Andrew knew the place before but had never gone in, as he hated to visit pubs solo. It was modern and brash and with enough young people to give it some buzz. Andrew enjoyed himself there, and occasionally Steve introduced him to a friend, making him feel even more acclimatised to Passworth. It was no longer the cold unfriendly place of a short time ago.

But still Andrew felt he was missing out on something – and this was a girl friend. He continued to think and dream of Diane Seymour, but nice though she was, he felt her to be quite unapproachable. As he sat chatting with Steve in the Green Parrot, his mind – and eyes – wandered. There were plenty of nice girls around, but they were usually with a boy or part of a group. Mostly they looked like students, probably from the FE college just outside town.

After some visits Andrew began to recognize their faces especially on Saturday night. He was drawn to quite a few of the girls, but they took no notice of him, and seemed quite unaware of his glances. Steve found Andrew's staring very funny and didn't fail to tease him about it.

'Look at that one!' he chuckled, pointing to a girl at the end of the bar. 'Nice, eh?'

She was – and Andrew had seen her then – and on previous occasions. She was very pale with long dark hair down her back; her mouth seemed in a constant sulk which somehow made her the more attractive. A sort of Madonna style face, Andrew thought, and not the holy one!

'Why not speak to her, offer her a drink?' Steve urged with a grin. 'Go on, you want to, that's obvious!'

But Andrew couldn't bring himself to ask her, not with Steve there anyhow. To be turned down in front of him – and his cronies – was just too much. But Andrew thought about the girl a lot afterwards, and the next time they were in the Green Parrot, he immediately looked round to see if she was there.

'No such luck!' grinned Steve. 'You missed your chance last time, now it's too late!'

That girl became an obession with Andrew. He couldn't stop thinking about her – even at school. He started to go alone to the Green Parrot, and when she was there he covertly gazed at her across the bar. But she was always surrounded by friends, or talking to someone, and Andrew could find no way to make advances to her.

She'd noticed his stare, and turned towards him, a bit puzzled though it didn't show on her face. Andrew didn't quite fit in with the clientèle of the Green Parrot, he was too smart, too well turned out; he'd have been more at home in a posh wine bar down south. But it was obvious he'd developed a crush on her, he just couldn't keep his eyes away. In a strange fashion she was flattered.

But she wasn't going to let on she'd noticed Andrew's infatuation – at least not yet. She didn't allow him to see her look in his direction every now and again, and she kept her face averted as she chatted to her friends. Andrew was quite certain he didn't exist for her.

'It's useless,' he sighed. 'She doesn't see me at all.'

After three weeks of this, he was ready to give up – and just stop going to the Green Parrot; his frustration was too agonising as he kept dreaming of that girl. He hadn't seen so much of Steve either, because he'd found himself a girl friend, and on Wednesdays and Fridays he entertained her in his room.

But in spite of Andrew's conviction he was wasting his time, he was still prepared to give the Green Parrot at least another try. On Wednesday evening he went there alone to spend another half hour or so of painful yearning.

'I'm a real masochist!' he said to himself ruefully. 'But I can't help it.'

There she was sitting at the end of the bar, this time with a girl Andrew had seen a few times before. They turned quickly as Andrew came in, then resumed their conversation apparently quite oblivious of his presence about ten feet away; it was as if he wasn't there.

'The bitches!' Andrew sighed.

But as he drank his pint, his eyes were still magnetically drawn towards the girl, even though she carried on chatting to her friend.

Then suddenly the friend got up and went out of the room, leaving the other alone at the bar. Andrew's heart leapt; was this his chance? He couldn't believe it – but at least it was worth a try. Quickly he moved towards the girl and spoke to her, thinking as he spoke: 'If she snubs me, I'll never visit this place again!'" Aloud he said huskily:

'Can I get you a drink?'

She turned towards him, her face quite expressionless; it seemed a very long time until she replied.

'Don't mind,' she said in the local brogue. 'I'd like a vodka and orange.'

Andrew ordered, then remembering he turned.

'And your friend?' he said.

'She won't be back.'

'No?'

'I told her to go – at least for a bit.'

'You did?'

'To give you a chance...'

'I – don't understand,' Andrew muttered.

'Come off it. Everyone in this bleeding joint has seen you staring at me for weeks. I had to check and see if you are just a peeping Tom or have something else more interesting in mind...'

She lit a cigarette and blew the smoke in Andrew's face as he struggled to find an answer. She was quite something to look at in her tight black sweater and jeans that made every effort to show off her sinuous figure to full advantage. Her pale face, dark eyes, and sensual mouth now twisted to a mocking smile made Andrew tingle with nervous excitement.

'Have I something else in mind?' he repeated at last. 'Like what?'

'Well, maybe that's up to you,' said the girl, taking a sip of her vodka. 'Do you often pick up girls?'

'I don't! But I liked – like the look of you – and that's why...'

'That's why you approached me,' said the girl with a sudden smile. 'Well, that's nice of you. What's your name if you don't mind me asking?'

Andrew told her. 'And what's yours?' he asked a bit shy.

'Helen,' said the girl. 'Can I have another drink – or shall we go somewhere?'

Chapter Two

THEY had a second drink, Helen keeping to voka and orange, Andrew to lager, but the girl didn't say much. He began to feel a bit uncomfortable, wondering if he was doing the right thing; maybe he should have said 'Let's go' at once, accepting Helen's alternative proposal. But he'd held back instinctively, remembering Mrs Reynold's bar on female visitors, for he couldn't think of anywhere to go but his room.

Then it clicked. Of course! Mrs Reynolds would be out – Andrew had seen her departing soon after he left the house about an hour ago. It would be worth taking a chance for on the rare occasions when she did go out she was usually away for the whole evening. He put down his glass and with assumed nonchalance he said:

'We can go now if you like.'

The girl stirred a little, visibly relaxing. Before she'd just sat there, very still, sipping her vodka, smoking, her mouth sulkier than usual; now she turned to him and got off her stool.

'Okay, where to?' she said.

'There's my place...'

'Where's that?'

'Just round the corner.'

'Fair enough.'

Andrew led the way somewhat awkwardly, and they didn't speak until they reached his place.

"Christ!' said the girl. 'A toff like you in a council house. I can't believe it.!'

'You don't have to come in,' said Andrew somewhat offended.

'I'll come in,' said the girl. 'You interest me. What's a swell like you doing in a dump like this? It's no better than mine...'

After a quick peep through the window to see the old bat was still away, Andrew opened the front door and led her to his room. Helen peered around.

'A bit basic!' she said, eyeing the spartan décor.

'Have a seat. Sorry, it's either the armchair or the bed...'

'The bed's good enough for me,' said Helen with a grin. 'Cor, it's solid, isn't it? She tried to bounce on it with a simulated grimace of pain. 'If I did that much more, I'd really have an ache on my you know what!'

Andrew smiled too. 'There's coffee if you like, but not much else I'm afraid.'

'Is all your cooking done at that?' Helen asked incredulously, staring at the tiny stove.

'I often eat out. I used to cook but it got too much effort.'

'I'm not surprised. Yes, I will have a coffee, thanks!'

Helen got up and looked into the bathroom. 'Good thing you're not too fat or you'd have to go in sideways.'

Andrew smiled again as he put two mugs on the table and scooped out some coffee. 'It is pretty grim, I know,' he agreed, plugging in the kettle.

The girl returned to the bed and sat down again; she looked at Andrew puzzled.

'Why stick it then?' she asked. 'I mean, a nob like you, can't you find something better than this?'

'There's not a lot of choice in Passworth; didn't you know?'

'There are good places south of town...'

'I can't afford them.'

'Can't afford them? I don't believe it; what d'you do?'

'I teach,' said Andrew apololetically.

'You teach. You're a bloody teacher?' cried the girl.

'I'm afraid so.'

'Crikey! Oh well that explains it, teachers can never afford anything.'

She got out her cigarettes and offered one to Andrew, but he shook his head.

'I suppose it's your vocation; that's what teachers say when people get at them. Is it yours?' She lit her cigarette and inhaled.

'No!' said Andrew fervently.

'No? Well, why do it then?'

'I thought it was.'

'And now you find you've made a mistake. I've heard that one before. Where d'you teach anyhow?'

'Passworth Community College.'

'Passworth Community College? I don't believe it! How did you end up there?' Helen's face was a mask of astonishment.

Andrew explained everything, sparing nothing, mentioning even the opposition of his family in Surrey,

'So now I put up with it, that's all.' he ended with a wry smile.

'I'm sorry,' said Helen after a silence, while she tried to understand this guy; he had her completely beat. 'How long will you stay?'

'I don't know; probably till the end of the year.'

Helen shook her head; Andrew was beginning to interest her. When she saw his room, she'd almost turned round and said: 'No thanks!' She expected from this "gent" something a bit better than a cramped bed-sitter in a Council house. Now she looked at him, so incongruous here, she felt she wanted to know him better, to find out what made him tick, what drove him to a school – voluntarily – which many would have avoided.

'I didn't mean to be rude about your room,' she said at last. 'It's not so bad.'

'You were disappointed,' Andrew smiled. 'I'm not surprised.'

Helen grinned in return. 'I'm not so hot myself, I'll tell you ... By the way,' she broke off. 'We never had that coffee.'

'You're right.' Andrew got up and went to the kettle. 'The water's hot anyhow.'

He gave Helen her coffee, and sat next to her on the bed; she smiled a little, noticing his increasing confidence.

'Tell me about yourself,' he said. 'Where d'you live?'

'With my Mam and Tom, my young brother, in a council house not so far from here...'

'What do you do?'

'I study sociology at the FE college ...'

'Do you like it?'

'It's all right, a bit of a doddle, I don't do much work... I had to do something and it's as good a way as any of meeting boys. When I find one I like I'll set up a place with him...'

'Are you fed up of home then?' Andrew had to ask.

'No,' said the girl restlessly. 'But my Mam's a widow and she can't really afford to keep me ...'

'Why don't you get a job?'

'I've had a few jobs but they didn't lead nowhere. Waitress jobs, that sort of thing. Then Mam said I'd be better off with qualifications so she got me to enrol at the College. That suited me, I never got to meet anyone interesting in my jobs. It was just work, bloody work. At least at the College you can have a good time.'

'What happened to your father?' asked Andrew a shade uneasily.

'He died of cancer – last year,' said the girl, her face had gone a bit blank.

'I'm sorry.'

'So were we. They said he got it from smoking but it wasn't that at all. He got cancer because he hadn't a job. He was made redundant after twenty five years and at forty five you're not going to get another job – not in Passworth.'

'What was his job?'

'He was an engineer in a small foundry. Then Passworth Electrical Engineering took it over – and Dad, with a good many others, was made redundant. He got a golden handshake he spent pretty soon and died a year later.'

'That's tough,' said Andrew helplessly. 'I wish I could do something.'

'We cope, you have to! But you can see why I felt pretty let down when the gent who picked me up in the Parrot turned out to be ...'

'Just a bloody teacher!' said Andrew with a grin. 'You had hopes I might be your knight in shining armour ...'

'Something like that. Not really,' said the girl. 'But one always lives in hope, and you looked interested...'

'I still am.'

'Well, I dunnow,' grinned Helen. 'I'm just a bleeding worker, remember, none of your Surrey silver spoon shit!"

'You can be pretty crude, I've noticed,' said Andrew not quite disliking it.

'I'm not so crude, but sometimes a short sharp shock or a kick in the balls works wonders. You should try it, especially on those kids at your school.'

'Can I see you again?' said Andrew after the long kiss that last speech had led up to.

'Are you sure?' whispered the girl in his ear. 'I'm a real bitch, you know...'

'I think you're terrific.'

'Glad someone does.'

They kissed even more passionately, lying on the bed mouth to mouth, clasped together, their legs interlocked. Andrew felt his senses completely engulfed.

'Do you want to have sex?' gasped Helen at last pausing for breath.

'Do you?' asked Andrew still holding her. 'I mean we only met today...'

She sat up on the bed, staring at Andrew, unable to make him out at all. What else was a pick-up for except to have sex? she reasoned to herself.

'What's the matter, stupid?' she said impatiently. 'Don't you have a condom?'

'Well no...'

'I've got one. Try it on.'

And so they made love; which was rather unfortunate because just as they had finished, the vast bulk of Mrs Reynolds came into the room. It was as well that they were marginally decent as she opened the door....

As quick as lightning, Helen was off the bed and nimbly ducking Mrs Reynolds' clutching hand. A quick but powerful shove which almost overturned her and the girl was through the door and rushing down the stairs two at a time.

'Stop!' shouted Mrs Reynolds but in vain. Helen had already flung the front door open and was haring off down the street. Poor Andrew was left staring into Mrs Reynolds' furious eyes. There was a silence while the lady tried to control herself, and when she spoke at last it was in quiet tones.

'Andrew,' she said. 'There is one thing, and one thing only I wish to make clear to you. This occurrence is not to be repeated. I will not have women in my house. This is a respectable house, not a BROTHEL!' she suddenly shouted.

Andrew was crimson with embarrassment – and anger. For the first time since he arrived at Mrs Reynolds' establishment he lost his temper.

'That's rubbish!' he exclaimed. 'Why shouldn't I have a friend in my room if I like? Your rules are impossible.'

'Impossible they may be but you *will* keep to them – or go!' snapped Mrs Reynolds. 'You have full permission to get yourself your own place whenever you like.'

'You know I can't afford a flat.'

'Do I? Well, if that is so, it's unfortunate. While you stay here, you keep to the rules that are made for your protection.

'I'm old enough to decide my behaviour!' Andrew exclaimed. 'It's none of your business!'

'While you are here, Andrew, I'm afraid it is my business. Do I make myself clear?'

Andrew said nothing, he just turned away, and started going up the stairs.

'Do I make myself clear?' Mrs Reynolds said in a louder voice.

'Yes!' Andrew was forced to reply.

Chapter Three

HE was unable to sleep that night until the small hours; he tossed and turned in his hard, narrow bed, torn with guilt and anger. Guilt at the word 'brothel', used so vindictively by Mrs Reynolds, anger that he felt guilt.

And suddenly he had doubts about Helen. What did he know about her really, except she was insidiously attractive and had seduced him? He'd made love to girls before but it was he who decided the time, and it was on his own terms. Why, she had even had to provide him with a sheath. That was not really on, Andrew was sure about that.

Then she had run away leaving him to face the music. Not that there was much she could have done if she had stayed, but even so. Andrew wasn't in the least pleased about the whole situation, and he had serious doubts if he would ever see Helen again, or wanted to...

Instead he decided to turn his attentions elsewhere, and to who other than Diane Seymour? Even during his infatuation with Helen, he'd always considered her sympathetic. They'd chat away during lunch breaks, or more briefly when she had a spare moment. Which wasn't so often because she always seemed to be busy, carrying piles of books from place to place, or attending endless meetings in addition to her normal teaching.

Andrew, after his liaison with Helen, now felt considerably bolder in his attitude to women. He felt, if not more attractive to them, less bothered at possible rejection; he decided he'd make an attempt to get to know Diane outside school as soon as possible.

She'd have certain advantages too. He could take her out to a meal or a show, he'd not be expected to take her to his room. She knew where he lived anyway, and though she didn't talk about it, he was certain she was aware of what kind of set-up it was – and its restrictions. So all in all, she had every advantage over Helen; Andrew felt very little remorse about forgetting her and setting his cap at Diane.

But now he'd decided, he found this incredibly difficult. He could never catch her when she wasn't busy, and rapidly the days went by without giving him a chance to ask her if she'd come to a meal with him. He knew of a pleasant Chinese restaurant in the residential part of Passworth, and as none of the school's pupils lived there, it would be the perfect setting for his first date.

In order to make sure he asked her, he had rather unwisely booked a table for two at the Jasmine, and though he allowed plenty of time, he suddenly discovered the booking was two days away.

'It's now or never!' he said to himself. 'I've left it almost too late; she may refuse because of short notice...'

He made a point of waiting for her after school; she was usually delayed in her classroom and didn't go home till some time after the bell. This time she was keeping a child in so Andrew had to wait long minutes outside her room until the culprit was dealt with. While he waited he considered her position somewhat enviously; although she had very few class problems, she did occasionally mete out punishments, and unlike Andrew's, these were never questioned by Terry Parsons, Jones, or anyone else.

At last she came out, the child skulking off in another direction. As usual she looked charming, elegant, completely in command. She was dressed today in a flaired crimson skirt and matching jacket, her fair hair loose and hanging about her shoulders, a most attractive sight for Andrew's jaded senses at the end of a long day. 'Hallo!' she exclaimed. 'Do you want me?' She looked quite surprised, though as usual pleased to see him.

'Yes,' said Andrew, a bit shy now the die was cast. 'I wondered...'

'What?'

'Would you like to have dinner with me at the Jasmine Restaurant? I'm sorry it's Friday and short notice but I've been trying to speak to you for ages and you never seem to be free...'

Andrew ended his speech a little breathless. He'd felt pretty nervous as he spoke, and he delivered it in an almost machine-gun staccato. He was very relieved Diane was still smiling when he stopped.

'It's kind of you to ask me, Andrew,' she said. 'And I'd love to come. But I can only stay until 9 o'clock. We're having a social at home and I have to get ready for it.'

'My invite doesn't matter!' Andrew exclaimed. 'I can see it's badly timed; we can easily go to the Jasmine some other day, that is if you want to...'

'Oh no! You've booked a table I'm sure, you have to at the Jasmine. What time is it booked for?'

'7 o'clock,' said Andrew, although he'd booked it for eight; he decided quickly he could change the time without any problem.

'That's fine then, I look forward to it. Do you want a lift now though? I'll run you home.'

Andrew's resources not yet extending to a car, he was glad to accept Diane's offer, and he thoroughly enjoyed their talk on the way back to Mrs Reynolds' domain. Diane's new red Metro nipped smartly through the Passworth rush hour without any need for Andrew to give directions.

'What's your room like?' Diane asked, looking doubtfully at the little council house.

'Awful!' said Andrew bluntly.

'Can't you manage a flat?'

'They're too expensive, I'm afraid ...'

'I'll look out for one. I know this area better than you.'

'That'd be great if you could! But on my pay it can't be too plush, I'm only in my first year, remember, and Jones didn't see fit to give me an allowance.'

'I'll look around,' she promised.

'The best thing I ever did,' thought Andrew after she'd gone, 'was to leave Helen and take up with Diane.'

But even as he thought this, he couldn't forget her pale face, those dark eyes, and her sulky sexy mouth. He was glad to have left her, he said to himself but he wouldn't have missed knowing her for worlds; would Diane ever excite him in the same way?

The next two days – and nights – seemed endless, but somehow Andrew got through them. At last Friday afternoon and 4H were behind him without serious mishap. 4H had been less lethal, Andrew thought, or maybe he was so used to them, they only seemed to have improved. At all events he wasn't in quite his usual state of exhaustion this time. He had a treat too, Diane having promised to collect him at his place because the restaurant was a long bus journey away.

He was ready in good time, waiting in front of the house. He knew Mrs Reynolds was looking through her window at him, but he didn't care; she couldn't stop him meeting a girl outside.

Diane was even more swish than usual. She was wearing a cream dress that matched perfectly her long fair hair; the dress considerably more revealing than what she wore to school as Andrew noticed when he got into her car.

'You look very smart,' she smiled, eyeing him admiringly.

'Oh, thanks,' he said, glad she'd noticed the suit he'd bought specially the previous day. 'And you look smashing yourself – but then you always do!' She laughed.

The restaurant was almost empty as it was early; Andrew was glad in a way, he liked to feel he had Diane to himself. They chose a corner table, from where they could look out over the green in front of the Jasmine, one of Passworth's few beauty spots. Dusk was falling but they could still see youngsters playing in the last moments of daylight. The atmosphere was extremely pleasant.

The Jasmine was attractive too. It was light and freshly coloured with Oriental pictures on the ceilings and walls, and as ever the staff were courteous and unobtrusive. Andrew ordered from the wide range of dishes; they took dry sherry for their aperitif.

Diane was an excellent talker and listener and as they drank their sherry and waited for the meal, Andrew had never felt more happy or relaxed since he came to Passworth, certainly not with Helen. With her, he'd felt a great many things, but relaxation wasn't one of them.

Almost without realizing it, he was revealing everything about himself to Diane, in a way impossible at school. About Camberford, his Surrey town, his home and family, and as he spoke she encouraged him more and more. She liked listening to him, for when he was at ease he was a good and interesting talker, intelligent and cultivated, in a fashion quite different from most of her colleagues. This was what had drawn Diane to him from the start, he was a '*gentleman*' but not in the way Helen saw him, something snobby and aloof but a person of taste and sensitivity. Helen admired him in a way but didn't understand him, Diane was attracted to him because she felt they had a lot in common.

The two hours went by almost instantaneously. It had been an excellent meal, prawn chow mein with sweet and sour pork, and a light nectarine dessert, accompanied by a medium dry Bordeaux. It encouraged the talk even more, and Andrew had a distinct singing sensation in his head after his second glass.

But all too soon it was 9 o'clock and Diane looked at her watch.

'I have to go,' she said regretfully. 'But,' she added after a pause, and looking at Andrew in a slightly different fashion. 'Would you fancy coming to this social? The one I've got to go to...?'

Andrew stared at her quite at a loss; he just didn't know what to say. Diane completely misinterpreted his expression for she went on quickly:

'Don't feel you've got to to come; it'll be a bore really. A lot of Father's business acquaintances and hangers-on, you probably know the sort of thing back at Camberford. But I would appreciate your company...'

'I'd love to come!' exclaimed Andrew. 'I haven't had that sort of do for ages – it'll be a great change from Mrs Reynolds' rooms.'

Diane smiled. 'I'm glad. I checked with Father so it *is* quite all right. And lucky you've got a nice new suit on; you don't even need to change. We can go straight home without bother.'

'Where do you live?' asked Andrew. 'You never told me ...'

'Didn't I? Oh it's about three miles out in the country.'

'Sounds nice.'

'It's not too bad; rather too many socials for my liking but I do have my own room when it all gets too much.'

Andrew settled the bill and they drove off immediately into the darkness, a feeling of excitement and anticipation making Andrew shiver slightly. The talk went on and he was even more certain than before he was experiencing a happiness of a kind he hadn't known in years. Not only did he find Diane tremendous company, but there was an unknown element about her, quite different from Helen's, which gave her a kind of magic.

Where did she live for a start? Out in the country – that could mean anything, he had to ask her more directly.

'I'm surprised you don't know,' smiled Diane. 'But it's one of your endearing traits, your unawareness. You must be the only teacher at our school who doesn't know about me.'

'I haven't the faintest idea what you are talking about!' Andrew protested. 'Where *do* you live? Is it special – like Buckingham Palace?' he ended, driven desperately to sarcasm.

'You're not so far out; do you know who lives at Carnforth Grange?'

'Of course, it's the millionaire owner of Passworth Electrical Engineering.'

'Do you know his name?'

'No.'

"Well, he's called George Seymour and he's my father...'

'What!' Andrew couldn't help exclaiming.

'And you must be the only one in Passworth who didn't know it...'

Andrew was quite dumbfounded. He'd never have imagined a teacher at his school could be a millionaire's daughter, but then he wasn't endowed with a great deal of imagination. If he had been, he wouldn't have taken on his present job.

But as he carried on thinking, it all seemed to fall into place. There'd always been something different about Diane that separated her from the rest of the staff, a brightness, a detachment, a charisma even, that gave her a special quality. Now he knew what it was! But no wonder, he couldn't help thinking cynically, she had no problems with the kids; who was going to annoy the daughter of George Seymour who employed most of the kids' fathers – and many of their mothers?

'You're very quiet,' said Diane at last, a faint sign of concern on her face.

'I was thinking,' Andrew answered quietly. 'What you've told me must make a difference, I can't help feeling that.'

'I suppose so. But you don't mind, do you? I mean, you should be pleased...'

'I am!' Andrew exclaimed. 'Of course! And very flattered a girl like yourself should have any interest in me, especially as I didn't even know who you were! I can hardly believe it!'

'Can't you see? It's because you *didn't* know about me I took to you; that and your elegant manners,' she said facetiously.

'They don't go down very well with the kids,' Andrew sighed.

'Maybe not, but you wait, you'll sort them out, I'm certain!' Diane said emphatically. 'And here we are, arriving at Carnforth Grange.'

The car turned off the main road and into the blackness of the wooded grounds. Andrew held his breath as the car advanced along the twisty drive, and he waited for Diane's mansion home to appear. Then, the car turning round the final bend, there it was, a dark square tower, rising into the moonless sky, ablaze with a thousand lights.

'Fantastic!' he breathed.

'You like it? said Diane, not without pride. 'It's worth seeing in the daylight too.'

'How old is it?'

'Father started building it about ten years ago; they haven't finished it yet.'

'Like a cathedral going on year after year...'

'Well, Father's hardly religious,' said Diane, parking the car in the vast garage where four limousines were already standing. 'Come on, the social will be starting shortly, and you must meet Mother and Father first.'

They rushed into the house, were relieved of their coats by a discrete domestic, and almost immediately they were greeted by Diane's parents.

Mrs Seymour came first. She was a tall, willowy lady, in her mid-forties, fair like Diane, and both imposing and beautiful; George Seymour was almost dwarfed by her in height.

He came forward with a smile, a large cigar, and some effort because of his stoutness, and Andrew recognized him at once. He was the Chairman of the Board of Governors of Passworth Community College.

Chapter Four

'Good evening, young man,' he said. 'I've heard a lot about you from Diane – and Arthur Jones, your headmaster....'

Andrew was too embarrassed to say anything; it was fortunate Mrs Seymour came to his rescue.

'Now, no shop, George,' she said chiding him gently. 'I'm Mary Seymour, Andrew. Welcome to Carnforth Grange. It's your first occasion here, isn't it?'

'Yes,' Andrew managed to reply. 'It's a beautiful house, Mrs Seymour.'

'Please call me Mary, won't you? Yes, it *is* a nice place. Diane, would you fancy showing Andrew some of it? There's still about half an hour until people arrive ....'

'But shouldn't I change?' Diane said. 'That's why I came a bit early.'

'You don't need to, darling, you look fine as you are,' said her mother.

''Yes, go ahead, show Andrew round,' said George, waving his cigar magnanimously. 'We'll be in the hall when you've done.'

'All right then,' Diane agreed. 'Come on, Andrew, and you might like to see my room as well...'

She led the way, and they started their tour; Andrew was quite overwhelmed. The whole mansion was designed on neo-classical lines with beautiful Greek arches over marble corridors. The parquet flooring gleamed like mirrors, and the rooms were furnished simply but in perfect taste, whether with genuine or reproduction Sheraton, Andrew wasn't expert enough to tell. While on the high white stucco walls hung artistic masterpieces, many of which Andrew recognised from galleries in London, Paris, and New York.

'They're copies of course,' said Diane. 'But all the exact size and tone of the originals. And we do have some genuine masterpieces, Father buys them as investments in case of a rainy day.'

'They're wonderful,' Andrew sighed.

'Father had nothing to do with planning this house,' Diane went on.

'He left all that to Mother; she has a tremendous sense of design and Father's good at recognising talent in others.'

'He made a slip about me!' Andrew couldn't help exclaiming. 'At my job interview.'

'I don't think he did!' Diane said emphatically. 'You undervalue yourself, that's what's wrong with you! Anyhow, about this house we've a library too with a couple of thousand volumes, from the classics to the latest best sellers. Again father didn't choose anything. "I leave it to Mary," he says. "I know I'm a bloody ignoramus." She laughed as she mimicked accurately her father's strong Lancashire accent.

'Are we going to look at it?' Andrew asked, feeling increasingly out of his depth.

'Not enough time – it's nearly ten, we'd better start making tracks for the hall...' She turned to go that way, then suddenly remembering, she changed direction and said instead: 'But there *is* one room I'd like you to see, and I think there's just time...'

'What's that?'

'My room, I told you I wanted you to see it, come on!'

Quickly she led the way up a nearby staircase, climbing rapidly while Andrew followed, almost out of breath; he wouldn't have guessed Diane could move so fast. They reached the third floor and taking out a key, Diane unlocked the little door in a dark corner.

'I like my privacy,' she smiled going in.

Andrew followed and looked round in absolute amazement, he'd never have imagined Diane's room could be so different from the rest of Carnforth Grange. It was very small for a start with a plain single bed and basic furniture, the only luxury item an enormous white wardrobe. Andrew couldn't help smiling as he looked at it, Diane had to have her one extravagance, the pleasure of a new outfit every morning! But he stopped smiling as he realised something else, the room was hardly any different from his own!

'D'you like it?' Diane asked, sitting on the bed – in quite a different way from Helen. 'I need somewhere to escape to – and this is it! My sanctuary in times of trouble.'

'It's very like my room,' said Andrew slowly. 'There's just one difference.'

'And what's that?'

'You *can* have your privacy.'

'Don't worry, Andrew.' said Diane getting up. 'I'll find you a flat and that's a promise. Now come on, they'll be waiting for us.'

She held out a hand and led him onto the landing, locked the door, and the two quickly ran down the steep staircase. Andrew was wondering nervously what the social would be like; he was used to them for his father entertained quite often at Camberford, but certainly nothing on the scale of Carnforth Grange. He hoped he'd be up to it – and was glad he'd lashed out the previous day and bought himself a new suit.

'Here we are,' said Diane, after a considerable walk through yet more corridors, and they found themselves gazing into the hall. 'We're on time, not many have arrived.'

About six couples, all in lounge suits Andrew was pleased to see, were chatting near two long buffet tables at the far end.

'Now for it!' Andrew said to himself. 'I've got to cross that vast expanse of floor with all that lot staring at me...' He almost wished he was back in his room.

'Just relax,' came Diane's whisper as she sensed his unease.

'I'm trying to!' he exclaimed, relieved to see Mary Seymour coming towards them with a welcoming smile.

'Did you enjoy your tour?' she asked. 'If that's not too grand a word?'

'It was wonderful,' Andrew replied. 'I'd like to see the rest – during the day...'

'So you shall,' said Mary. 'You're free to come any time you wish. Now, you must meet some of our friends,' she continued. 'But first what can we offer you to drink?' She indicated one of the tables, sparkling with its vast array of glasses filled with beverages of every kind.

'Diane?' Andrew invited, just able to keep his presence of mind.

'I'll have a vermouth, thanks,' she smiled.

He handed her a glass, then chose for himself a medium sherry, savouring the clean dry taste.

'Excellent!' he said approvingly.

'It's vintage,' Diane said. 'Father has a wine cellar second to none round here; he visits Jerez every year to find out the best choice available.'

'Now Andrew,' Mary went on. 'I'd like you meet Peggy and Malcolm;

Malcolm's a sales representative. Andrew's a teacher,' she smilingly informed them. 'If you'll excuse me,' she apologised. 'I must go and welcome new arrivals, I'll try and see you all later, once things things are more settled....'

With a parting smile she moved away, chatting to couples as she went past, checking all was well, the perfect hostess.

'Nice woman!' said Malcolm wih approval, eyeing her departing back. 'So you're a teacher,' he went on. 'What d'you teach?'

'Languages,' said Andrew, wondering what would be the response; he was soon to know in no uncertain terms.

'Languages, eh?' Malcolm barked. 'Languages ain't my line, no fear! I've been in sales since I left the army back in 1980. Not that I wouldn't have appreciated a spot of *français* or even *español* now and again, just to get me out of an awkward *fracas*. Still never mind, I've always discovered a fistful of dollars just as good, so why worry?'

He laughed boisterously and sipped a venomous looking cocktail, Andrew laughed too out of politeness though he noticed Diane wasn't quite so enthusiastic, neither was Peggy. He looked askance at Malcolm, observing the stocky figure, the tooth brush moustache, and the jarring military accent.

'Ignore him,' Peggy smiled. 'He's incorrigeably insular; in his opinion the British Empire didn't die, it moved to the Costa del Sol.'

Andrew regarded Matthew's wife with interest. She wasn't bad looking at all, even though not in the first flush of youth. The early thirties, he decided; but her blue eyes were a definite plus, so was the scarlet mouth, clenched most of the time to a black cigarette holder; she hardly took it out even to speak. And her gown; Andrew couldn't help noticing what the plunging neckline made very little effort to conceal. Of course she saw his look and her smile became the broader, as he quickly turned away, embarrassed.

'I see you approve of my dress,' she said mockingly. 'Striking, isn't it?'

'Oh yes!' Andrew agreed with enthusiasm, blushing a little. 'I must say, all the ladies tonight are – quite stunning!'

'You mustn't see too many '*stunning*' ladies,' Diane advised with a smile. 'I might think you've got a roving eye...'

'And why shouldn't he?' Malcolm barked. 'The idea that man is monogamous is so much – eye wash, to put in politely. Man is – and always has been – instinctively polygamous. He is one of the few species that can make love whenever he feels like, and not by the order of the season – or anything else!'

'So where do Adam and Eve fit in?' Andrew asked.

'They don't! They're just a convenient idea proposed by society, to persuade us of the value of family life, – that's all!'

'Interesting,' Andrew replied, beginning to enjoy this.

'More than interesting, true!' Malcolm took another sip of his poison.

'Off he goes own his favourite hobby horse, sex!' Peggy smiled.

'It's everyone's *hobby horse!*' Malcolm growled.

So the chat proceeded and soon Andrew noticed the numbers had reached maximum, about thirty. Mary Seymour was constantly on duty, checking that all was well with the guests, while George remained with one group fortunately some distance away, Andrew was relieved to see, not having recovered from learning George's educational identity.

But now there began a noticeable gravitation towards the second buffet table, loaded with food. It was clear that minds were becoming increasingly concentrated on the dietary part of the evening. Andrew's mind was even more concentrated than most, as the Chinese meal, delicious though it had been, remained nothing more than a sweet memory.

At last Mary announced starter's orders, and the guests heaved a silent but unmistakable sigh of relief. The sight of all those succulent quiches, pâtés, chicken salads, and sea food had become no longer a decorative pleasure to behold, the kind of torture Tantalus had to endure, but were now accessible. In next to no time a queue had formed, and Andrew found himself urged by Diane to get a place before he was relegated to the back.

'Here's a knife and fork!' she hissed. 'And a serviette...'

'Thanks!' he gasped. 'Doesn't the food look good!'

At last the pair were sitting down and eating with hearty appetite pâtés with French bread, washed down with cold Moselle.

Andrew now felt more relaxed and even began to enjoy himself; he was able to look round and see what was going on. Still George Seymour mercifully kept his distance, seemingly concentrating on some business deal with various big-wigs, for he was chatting away nineteen to the dozen and gesticulating with his cigar. For once Mary had vanished, probably to the kitchen or some such place to liaise with caterers; maybe she was even have a rest!

'Penny for your thoughts,' said Diane, breaking into his reverie. 'Here comes Elizabeth, one of my best friends from school, just to liven you up!'

A red haired, svelte, and very attractive girl sat down next to Diane.

'Enjoying the party?' she asked Andrew, after they were introduced.. 'Rather overwhelming this place if you're not used to it...'

'And even if you are!' said Diane before Andrew could make some kind of polite reply. 'Father allows me a quota of personal friends for these affairs for that reason; I wouldn't come at all otherwise! When the proceedings get too much, we can always go into a huddle or remove ourselves to the kitchen.'

'When does all this take place?' Andrew asked curiously. 'I thought you had to make an act of presence.'

'Only till the buffet! After that, no one has the faintest idea who's here, they certainly won't miss little me ...'

'Will you vanish tonight?' asked Andrew rather concerned; he didn't wish to be left stranded just then, even in the attractive company of Elizabeth...

'Don't panic, Andrew! If I went off, you'd come with me of course! But maybe we'd better not this time, Father's got his eye on you, I'm sure, and you'd better make a good impression on him for your first visit...'

'Who have you met so far?' Elizabeth asked. 'Anyone interesting?'

'Peggy and Malcolm...' Andrew began.

'Those two? What a pair! Did Malcolm tell any sexy stories?'

'Not really; only that Adam and Eve were planted in the Bible to encourage family life; at least that's what I think he said.'

'The truth is,' Diane remarked with a grin, 'while Malcolm was delivering his spiel, Andrew's mind was elsewhere...'

'Elsewhere? What do you mean?'

'He made a vast compliment to all the ladies present – which proves he was far more interested in them than Malcolm's peroration!'

'I'm not in the least surprised if Andrew's mind was far away,' said

Elizabeth. 'Malcolm's quite fun – for a couple of minutes; after that you feel you've heard it all before.'

'Actually,' said Diane, giving Andrew a quick, mischievous glance. 'There was a little more to it than that...'

'There was?' said Elizabeth with an expression of great interest.

'What really happened was Andrew had noticed Peggy's plunging neckline – even more plunging than usual – and he made his little compliment to put us off the scent...'

'So you knew,' Andrew sighed. 'I thought I'd done it rather well.'

'You did – it more or less put Peggy in her place! But we'd all been expecting something to happen. She tries it on with all the new faces, mentioning her dress directly just to embarrass them!'

At that Diane giggled loudly, quite different from the poised young lady at school. Andrew suspected the Moselle had gone to her head, or else she was letting go to get through the usual boring evening. He decided a change of subject was necessary, and turned his attention to Elizabeth.

'What do you do?' he asked her. 'I take it you're not still at school...'

'Hardly!' she laughed. 'No, for my sins I work for the Inland Revenue.'

'A difficult job in Passworth ...'

'Yes, tax evasion and moonlighting are growth industries here, but half the time we keep a blind eye, the average wage being so low ...'

'She doesn't cope with hard cases,' said Diane. 'She also sorts out the better off; she's coped with some of Father's taxes a few times.'

'Only the very simplest,' said Elizabeth modestly. 'But he has asked me my advice; whether he took it or not I wouldn't like to say...' She smiled as though she doubted if George took anyone's advice on anything.

Andrew in turn explained his own predicament, as evasively as possible, he was glad Elizabeth asked no awkward questions, and Diane this time kept tactfully mum. Soon after, Elizabeth left, saying she had to go early, which Andrew considerably regretted. Especially as in her place came other guests, not quite as appetising as she was. Noticing a strange face, they tested fully all Andrew's powers of diplomacy and stonewalling with their courteous inquisition; just then he envied greatly Diane's skill at blocking awkward questions with a smile.

During a reprieve, after Andrew had presented for the tenth time his edited version of life at Passworth, he expressed these sentiments to Diane

– in no uncertain terms.

'Don't worry,' she replied, now completely changed to her familiar self, much to Andrew's relief. 'If you're really desperate, just lie, they won't remember what you tell them anyhow. Actually you are doing rather well, they all think you're fascinating, they've discovered so little about you.' She stopped then and noticed there followed a silence. 'You're tired, I can see,' she said, more gently. 'I'm sorry I teased you just now.'

'Oh, I didn't mind,' said Andrew with a smile. 'It was quite funny really, the whole scenario...'

'I don't know it *was* so funny,' said Diane reflectively. 'These completely artificial *dos* get on my nerves; at that point I could also see you were a bit bored, and I thought, why not play around a bit just to liven things up? I didn't mean to embarrass you...'

'Forget it; you didn't!' said Andrew. 'I liked Elizabeth anyway, she's a peach...'

'I agree, we've known each other since school. She helps no end at these socials if I get moody.'

'I'd never have imagined you moody from school!' Andrew said astonished. 'You always look so – alive! How can you – in that place?'

'It's all a bit of a front,' Diane admitted. 'Though actually I do like '*that place*.' It's far better to be there, living one's own life and being my own woman, than here where I'm just my father's daughter...'

'I understand,' said Andrew, and he thought he did. Even so he couldn't suppress a yawn, the evening having taken its toll on him.

'D'you want to go?' Diane asked. 'I can see you're tired.'

'I wouldn't mind,' he admitted. 'Friday, you know, and 4H. But isn't it still early?'

'People are starting to drift off, this isn't meant to be a late night show. I'll take you back, so you don't need to worry about that...' Diane stood up, Andrew following suit. 'Let's go then, okay?' He nodded silently and they moved towards the main door of the hall.

'I'd better thank your mother,' Andrew said, seeing Mary Seymour, now returned, busy talking to a couple who were clearly leaving. He went towards her, and she smiled as she saw him approach.

'You're going, Andrew?' she said. 'I hope you had a nice evening. It was a pleasure to meet you, I hope to meet you again soon.'

'Thank you very much, Mrs Seymour – Mary; it was kind of you invite me, I've really enjoyed myself.'

'I'm glad. Is Diane taking you back?'

'Yes, if she doesn't mind.'

'Of course not Have you said goodnight to George?'

'No...'

'Is Andrew going?' As if from nowhere, the compact figure of George Seymour appeared. 'Well, young man,' he said, his dark eyes boring into the lad. 'Sorry not to have been able to talk to you...'

'I could see you were busy..'

'I was; masses of shop at these affairs, I'm afraid. Anyhow I could see Mary and Diane were looking after you.'

'Oh yes...'

'All right then, I won't keep you, but we must have a proper get-together soon. A dinner perhaps?'

'Yes – thank you ...'

'Diane'll fix it. Goodbye!' Quickly George shook hands and moved back to his group. As Andrew left the hall, he could still see the cigar and the quick gesticulations. What energy! he thought. Was George ever tired?

Once in the car, Andrew fell silent. So did Diane, uncertain of his state of mind. She knew what a traumatic experience the evening must have been, especially as he'd had no idea of what was in store until their dinner in the Jasmine. Diane couldn't help fearing his reaction would be against not in favour of the experience, in which case she would inevitably be the loser. So at last she decided to speak in order to forestall this possibility...

'All right?' she said, smiling even though she knew he wouldn't be able to see.

'Fine!' Andrew answered, but quietly.

'Thinking?'

'Well, yes...'

'Don't *worry*, Andrew,' Diane said gently. 'And let's not talk about this evening now. I realise it's all been a bit too much for you. What you need is to go away and get things more in proportion. You'll feel better in the morning...'

'Yes. Yes, you're right,' said Andrew. 'You've a marvellous home and your mother's lovely..'

'She *is* sweet, isn't she?

'But your father...'

'Yes?'

'I wish he wasn't Chairman of the Governors for our school.'

'I know. But as I said, let's not discuss that just for the moment. It really makes no difference to me anyway.'

'But it does to me! Especially as I like you a lot and will feel constantly your social position comes between us.'

'Don't worry about all that now,' said Diane. 'Here we are at your place,' she went on, parking quietly in front of the building. 'Goodbye, and see you Monday...'

'Goodbye, thanks a lot,' said Andrew, getting out and moving round the car to speak a few last words to Diane; she opened her window and leaned out. He could just see her beautiful face in the light of a nearby streetlamp. 'I did enjoy your social, really!' he said, trying to allay his doubts.

'I'm glad,' Diane replied, looking at him. 'Are you going to stop talking and kiss me now, or isn't that why you really walked round the car?'

Shyly Andrew stooped and kissed her on the lips. Later when he was lying on his bed, it was of that kiss he was thinking, not Mrs Reynolds who had opened her door as he crept quietly past. He knew she'd speak to him in the morning, but he didn't care; all he was thinking about during the last moments before he dropped off to sleep was Diane's sweet lips.

Chapter Five

THE following morning Andrew was relieved he had no immediate assignations with Diane; he needed time to think. His first decision was to find out a bit more about Passworth Electrical Engineering – and George Seymour. He knew very little about either, a somewhat strange fact when one considered how they dominated the region, and the fathers of a large proportion of the kids at Passworth were employed by him.

Immediately after school on Monday, Andrew went to the reference library to go through a few local directories; Passworth Electrical Engineering appeared conspicuously. It had existed in some shape or form for nearly half a century, in its early days on quite a limited scale, supplying machinery and plant for Manchester industry. But gradually it began to widen its scope until by the eighties, not only did it manufacture plant, but it had also secured a foothold in computers and electronics. Only the name remained unaltered, for George felt rightly that people have a soft spot for what at least appears familiar.

But with the changes in purpose came changes in personnel. Whereas at the beginning, Passworth Electrical Engineering had employed a high proportion of unskilled labour, now the situation was quite different. It began more and more to limit its recruitment to those skilled in electronics and computer technology, so that ironically although George Seymour remained Passworth's biggest single employer, the organisation which provided sustenance for even more families was the Department of Health and Social Security.

To discover George Seymour's personal origins wasn't quite so easy. Andrew at last succeeded in building up a picture through old newspapers as well as biographies; the newspapers on the whole were more accurate, and what Andrew discovered was astonishing.

George Seymour was effectively a glorified entrepreneur. He was a specialist in nothing, and began twenty five years ago as an apprentice school leaver with basic qualifications. But although he started at the bottom rung of the ladder at Passworth Engineering Works, very soon his ruthless determination pushed him rapidly upwards; by the age of forty some five years ago he was indisputably the boss.

His great skill lay in manipulating others and using their talents. He was also aware that the secret of success in the ruthless world of business and manufacturing was adaptability and foresight. These skills he had in plenty, and in addition he was a good mixer, able to make people feel that in any deal he was concerned with, they too would reap the benefits. Sometimes this actually occurred for George knew the importance of having support from people he could trust – and who trusted him.

But his true triumph was with the arrival of electronics and the microchip – about which he knew virtually nothing. Even so he sensed at once they would be essential elements in the future, and if wanted to survive and prosper, he had to be in on the act. He made it an immediate priority to consult experts in those fields and give them jobs.

But although this was the beginning of George Seymour's phenomenal success, culminating in his mansion home, Carnforth Grange, it was also the beginning of the end for many of his employees. Those who couldn't adapt to new demands became redundant, many were dismissed anyway for the modern factory didn't require nearly as large a workforce as previously. And in order to fill the inevitable spaces with people owning the necessary skills, George Seymour recruited from elsewhere, bringing in people from Manchester – and beyond.

This was why so many of the children at Passworth Community College were unsettled; their fathers had come to Passworth in answer to advertisements and it was Passworth Electrical Engineering that had called them. What the town had now was a monopoly, stiffling other smaller concerns – like the steel foundry employing Helen's father for twenty five years – and then snuffing him out of existence.

Andrew was feeling quite dizzy when one and a half hours later he emerged from the reference library; but he was considerably wiser.

All he could think now was where Diane stood in this, and where their friendship stood, it kept him awake that night. But in the end, in spite of eight hours of agonizing, he decided to let things ride. He was very fond of Diane, and she clearly didn't go along with her father's ethics completely, hence her job at Passworth Community College and her bedroom. Her sole concessions to luxury were her new Metro and an inexhaustible wardrobe of clothes.

They began to go out to places, the theatre in Manchester, concerts, drives in the lovely Pennine countryside not far from Passworth and Carnforth Grange. And as promised, Andrew was able to visit the mansion during the day at weekends, finding it even more luxurious than on that Friday night. In addition to the magnificent interior, there were the grounds, beautiful and wooded with two small lakes, grottos, and a botanical garden filled with rare shrubs. And even after a day wandering round these places with Diane, Andrew still felt he'd only experienced a fraction of the whole.

Diane meantime was very careful in her attitude towards him; she knew it would be unwise to make too many demands, at least not yet. They chatted only about everyday things, but having a limitless supply of small-talk, she was easily able to make time pass smoothly by. There were few silences in their interchanges, and Diane knew – with some complacency – that Andrew found her a fascinating companion. Even so, although he tried to hide his unease, he couldn't help being continually aware of the vast pressure of the Seymour empire weighing heavily upon him.

Meantime, Diane had her problems, though she was more skilled than Andrew at concealing them. She was an only daughter, and the more valued therefore by her father. He had accepted very unwillingly her teaching at Passworth Community College, considering her decision misguided. And now she was developing a friendship for this youngster, who was not only an outsider from down-south, but a constant reminder to George that he'd made a mistake in backing him for his job.

As the friendship continued, George's anxiety increased, until at last he could keep silence no longer. One morning at breakfast when he had Diane to himself, his wife having gone out earlier to one of her many conferences, he decided to have it out with his daughter – once and for all.

'Are you – keen on Andrew?' he asked bluntly and uncomfortably, hiding his embarrassment behind a cup of coffee.

Diane looked at him with an appearance of surprise. 'I think so,' she said in a careful tone.

'How keen, may I ask?'

'I don't know, Father, and I'm not sure it's any of your business!' she answered, a spark of fire in her voice.

George said nothing to that – for the moment; he had no wish for a row with Diane, especially as he knew she'd win in any confrontation. After a pause, he smiled and said quite mildly:

'I'm sorry, Diane, I didn't mean to interfere. But I *am* your father, you know...'

'You only say that because you have a guilty conscience!' she snapped; George smiled at her plain speaking.

'You're probably right, lass,' he admitted. 'Even so, may I put you one more question, and I promise you can leave the witness box – for good?'

'Ask anything you like,' Diane answered coolly. 'But I can't promise to answer...'

'If you felt you loved Andrew, would you be prepared to go ahead with your friendship – even to marry him?'

'That's very simple, Father,' said Diane. 'The answer is "Yes"; and why not? He's an intelligent boy, sensitive, gentle, he has a lot of interests that I share; and he's much better than those fortune hunters who are only interested in my body and your money. Andrew, I can tell you sincerely, has shown no special interest in either...'

'Then he's a bloody fool, and probably a queer!' George exploded, completely taken aback.

'That's offensive!' exclaimed Diane, standing up, flushed with anger. 'I demand an apology or I promise I'll leave this place, I'm near to leaving already...'

'Sit down, sit down, Diane,' muttered George, aware he'd gone much too far. 'I'm sorry, I *am*, I didn't mean what I said, you know me and my quick tongue...'

'I think you did mean it, and that's the trouble!' said Diane, sitting down again, her face averted so as to hide a tear.

'I'm sure Andrew's all right and I know I'm a bastard,' said George. 'It's only I meet so few – good men about, that when I meet one I can't believe it's possible...'

'Father, Andrew is a good man!' said Diane, moving round the table. 'Why else would he take on a completely thankless job like teaching at our school?'

'*You're* teaching there...'

'You know it's different for me; I have your support so I manage. And even so you don't like it...'

'You're right, I don't! But I did back this lad at the interview on account of you. I felt if I'd let my daughter go ahead and make a fool of herself, why should I oppose this young fellow?'

'Does that mean you don't oppose him now, Father?' Diane asked, her arms around him.

'How could I oppose anything you wanted, lass? I love you!' said the little man.

' And I love you!' said Diane giving him a kiss.

'You could have saved yourself a lot of trouble, by keeping out of it entirely,' said Mary after George had told her what had occurred. 'You know from your experience it's easier to manage a thousand employees than a daughter...'

'Or a wife.' said George with a grin.

'And don't forget you married me against the wishes of my family.'

'I'd do it again!' he said, standing close to her, his face level with her chin.

'They said you weren't good enough for me, uneducated, common,' she smiled, knowing these words far from hurting, pleased him, for he felt that having won her completely they were rendered meaningless.

'I loved you,' he whispered.

'And I loved you, which is why – if Diane does love this boy, we won't oppose him, whatever we think...'

This victory was the prelude to yet another success in Andrew's meteoric rise to fortune; Diane found him a cheap flat in Passworth's residential area.

'I don't believe it!' he exclaimed when she told him the rent was little more than he was paying Mrs Reynolds.

'But it is!' Diane insisted. 'To be honest it belongs to a friend of ours and she's quite happy to let it out for that amount. She doesn't need the money but likes having the flat occupied. It saves her anxiety about burglars, damp, and so on if it's empty.'

'Is there anyone in it now?'

'Yes, but she's moving out at the end of the month; she's getting married and it's really only suitable for one person...'

'Who do I pay the rent to?' Andrew asked, still convinced this was all far too good to be true, a scepticism that seemed to be confirmed when Diane said:

'You can pay me; I see Mrs Symonds regularly and that would be the most straightforward method.'

'It'd be the most straightforward method for you to subsidise me!' muttered Andrew, after a pause while he thought it over – not entirely pleased at the possibility.

'That's nonsense!' Diane exclaimed, almost angry. 'You *are* foolish, Andrew, will you never take advantage of good luck?'

'I do if it *is* good luck...'

'All right, I *shall* be subsidising you!' Diane admitted irritably. 'If that's the way you want to put it!' Then more gently she went on: 'But you *can't* carry on in your present set-up, you know that, not now we're friends. This flat is quite independent, no interfering landlady on the premises...'

Andrew was silent at that; it made a vast difference, independence, in fact without it, no way would he have even considered Diane's offer; as it was he saw no way he could refuse.

'I'll take it,' he said though still quiet, Diane watching him was almost nervous, secretly angry at his pride. Why couldn't he have just accepted her explanation instead of having to dig out the truth? She shook her head, controlling her impatience so Andrew saw only her smile.

'Don't you want to look at it before you really commit yourself?' she said.

'I'm sure it's fine, it'll be a lot better than my present room, and even yours!' he said.

'Definitely mine! All right, we won't bother, at least not now, the girl's still there anyway; but we'll look at it as soon as she moves out, I promise you, you don't need to take it if you don't like it, I can always find you somewhere else.'

'It'll be fine!' Andrew repeated.

And it was; not even too smart, which was what he'd mainly feared; he'd have hated a luxury flat at a ludicrously low rental and would have felt even more of a toy-boy. As it was, it had everything he wanted, a separate kitchen with a proper cooker, reasonable furniture, and a bathroom you didn't have to enter sideways, as Helen had put it. But the insuperable advantage of the place was its independence – and this did much to make Andrew forget his morbid feelings of guilt.

'It's great,' he sighed after they'd gone round it and inspected every nook and cranny. 'Thank you, Diane, you are good to me; *and* it's got a phone.'

'You deserve it,' she said, pleased and relieved at the reaction, she felt she'd won that battle at least. 'Now I can see you whenever you wish...'

'The only reason I took it,' Andrew said, looking at the girl as she stood close to him, as attractive as ever. Today her dress was a strawberry pink, matching perfectly the gold of her hair.

'What are you waiting for?' Diane asked moving even closer. 'Do I always have to ask you for a kiss?'

At the end of the month Andrew left Mrs Reynold's domain with literally no regrets at all. He'd found it hard to give her his notice prior to that without telling her plainly what he thought of her, he had yet to forget her offensive complaints about the night he arrived late from Diane's social. In spite of them, he was able to confine himself to telling her he was going and when, and to leave it at that. Or he would have done, had Mrs Reynolds let him, but she had no intention of allowing to get away so easily.

'It's that girl you were out with till all hours, is it?' she sneered.

'I don't know what you mean,' said Andrew politely.

'Are you going to co-habit with her?'

'I am not, as a matter of fact, but I can say without fear of contradiction, that in this case what I do is none of your business.'

'It may be true I cannot stop you behaving as you wish once you leave here,' said Mrs Reynolds malevolently. 'But I am still free to express my opinion about your behaviour which I consider to have been quite unethical for a school teacher and I intend to mention it to your headmaster and see what *he* thinks of it.'

'You can do what you like, Mrs Reynolds,' replied Andrew icily. 'Now will you kindly go, I have things to get on with.'

But after Mrs Reynolds vanished, he felt slightly uneasy; he wondered what complaints she might make about his behaviour and if they could be used against him. He didn't see how, because there was very little she could prove apart from the fact a girl had been in his room on one occasion, hardly a criminal act in itself, and she had seen nothing of what actually happened... She might guess but that was a long way from proof. Even so, Andrew was left with a definite cloud of anxiety hanging over him; he decided to mention Mrs Reynolds' threats to Diane.

'It's disgraceful!' she exclaimed. 'She has no right at all to say that to you; I'll mention it to Father.'

'No, don't, don't bother!' Andrew protested. 'She won't complain, I'm sure, and even if she does, there's nothing really she can say against me.'

'There was this girl,' said Diane. 'Who was she anyway? Do I know her?'

'Oh, she's just someone I met and invited round for a coffee,' he said, feeling the whole truth wouldn't be very expedient here. 'It was our bad luck Mrs Reynolds happened to see her as she was going...'

Diane said nothing to that and the subject was dropped, though Andrew couldn't help wondering if she suspected there was a little more to his meeting with this girl than he had stated. Still, he wasn't seeing her any more so Diane had no reason for concern, and he was able therefore easily to push Helen to the back of his mind, soon forgetting about her completely; at least for the time being!

On the surface all went well. Andrew heard nothing further from Mrs Reynolds, he settled happily into his flat, and it was just as agreeable and independent as he could have wished. His relationship with Diane became closer too, but it was careful and controlled, and he rarely went all the way with her. When he did, she made sure he was wearing protection, telling him from the start she wasn't on the pill, and had no desire for it; neither did she like the other contraceptive methods, finding them at best awkward and at worst calculating. If a man wanted to make love to her, she felt it was his responsibility to look after her, not hers to defend herself. Andrew respected her for this and acted accordingly.

All this time they kept as low a profile as possible. No one at school knew they had any contact with each other outside the staff room, at least Andrew assumed that; Diane's wider personal experience made her suspect otherwise. She was to be proved quite right, for Andrew soon discovered with brutal suddenness that not only his colleagues knew exactly what was going on, but also the kids.

'Had it off with her, sir?' Kenny of 4H shouted out of the blue.

A silence followed, of shock on Andrew's part, and expectation from the kids.

'What on earth do you mean?' Andrew demanded at last, very red in the face.

'You know what I mean,' grinned Kenny. 'You and Miss Seymour, you're *friends*, ain't you?'

Andrew continued to stare, not just at Kenny whose cheeky freckled face was one enormous grin; but the rest of the class too, all filled with a mixture of excitement and triumph, as they always loved it when they discovered something personal about a teacher.

At last Andrew spoke, anxious to stem this outburst before it went totally out of control.

'As usual you're talking rubbish!' he said, filling his reply with contempt. 'Miss Seymour and I have nothing to do with each other; where did you get hold of that idea?'

'Where?' said Kenny standing up. 'Why, it's common knowledge! Everyone knows you've been after her so we was just asking, an' you 'aven't yet replied, 'ave you 'ad it off with 'er yet?'

This last piece of offensiveness seemed to be a signal to the rest; the brief silence that followed Kenny's was succeed in turn by desk moving. At first the kids moved them slowly but carefully together, but gradually they quickened the pace until soon the whole room was overwhelmed by wave upon wave of movement.

Andrew meanwhile had been staring at Kenny as though hypnotised; the boy was moving his desk with one hand while he made obscene gestures with the other. Suddenly something snapped in Andrew's brain.

'You disgusting creature!' he gasped, rushing towards him. He caught hold of the boy and dragged him from his desk, giving him at the same time an almighty slap on the side of the head.

'Fuckin' bastard!' yelled the boy, more in shock than pain. 'I'll report you, I'll get you sacked for that!'

'Good!' panted Andrew; he dragged the boy to the door, opening it with his free hand, and launched him out of the room into the yard. Then, slamming the door shut, he turned to face the continuing pandemonium.

A couple of girls, old enemies of Andrew, had started a fight, the bigger of them having her victim pinned to a desk while she slapped her repeatedly on the face. Meantime the desk moving continued and the noise was quite unimaginable. Andrew, ignoring the desk moving for the moment, went up to the two struggling girls and dragged them violently off the desk, then they were both sent flying out of the class to join Kenny outside. And finally he caught hold of another fighting couple, boys this time, banged their heads together, and they too were thrown out.

Andrew was now at the point of total nervous and physical exhaustion, and had to lean against the blackboard, panting audibly. A great pressure bore down on his chest, and he was unable to say anything for he couldn't trust his voice to remain steady. But the expression in his eyes and face demonstrated such anger and hatred that the youngsters stared at him, now quieter and rather frightened at what their behaviour had provoked. No longer did they feel like desk moving, that was over.

It was at this point that Terry Parsons stepped into the class, quickly putting away his notebook. The kids fell completely silent as he came in, some looking guilty and ashamed.

'You may leave, Mr Makepeace,' said Parsons briskly. 'I'll deal with this; may I see you at 4 o'clock?'

Almost weeping Andrew went to the staff room, fortunately unoccupied, and he collapsed into an armchair. He knew he'd had it now, he'd lost his job, even though he wasn't aware of the huge dossier already compiled against him, and just then he wasn't in the least sorry. He didn't care a damn if he never saw those kids or this school again. All he wanted at that moment was to go back to the privacy of his flat; he didn't even want to see Diane, her least. He wanted to be well out of Passworth Community College and all it represented – for ever!

Chapter Six

'I'm afraid this is serious, Andrew,' Jones stated in neutral tones as he turned over the pages of a thick dossier lying on his desk in front of him.

At 4 o'clock as promised, Parsons had returned to the staff room and immediately ushered Andrew to the head teacher's room.

'Oh well,' Andrew was thinking. 'At least the execution will soon be over.'

Now he was facing Jones across his desk – and the dossier – and Jones was delivering the ultimatum, with Parsons a silent observer.

'I have to say,' the head teacher began smoothly, 'I have not been at all happy about your performance since you arrived.' He continued to turn over the pages of the dossier. 'I won't go into detail now, it would take too long,' he said. 'But numerous reports here testify your inability to manage the children in your classes. In addition we have received complaints from parents, and we have recently had a report from Mrs Reynolds your former landlady about your behaviour *outside* the school.' Jones paused. 'It's not good enough! We shall have to hold an enquiry into all this, culminating in your disgraceful behaviour this afternoon when you laid hands on at least five of your pupils! Have you anything to say?' he asked, waiting a moment as a matter of form. Andrew shook his head, knowing it was pointless for him to make any comment, the whole affair being neatly cut and dried in the thick folder on the desk.

'You need not come to school after today until we advise you,' Jones went on. 'You are suspended, at the moment on full pay, but if it is decided at the Board meeting you do not merit it, this pay may be reduced – or possibly terminated.' Jones stopped again, going on to say slowly and finally, 'That'll be all, Andrew, I'm sorry it's come to this...'

Andrew left Jones' room, still in silence, shutting the door behind him without looking back. Tears pricked at his eyelids but in a way he felt more relieved than anything else; this would probably be the last time he was to see Passworth Community College, for which blessing he thanked

God most sincerely. As for Diane, he didn't think he could bear to see her again either. She might telephone him, she was bound to hear all of this, but he was determined to be politely evasive and not see her, he was sure she'd understand and accept this.   .

He debated whether to hand in his notice prior to the enquiry but decided against it; let them dismiss him! he thought bitterly. Why should they have the satisfaction of an enforced resignation? He'd attend the hearing, listen to the muck they'd been piling up for nearly a term, and then, before they let the axe drop, he'd have his own say.

He had clearly planned in his mind the shape this reply would take, about the corruption in the school, the hypocrisy, the double standards, and the devious spying and tale bearing that permeated the place. This would get him nowhere, he realised that, but at least his resentment, his sense of unfairness would be off his chest, and they hadn't got rid of him without some retaliation. Having decided all these points, Andrew felt a lot better, almost happy, and he actually looked forward to the hearing with a sort of martyr's joy.

Surprisingly enough, Diane didn't telephone, Andrew was glad about that, for he didn't have to make excuses not to see her. When the phone did ring at last it was three days later at 9 am; he had more than half a mind not to answer for he was pretty certain it'd be not Diane but Jones informing him when the hearing was to be held. He answered in the end, deciding what the hell? He might just as well go ahead and get the miserable business over with.

'Hullo,' he muttered.

'Arthur Jones here; is Mr Makepeace available?'

'Speaking.'

'I've good news for you, Andrew,' Jones went on. 'But I'd prefer you to come to school so I can tell you personally...'

Andrew shook his head. Good news? What good news could there possibly be – at least for him? What on earth was going on? He remained silent, completely baffled, and Jones raised his voice a little to check he was still there.

'Did you hear me, Andrew?' he squeaked.

'Yes, but I don't understand; what d'you mean, "good news"?'

'It's a bit awkward on the phone,' said Jones. 'But I can say this; will you accept my apologies for having disturbed you, and could you come and see me as soon as possible?'

"Apologies"? This was becoming increasingly bizarre; by now Andrew was longing to discover what was going on. Furious though he was with Jones and reluctant even to listen to any apology, he had to go and see him, if only to discover what had caused this complete U turn... So without any further questions he agreed to be at the school at 11 o'clock that morning, and then attempted to get ready in some sort of calm fashion. One and a half hours later, shaved and reasonably smart, he was knocking at Jones' door, still agog with curiosity.

'Come in, come in!' cried Jones, as Andrew entered; he leapt up and went to the cupboard at the back. 'Would you like a sherry?' he oozed. 'Sorry I've only a medium...'

Dumbly Andrew nodded at this incredible, fantastic turn of events, and while he sipped sherry, he stared at Jones' thin bearded face and waited for an explanation.

'Lovely!' said Jones, smacking his lips in appreciation. 'Straight from George Seymour's cellar; some beautiful sherries he's got, I must say!' He continued to smile ingratiatingly while Andrew waited in silence. 'Now then,' Jones said, feeling he ought at last to come to the point. 'As I said on the phone, Andrew, I have some good news for you...' He paused, looking slightly less comfortable.

'Yes?' said Andrew, sensing a prompt was necessary.

'It's all very simple,' Jones went on with a brave attempt at nonchalance. 'Terry Parsons and I have discussed in detail the incident in your class the other day, and we have decided that you were in no way to blame for it. The children's behaviour was quite offensive, they themselves have admitted that, and you were completely justified in taking action...'

Andrew was staring at Jones in open disbelief. What was all this? How could this man who three days ago had been after his blood now be apologising and eating humble pie with apparent relish? It couldn't be happening, Andrew was certain of that; in two minutes he would wake up and find out this was just some extraordinary dream. For the moment however, he would play along with Jones if only to discover whether this dream had any reality.

'There are still a few things I don't follow,' Andrew said slowly. 'That dossier, for example, you told me it was full of complaints...'

'Did I? I think you misunderstood me,' Jones smiled. 'All teachers here have personal files, this is yours. It's no worse than many others, and for a beginner, it's not bad at all...'

'Oh,' Andrew sighed, wondering in spite of himself, whether his confused state after 4H had caused him to believe things to be worse than they were. 'But what about Mrs Reynolds?'

'Ah, Mrs Reynolds,' said Jones smoothly. 'I spoke to her yesterday, and she admitted that her rules are a little too ... rigid?'

'They are!' agreed Andrew with emphasis.

'So really,' Jones continued, still smiling. 'I don't think there's any more to discuss. I'm only sorry the problem arose in the first place and glad we now have it nicely settled.' Jones got up, the picture of good humour, a hand stretched for Andrew to shake. 'Goodbye,' he said. 'Thank you for taking it so well. You can resume teaching tomorrow, if that's all right, you'll need this afternoon, I expect, to get things straight. I'm sure you must still be disturbed by this unpleasantness. Have an evening out and relax, dear boy!'

The interview heralded a new era for Andrew; the next day he could hardly believe his classes were the same as previously for even 4H seemed to have become enchanted. The kids' behaviour was perfect, their attention so concentrated Andrew could actually hear into the next classroom, something he'd never experienced before, not even on his first day at the school.

His friendship with Diane was now able to continue as before – after the three day gap. She explained she'd been called away without notice to an education conference in Birmingham, which was why she'd not telephoned him during that time. Andrew was in fact relieved by all this; he had no desire to talk about that period of time, and was pleased she'd been away when his classroom drama had occurred. He did mention even so how happy he was his classes had suddenly improved – at which Diane, almost unaccountably, seemed little surprised.

'I always thought you'd win in the end,' she remarked. 'I'm glad to be proved right.'

Andrew looked at her a bit more closely, wondering at the lack of astonishment; he didn't pursue things however, content this time to allow sleeping dogs to lie undisturbed.

They weren't allowed to remain thus for very long, unfortunately, Andrew's fellow teachers saw to that! They soon began a campaign of whispering and gossip, that he didn't notice at first but rapidly reached the stage where they were not satisfied to talk about him behind his back, instead carping almost openly. In the end when the word '*bootlicker*' came to Andrew's ears as he was entering the staff room one lunch time, it proved the last straw, and he rounded on Frank Stephens, his German colleague who'd said it, asking him directly what he meant. The half dozen teachers in the group fell silent but Stephens did not look in the least embarrassed.

'What did I mean, Andrew?' he repeated innocently, 'Don't you know what a '*bootlicker*' is?'

'You were talking about me and I want to know why...'

'Listen, young man,' said Stephens reprovingly, although he was only a couple of years older than Andrew. 'If you must eaves-drop, you can expect to hear things you don't like...'

'I was not eaves-dropping!"

'Assuming you really don't know what has happened, and I find that hard to believe,' Stephens continued. 'Maybe you'd better ask Diane Seymour...'

'Diane?' Andrew was filled with astonishment. 'What has she to do with it?'

'Ask her, she'll have all the facts,' said Stephen with smooth irony. 'I'm surprised she hasn't told you already.' He put a hand to his mouth to ill-conceal a smile and a titter rippled round the staff room.

Andrew turned abruptly away, his face red hot, and he set off immediately in search of Diane and an explanation of what was going on.

'Hullo!' she exclaimed as he came quickly into her class room, his face still flushed. 'What's the matter, has something upset you?'

'Everything's the matter!' Andrew said bitterly. 'And you know why! Listen, I must speak to you but not here, tonight, at my place...'

She stared at him, suddenly pale.

'You know then,' she whispered.

'I half know – but I want the whole truth, not just innuendos! That

bastard Stephens called me a *'bootlicker'*, I must know why!'
'The envious swine!' Diane muttered. 'All right, darling, I suppose you had to know. But don't worry, it's okay, it really is! There's nothing at all you need be ashamed of...'

So that evening at Andrew's flat, the whole story came out; and what Diane didn't describe in detail, he was able to picture with technicolor vividness. Of course there'd been no conference in Birmingham, Diane was so distraught by the news Andrew faced the chop, she couldn't bring herself to speak to him until matters were settled. For her it all began the evening following Andrew's confrontation with 4H and Jones; like many a holocaust it began fairly quietly.

The telephone rang in George Seymour's study at Carnforth Grange; it was 6.30 so he was preparing for supper with his customary libation, a glass of brandy.

'Jones here,' came the voice of the head teacher, and the the whole story was unfolded – in suitably melodramatic fashion. George said nothing while Jones held forth, he knew the value of the occasional silence, and Jones' eloquence eventually petered out.

'I'd like to see you at school first thing tomorrow morning,' George then said in level tones. 'Have you repeated this to anyone else on the Board?'

'Of course not. I'm naturally informing you first...'

'Does the Town Hall know of any of the previous incidents?'

'No. I felt it best to wait until Makepeace had been given a reasonable amount of time, after all he might have established himself. But this afternoon's incident proves he isn't able to...'

'A reasonable amount of rope to hang him,' George was thinking; aloud he said: 'I'll see you at 10 o'clock; meantime, talk to no one about this, no one! Will Makepeace be coming in to school tomorrow?'

'No, I said he was suspended on full pay for the moment.'

'Good,' George replied. 'See you tomorrow.'

George's next action was to discuss with Diane these developments, it wasn't a task he looked forward to; in order to avoid spoiling his dinner, he postponed the evil moment until afterwards. Then just as Diane was slipping from the dining room to phone Andrew, he intercepted her and asked her to come to the library.

'Why?' she said suspiciously, for she knew George only invited anyone to his sanctum in situations of emergency.

'I'll tell you there,' George answered, leading the way, Diane followed not very willingly and looked towards her mother to check her reaction. She was sitting very still at the end of the table and smiled a little in an attempt at reassuring her, but she was content to keep silent for the moment.

'What is it, Father?' Diane asked anxiously as soon as the library door was closed behind them. George didn't answer for the moment, he was occupied pouring himself a glass of brandy and lighting a cigar.

'It's quite simple,' he replied at last, sitting down with each in either hand. 'Your boy friend faces the sack!'

'The sack? But why?'

'He struck five of the kids in one of his classes.'

'Five? Oh no! I can't believe it! Which class?'

'4H.'

'But they're awful, the worst in the school, you know they are!' Diane sighed 'Do you know why he hit them?'

'Jones didn't mention that unimportant detail,' said her father ironically. 'He simply recited what young Andrew did; apparently he struck one boy and threw him out of the class, threw out two girls, and knocked the heads of a couple of boys together before he threw *them* out.'

'And I bet they deserved it, the little swine! It's unfair, Father! Andrew's had one hell of a time with those kids, I don't blame him for getting sick of them in the end. He never had any support either, Jones has been waiting for this to happen just so he could get rid of him!'

'Yes, I did know that,' said George thoughtfully. 'He told me the day I backed him for the job, he was certain I was making a mistake; I suppose he's pleased to be proved right. And he *is* right, lass, we've got to admit it, Andrew doesn't fit into your school at all.'

'Neither do I, Father, if we're honest; I'd have had problems without my position...'

'But that's the point, in a nutshell!' George exclaimed excitedly. 'You're my daughter, he may be somebody in Surrey that he should never have left, but he's nobody round here, you can't alter that!'

'Why can't you alter it?' demanded Diane. 'He's nobody at present but he could be somebody if you'd give him your backing! Why haven't you up till now?'

'Because I can't go backing every young fool I come across,' snapped George. 'Jones is in charge of that school, not me...'

'But Andrew's not "every young fool", he's my friend!' cried Diane. 'You've got to help him, especially now, please, Father!'

George looked at her for a while, still standing in front of him, her eyes flashing; he drew on his cigar, took a sip of brandy, and knew he was beaten – as usual. He smiled a little because in truth he wouldn't much have enjoyed winning this battle.

'I'm speaking to Jones tomorrow, it's already arranged,' he said at last. 'He's promised meantime to keep this under wraps until I've seen him.'

'Oh, Father!'

'But if your boy friend lets you down after this, I'll want to know the reason why!'

Jones was lucky he knew nothing of what was lying in store for the morrow – or he'd have got as little sleep that night as Andrew did. When George entered Jones' office at 9 am prompt, the enormous dossier was lying on his desk with the head teacher almost hidden behind it. He rose quickly as George advanced, and made for his wine cupboard.

'A sherry?' he invited affably.

'Don't bother,' George replied sitting down. 'You may not feel like drinking in a moment...'

Jones ceased to look so cheerful. 'What's the matter?' he asked. 'Has something happened?'

'No, and it's not going to, at least not to young Makepeace,' the little man stated with a grim smile.

Jones gasped in disbelief, almost unable to speak.

'But I told you what he's done!' he stuttered. 'He assaulted five of his pupils, including girls!'

'I know what he did, and I also know what you didn't do, back him, give him the support he needed, it's your standard procedure for getting rid of someone you don't like.'

'He's had every support available!'

'Come off, it, Jones, look at that file, does it look like belonging to someone you're keen on?'

'There's nothing in that file that's invented, Makepeace himself would admit to what's in it, but he didn't even talk about it, just accepted what I said like a lamb! He knows he's no use here!'

'He thinks he's no use because you've undermined his confidence. Now you've got to reestablish it – and quickly!'

'I can't, it's out of the question! This is my school! We should never have taken Makepeace in the first place...'

'You had the chance to veto him then – and you didn't take it, now you've got to support him!'

'But it'd create a precedent, can't you see that? I know your daughter's interested in him, but there's a limit...'

'I'll be honest with you,' said George blandly. 'If Diane wasn't so keen on young Makepeace, you could sack him tomorrow! Not because I think you're right, in fact I know you're as twisted as a cork screw...'

'Thanks.'

'But I can't go bailing out every young fool who gets himself into trouble. Diane however makes a difference; she likes the lad, might even love him, and I can't have my daughter involved with someone who's a victim of your little schemes!'

'He's not a victim, you agreed he shouldn't be here!'

'All right, he's not best suited to this place, but who is? Only a handful of your staff I know for a fact; and the rest, you for example, stay behind closed doors while war rages outside. Listen, Jones,' George said, his voice hardening. 'Andrew's got to be reestablished *now,* and given proper status.'

'That'll take some doing considering what he's done,' Jones muttered sulkily.

'Come off it, you old hypocrite, what has he done? Given half a dozen kids the treatment they deserved – and were begging for!'

'But their parents, it won't be your door they'll come banging on, it'll be mine! And worse still they might complain to the Town Hall, and you know that reflects against me.'

'That's why we've got to act quickly, nip this business in the bud! The kids know Makepeace isn't in today, they'll be assuming they've got him on toast; their parents will be eagerly waiting for the axe to fall on yet another teacher's bleeding neck! We can cash in on that, *you* can take the intitiative, get 4H together this morning and frighten the hell out of them...'

'What'll I say?' asked Jones in sullen resignation.

'You know as well as well as I do!' George grinned. 'Just make it clear that if Andrew's not given a fair deal, there's going to be a sudden increase in redundancies at Passworth Electrical Engineering, that'll fix 'em, and it'll fix any parental complaints too. They know I mean what I say, I've done it before!' With his usual awkwardness, George got up. 'Is that clear?' he said at the door. 'I'm promising you, Jones, and I mean this as well, if I don't hear better things re. Andrew from tomorrow, you'll be for the chop too, Town Hall or no Town Hall!'

Andrew sat very still after Diane had told him all that; he could picture clearly Jones' ultimatum to 4H, their silence, their capitulation. He had no conscience about that, they deserved to be intimidated just as they'd intimidated him. But he was revolted by Jones' hypocrisy, by the fact that only George Seymour's threats and enforcement had made him intercede on Andrew's behalf. The whole thing stank! Diane stirred a little, uneasily, seeing only too well what was passing through his mind.

And worse was still to come! Andrew could also visualise himself under even more obligation, not just to Diane but to the whole Seymour clan. He had nothing against George personally, he couldn't help admiring the man, his energy and dynamism; but he didn't want to be owned body and soul by anyone or any family. He had a very real fear just then that if he accepted all this, there'd be a price to pay, and he was by no means certain it was a price he could afford.

'You had to know,' Diane sighed at last. 'But I wish you didn't! I'll go now,' she said more briskly. 'I've talked too much anyhow, you need time to think, to get used to the situation, I'm in the way, just now.'

She stood up and Andrew stirred, glad she'd made that move.

'Yes,' he muttered. 'Thanks for telling me, it must have been tough for you. And thank your father for saving my job...'

'That was nothing,' Diane smiled. 'He enjoyed putting Jones in his place.'

She went out, and when the door closed behind her, Andrew heaved a sigh of relief. But as he stared round his flat, he almost wished he was back with Mrs Reynolds. He had a strong suspicion he'd escaped from one prison, only to exchange it for another.

Chapter Seven

LIFE for Andrew after that became kaleidoscopic; the teaching was marvellous, his friendship with Diane less so, for there loomed continuously over them the shadow of the Seymour empire. Although Andrew rarely went to Carnforth Grange, entertaining Diane in his flat or taking her to places roundabout, he was never able to forget he owed his present good fortune to her.

Ironically he was happier at school than out of it. Even in the staff room things had improved, as after a while his colleagues felt they'd better treat him with at least the appearance of cordiality; you never knew, this fellow *might* be promoted and then use his increased powers to settle a few scores.

But Andrew's classes puzzled him. He actually enjoyed them and couldn't understand why, if the kids only co-operated for fear of reprisals. He was starting to know them better as individuals, and they often talked to him about themselves, their families, and their problems. He learnt how much they'd hated being moved from their previous homes in streets and districts where they'd been born. They resented having to go to a strange school and were determined to make life tough for anyone who let them. They'd found Andrew easy meat, and got a perverse pleasure from torturing him.

Now things were different. The worm had turned at last, and when the kids attacked Andrew on that memorable occasion, they found not putty yielding to their pressure, but a brick wall that hurt their knuckles, badly. After that they did the only thing they could, they treated the wall with respect. And gradually they found the wall was human, had feelings, and was something they could even like.

'You're not so bad, sir,' said Kenny one day. 'We thought you was a real tosser at first...'

'But not so much now, eh?' Andrew smiled.

'Nah, you proved you could be hard...'

Andrew nodded – but thought cynically of the true state of affairs. The fact was he'd been within an inch of the sack, and had it not been for Diane... He shook his head furiously at the thought, he had to stop thinking of these things, they were foolish, neurotic, the kids admitted he was accepted now, so why worry about obligations?

Once Andrew was able to persuade himself he had no reason for guilt, his feelings for Diane immediately grew stronger, and the Seymour shadow more distant. It was only a matter of time before the pair returned almost to the *status quo* prior to the 4H confrontation, when just being together had been idyllic; the difference now was that school had become a pleasure. Andrew only wished this blissful state could go on for ever.

Time unfortunately put paid to that. Already the autumn term was almost over, and Diane was trying to persuade Andrew to leave his flat and stay at Carnforth Grange for Christmas. In fact she was hinting he could move in with them completely. It would be a lot more convenient for him than the flat where a good part of the time he was on his own and having to look after himself. At the Grange he would have everything – including Diane – on tap!

Andrew drew the line at that – he wanted at least the appearance of independence and his flat provided him with that. Much though he liked Diane he welcomed rather than otherwise the gaps between their meetings, they gave him time to think and try to establish his sense of proportion. But his main reason for refusing to move into the Grange was his strong suspicion it would be the prelude to his engagement to Diane and subsequent marriage; and Andrew was far from ready to contemplate such a drastic development as total absorption by the clan Seymour.

As far as Christmas was concerned, Andrew managed to get out of having to stay with them by pleading his family as an excuse. He hadn't seen them since he went up to Passworth last September and his letters were somewhat infrequent. He had phoned his mother a few times, especially now his life at the school had improved, also about Diane though he said nothing about her background. So all in all, he felt he ought to spend Christmas in Camberford and keep his family more or less up to date about his activities.

He enjoyed Christmas at home; he was able to relax, be himself, and regale his family with for once a story of success instead of failure. They were duly surprised – and impressed, especially Deborah, his sister.

'I never thought you'd make it!' she exclaimed. 'And a girl friend too

– what's she like?'

'Beautiful with long fair hair...'

'A blonde, you lucky beast! You must get her to come and see us...'

Andrew said something evasive about that; he had no intention of introducing Diane to his family, it would be almost as involving as a move into Carnforth Grange.

It was his mother who worried him most for she had always the knack of digging out his secrets. But this time she seemed less curious than usual; she could see he'd grown up a lot since last September, and so she felt reluctant to ask too many questions in case he thought she was invading his privacy. She decided to wait until he approached her; instead she had a word with her husband.

'Andrew's changed quite a bit,' she said.

'I'd be worried if he hadn't,' Peter answered somewhat absently from the depths of his newspaper. 'He needed to change.'

'That's not what I meant, dear,' Catherine said patiently. 'I think he's got something on his mind.'

'What for instance?' Peter asked, now looking up.

'Oh I don't know. This Diane perhaps. He's very cagey about her.'

Peter returned to his paper. 'If there's anything amiss, we'll hear about it soon enough! Don't meet your troubles halfway,' he grunted.

So Andrew had no awkward questions – from his parents at least – only from Deborah, and he was a past master at fending her off, so that was no problem.

He returned to his Passworth flat and the new term, refreshed and relaxed, but unfortunately no more decided about his future. For the moment all he wanted was to keep things ticking over and in this agreeable if aimless fashion, the next few months passed rapidly by. At the end of them, the spring drew the pair back to their Pennine rambles and late evening walks but Andrew gave no indication to Diane of how he saw their future together.

She meantime had grown a little less happy about their relationship. She was certain now she loved Andrew and wanted to marry him, but realising her position as the daughter of a millionaire was still an obstacle, she'd gradually been inviting him more often to Carnforth Grange in the hope that custom would breed usage, so to speak. To sugar the pill she often asked him to her room to make love so that through enjoying every freedom, he might be tempted to leave his flat and move in with her.

Unfortunately none of these ploys worked, and at last Diane was beginning to get, if not impatient, certainly less serene than before. She now felt she had to show her hand more unmistakably and maybe exert a little pressure on her reluctant swain...

Andrew noticing that, began to panic. He still found George Seymour intimidating and Mary too much the *grande dame* in spite of her charm. To think seriously of them as in-laws was something he couldn't face, not yet, maybe not ever. And as Diane began to make her desires more obvious by attitude and even words, Andrew took steps to withdraw in the opposite direction.

He used the periods he had to himself in order to seek fresh company. He was now on better terms with a number of his colleagues and he visited them from time to time. He even went to dinner with Jones on one occasion, something he'd never have thought possible six months ago. And on a Wednesday evening when Diane was busy at an all-ladies social, Andrew made the most of his opportunity by visiting the Green Parrot to see if Helen was there.

The fact was during these last weeks, he'd often been thinking of her and wondering how she was. Increasingly he'd been picturing her pale anaemic face, her large dark eyes, and that melancholy sensual mouth; just the thought of her aroused him. Since that fateful evening when Mrs Reynolds had almost caught them in the act, Andrew had never tried to contact her or go near her district; but now his relationship with Diane had become a little less benign, he decided a visit the Green Parrot might be a good idea.

As he went into the pub, he felt with a pang how little it had changed – and in a way how much he'd missed it. It was still friendly and cheerful, filled with young people all enjoying themselves, and it was as though Andrew had been there only yesterday.

And in her regular corner sat Helen, chatting animatedly to the same girl she'd been with nearly six months ago when Andrew approached her for the first time.

But suddenly he had a moment of terror – he wanted badly to turn round and get out of the place; he no longer had any desire to speak to Helen, far from it, he was sure it would be a mistake. But in his moments of indecision it was too late to back out, for the girl had seen him and a look of recognition came immediately to her face.

'Well, hello, stranger,' she said with her usual mocking smile that was already giving him the old familiar tingle all over. She wore tonight a black outfit of trousers and sweater, both so tight the smallest movement revealed her curves, and he couldn't help staring at her as though hypnotised.

'What happened to you?' Helen went on languidly, drawing at her long cigarette with slow deliberation. 'I looked for you but they told me you'd moved out...'

'Yes,' Andrew said uncomfortably. 'It's a long story.'

'Has it a happy ending?'

'Can I get you a drink?' said Andrew quickly. 'And your friend?'

'Sandra.' said the plumpish, pleasant faced girl. 'No, thanks, I'm just off, my boy friend's meeting me outside in a few minutes.' She got up with a smile. 'Glad you're back, Andy,' she said pointedly. 'Helen missed you. Cheers!' She went off without a backward glance, leaving the pair silent for the moment.

'A vodka and orange?' Andrew offered, the girl nodded acceptance and blew out some more smoke.

'I suppose it's not on to go to your place,' she said with a grin. 'Our last encounter wasn't too lucky. What happened anyway? Did the old bat throw you out?'

'Oh no,' said Andrew hastily. 'She moaned but that was all. I only left because I found a better place.' He told her where it was.

'Posh, eh?' Helen exclaimed, sipping her drink. 'So that was why you dropped me – I wasn't good enough for you. What made you come back here then? Your smart lady give you the push?'

Andrew blushed at Helen's perception. 'I'm sorry,' he muttered. 'I'll explain it all later if you like...'

'Suit yourself!' Helen said coolly. 'But if your place is out...'

'It is a bit far...'

'You'll have to be satisfied with staying here. Unless ...'

'Unless what?'

'We went to my place...'

'Could we?' asked Andrew surprised. 'I mean, they wouldn't mind – your family...'

'Me Mam won't bite you!' Helen snapped irritably. 'She's not like your bleeding landlady. And I do have me own room!'

'All right,' Andrew agreed, wondering what lay ahead. 'How far's your place?' he asked.

'Near enough, said Helen briefly, slipping off her seat. 'Come on, finish your drink and let's go.' Immediately she made for the door with Andrew in train, ignoring the grins and nods from her acquaintances. 'Thank God we're out of there!' she cried as they stood outside the Parrot. 'Too much gossip by half from that lot!'

They quickly set off and in about ten minutes arrived at Helen's house. It was quite a superior council house, a semi of solid red brick and with an attractive garden; it could have been a lot worse, Andrew thought. Pity it looked a bit neglected thanks to a shortage of cash... Helen let herself in with her yale and they were standing in the little hall with a narrow staircase rising above them. They could hear sounds from the back of the house, and in a moment Helen's mother opened the dining room door and came in.

How nice she looked, Andrew took to her at once, but he couldn't help feeling a deep pity for the air of ingrained fatigue that pervaded her whole being. She looked as if her frail shoulders had borne some excessive pressure for years and she had only that to look forward to in the future. In spite of all this she was still able to give a welcoming smile to her guest.

'This is Andrew,' Helen said. 'You remember? I did mention him ...'

'Yes, dear,' said her mother vaguely. 'I'm sure you did. Would you like a cup of tea? It's nearly ready...'

Andrew said nothing but looked to Helen.

'Why not?' she said with a quick shrug. 'Thanks, Mam.'

They went into the crowded dining room and the couple sat down while Helen's mother made the tea in the tiny kitchen next door.

'We're a bit small, that's our main problem,' she called out. 'But we like it here, we've been in this house for nearly thirty years, since it was built in fact. When Albert – he was my husband – got his job at the foundry, this was part of the deal, brand new it was! We thought it was smashing then, we'd only just married and Helen wasn't even thought of, she didn't come for a few years when we'd put something by. We were sure our fortune was made in them days, funny how things can change so quickly, isn't it?'

She bustled in with the tea, and Andrew looked at her more closely. She was in her mid-forties and thin now, prematurely grey and worn, but still retaining a sympathetic warmth that had attracted Andrew from his first glance.

He now looked around at the colourful pictures on the walls, the plentiful cushions, and the cheerful lived-in atmosphere surrounding them.

'I like this room, Mrs...' he began.

'Curtis, dear. Yes, it *is* a nice room, we're quite proud of it. Didn't Helen tell you our name?' she continued. 'I'm surprised, but then young people are so casual these days...'

'What's in a name?' Helen said glibly. 'I don't know Andrew's come to that.'

'It's Makepeace.'

'Makepeace! It suits you...'

'Yes,' Mrs Curtis went on. 'We've been here a long time. Difficult to imagine anywhere else – even though I realise things constantly change and we don't get any younger.'

'Don't worry, Mam,' Helen said impatiently. 'I'll soon be independent – and that at least will be a relief to you.'

'Don't talk that way!' said her mother. 'You've got your education to get – we mustn't have you sitting on the shelf useless because you've no qualifications.'

'Qualifications!' Helen sighed. 'You've set your heart on them, but they're not that important, I'm sure...'

'Of course they are! If your father had been a bit better qualified...'

'Dad was perfectly qualified! It wasn't his fault they changed his job! Even if he'd had these *qualifications,* he'd still have been made redundant, I'm certain!'

'Maybe you're right,' Mrs Curtis admitted. 'Even so, you won't be any worse off with a few exam credits, you didn't get none at school! Would you like some more tea, Andrew?' she offered.

'No, thank you, that's fine,' he smiled, as Helen made a gesture towards him and began to stir.

'Come and admire my etchings,' she said, getting up. 'My room's a bit different from this.'

'A pleasure to meet you, Andrew,' Mrs Curtis smiled as he too got to his feet. 'I hope to see you again soon.'

'So do I,' Andrew replied. 'Thank you for the tea and the talk; it was very interesting...'

Moments later he and Helen had climbed the narrow stairs and they were standing in her little den.

It was completely in shadow. The grey curtain at the small window was drawn across, and almost diaphanous, its sole purpose clearly to subdue the light to a subtle dimness so that all the objects in the room were reduced to suggestive shapes.

'Like it?' asked Helen, standing close to Andrew, her face almost touching his. She put out her tongue and licked his ear, he immediately felt himself aroused by the warm wetness.

'It's different,' he muttered huskily. 'Have you a light – I mean, do you always keep the room as dim as this?'

In answer Helen stooped to the low table next to the bed and switched on the little lamp; Andrew was amazed at the hypnotic effect of the multi-coloured walls, a rich variety of shades in blue, green, orange, and yellow.

'Marvellous!' he sighed. 'Was this your idea?'

'Not quite. One of my boy friends at the College was an artist; he told me of the stimulating effect of colour and shade.'

'He was right; it definitely turns *me* on!'

'Not too much, I hope,' grinned Helen teasingly. 'Have a seat, I want to hear what you've been up to for the past six months.' She sat with him on the bed.

So Andrew gave the girl a version of the truth, carefully avoiding all mention of Diane. Instead he implied his absence was caused by their last encounter at Mrs Reynolds' establishment; it had so confused him, he just needed space to sort himself out.

'So there was no other girl?' said Helen teasingly. 'There must have been, or how could you afford to move to the district you're living in now? You told me you couldn't afford it, and I believed you. Come clean, Andrew,' she said challengingly. 'Someone's helping you, and it's either a rich girl friend, or your parents who I know are stacked. Which is it, come on, tell me, I must know...'

Andrew couldn't tell an outright lie. 'It's not my parents,' he began.

'A girl friend then. Congratulations!'

'It was nothing serious, I promise,' he lied. 'That was why I had to see you again; I couldn't forget you...'

'It must have been serious on her side,' said Helen. 'Noone's going to pay out quite a lot of cash for no reason, I'm certain of that.'

"Oh she's loaded, at least her father is,' said Andrew. 'She teaches at my school and she felt sorry for me...'

'Very convenient,' said Helen cynically. 'So out of pity she set you up in a luxury flat. I don't believe it, not in the pity anyhow... The girl loves you, you bloody fool, and now you're chucking her. Not only are you a bastard, Andy," whispered Helen again licking his ear. 'You're a bloody stupid bastard. Go back to her, she wants you, and I can offer you nothing. Nothing that is but sex.' She put a hand on his thigh and stroked it, enjoying the knowledge he was quite aroused.

'I don't love her,' Andrew protested. 'I liked her, I like her, but that's not love. I think I could love you,' he sighed.

Helen stopped playing with him and moved away.

'You don't know what you're saying,' she snapped. 'I'm nothing, I'm just trash, and trash without money. Go back to your rich girl – if she'll take you. I have nothing...'

'I don't want to go back to her,' Andrew sighed. 'I hate her wealth. I felt she was buying me with that flat, I hated it. I wish I could move out, even back to Ma Reynolds, really...' His mouth was close to hers, and this time Helen didn't move away, instead she kissed him, gently at first then with increasing passion until his senses were quite overwhelmed. All he could think of or want was Helen, and almost without realising it he was in her arms, their two bodies as one.

Chapter Eight

IN spite of Andrew's protestations to Helen that his relationship with the other girl was a thing of the past, in practice this was very far from the case. When it came to it, he was quite unwilling to leave Diane, not only because of his many obligations to her, but even if he wasn't passionately in love, he still held for her a very strong affection. She'd been his first friend at Passworth, and it was no easy matter to relinquish a girl who loved him and whose only fault was her family background. In addition Andrew was still enjoying the fruits of his relationship with her, and he knew deep inside the only way he could leave Diane would be to give up everything else at the same time.

But he found very tedious the double game he was forced to play. Anyone who has tried to keep one girl satisfied will realise that to keep two in that state is impossible, and so it was with Andrew. Fortunately Diane knew nothing of Helen's existence, but even so she was becoming increasingly keen for him to stop sitting on the fence and give himself to her entirely, in the shape of a formal engagement... When he persisted in his evasiveness, the tension between them grew, until only Andrew's quiet temperament prevented a wholesale row breaking out. Meantime Helen constantly teased him about his "posh lady friend" and although he was pretty sure her actual identity was a secret, he couldn't help wondering how much Helen guessed for he'd learned to respect the insight behind her mocking smile.

He went to her house on Wednesdays Diane's social night, and got to know Tom, her lively younger brother. He was shortish for his age about fifteen, thick-set and fair, quite different from Helen. Probably he was like his father, Andrew guessed. He was quiet in manner – until he got onto politics, his favourite subject, and then there was no stopping him, he'd talk for hours given the chance. He was a red hot Young Socialist and went to every political meeting for miles around, shouting support if it was his party and heckling furiously the opposition.

'The bouncers have thrown me out at least a dozen times in the past year,' he grinned. 'I'm a marked man, – and I have the bruises to prove it.'

'Won't they stop you going in?' Andrew asked curiously.

'I go to different places – they never remember...'

'You just be careful!' Andrew warned with good humour. He admired Tom's positive attitude to life even if he didn't agree with the lad. He had no interest in politics at all, voting Conservative like his parents simply because it had never occurred to him to vote otherwise. Now to hear young Tom ranting on, expressing ideas that would have horrified his family, made a refreshing change. And through all their talk, Helen said nothing, she just sat there quietly – and smiled.

'Come to the rally, Andrew,' urged the boy one time. 'You'll love it – Mike Dartle's speaking...'

Andrew shook his head doubtfully. The rally in the Town Hall that night was on unemployment – and though he was tempted, he didn't like to agree straight off, not without consulting Helen anyhow. He looked towards her.

'What d'you think?' he asked. 'Do you ever go to these things?'

'Rarely, I'm no politico! But I'll come this time if you're going, I like Mike Dartle...'

So did Andrew. Who could fail to be attracted to that bluff, tough, out-spoken Yorkshireman, shadow employment minister, but just as liable to attack his own party as the Conservatives if he felt it called upon. He was one of the best tub-thumpers in the business and with him on the platform, there'd not be an empty seat in the place. Andrew pointed this out.

'There's always standing room!' Tom replied. 'And anyhow there'll be plenty of loud-speakers onto the street. Just to be there and drink in the atmosphere'll be great, I promise!'

'Okay!' grinned Andrew. 'We'll go!' He looked at Helen who smiled back.

Half an hour later they were at the Town hall. There was no room inside, but as Tom had promised there were plenty of loud-speakers and the three of them stood in the street, completely surrounded by hundreds of people. They were mostly men in cloth caps, many obviously on the dole as they had anxious expressions and listened intently to what was going on.

The man bellowing away was the chairman for he named the speakers lined up, going on at great length especially about Mike Dartle, and on the whole, Andrew thought, he had a large number of words but not much else.

'A bit boring this!' Andrew whispered to Tom.

'Don't worry, Dartle's on pretty soon. He'll have to get away early so they're bringing him on first. This chap's going on because Dartle hasn't arrived yet.'

'How d'you know?' demanded Andrew. 'We're not even in there!'

'It's always the same! The main speaker arrives ten minutes late – or more – and he has to dash off straight after. Poor old Forster has to fill in – that's him now, he's all right, can't help being a bore.."

Andrew carried on listening. There were a great many generalisations and promises, all shouted very loudly, and he hoped more and more Dartle would arrive soon. But suddenly he was aware of Helen, standing close behind him. He looked round and smiled, glad she was there, sorry he'd forgotten about her for the moment. She started to lean against him which Andrew liked; still she said nothing.

At last Dartle arrived, and immediately the atmosphere changed – completely. For a start there was furious clapping inside the building which came through the loud-speakers in a roar, and soon everyone was cheering and shouting madly. It was fantastic! Andrew couldn't resist joining in, and clapped louder than anyone. It was marvellous!

Then the speech – it made Andrew's hair stand on end! He felt: that's it, I'm going to become a bloody Socialist! I can *never* go back to Diane now, or Carnforth Grange! He wondered with a shock if he could even go back to Camberford and his own family ... You could hardly hear any words, the noise was so great, applause breaking out every two or three minutes, but that didn't matter, it was the atmosphere that counted, as Tom had said.

Andrew tried to listen; he heard words such as "*brotherhood*", "*fight*", "*win*", and there was talk of the election bringing a miracle for all. Captivated and overwhelmed by the occasion, Andrew continued to applaud, much to Tom's amusement, and he shouted through the din:

'Good, eh? I said you'd like it!'

'It's smashing!' Andrew yelled back. 'I'm glad I came!'

The speech went on and the atmosphere continued to be electric; Andrew's hands were sore with clapping. But sudddenly in the midst of the excitement he was aware of something else, it was Helen!

That evening in addition to a long black skirt, she was wearing a tight sweater, red in honour of the occasion, and she was pressing her breasts against Andrew's back, as she was standing just behind him. She continued to press, and he couldn't help being aware she had nothing on under her sweater, and her nipples were erect. He wriggled in aroused frustration, and turned to see Helen's smile more tantalising than ever.

'Enjoying it?' she whispered in his ear. 'The speech I mean.' She giggled and Andrew continued to tingle as her fingers caressed his thigh. He moaned softly in sympathy with the continual stroking, the speech came to an end, and there burst forth from the hall a deafening riot of applause, at which Andrew sighed in sympathy, his body now quite relaxed.

'Feeling better, darling?' Helen mockingly asked; Andrew said nothing, but he didn't need to.

'Shall we go?' said Tom. 'We've had the best, there's nothing more to come.' Andrew agreed whole heartedly...

They turned but before they could escape from the morass, a loud high-pitched voice rang in their ears; it was one of Andrew's pupils, a small cheeky lad with carroty hair.

'Hello, *sir!*' he shouted, and with a laugh turned away, and at once he was lost in the crowd.

'4H!' murmured Andrew, looking after him. 'Nice lad!' He'd been one of his chief tormentors not long ago.

That evening heralded a real break-through for Andrew and Helen; from then on he felt quite committed to her. He ceased even to speak to Diane at school, avoiding her when possible, and he longed increasingly to leave his flat, associating it with her. She said nothing but Andrew couldn't miss the anguish on her face; still he hardened himself.

'To hell with it, I didn't ask for this flat! It was her idea – like my job!'

But uneasily he wondered how long it would be till she told her father. He was pretty sure she'd said nothing yet, but any time ... And once that happened, he had a definite feeling his secure position at school would vanish; he'd be back to how he'd been during his first term, an unwelcome foreigner. The prospect didn't bear thinking about.

In the meantime he enjoyed life with Helen, who amazed him continually with her variety of love-making. Her bedroom was the setting for their dalliance, and Mrs Curtis affected to be quite unaware anything was going on. She always treated Andrew with natural friendliness and he became very fond of her.

But Helen was incredible. She would tease Andrew to distraction even while out with him, wearing either tight jeans and sweaters that showed her body to maximum advantage; or long voluminous dresses concealing her figure completely. Their modesty however was completely destroyed when there was no one about for then she would lift up her skirts giving Andrew an all-too brief glimpse of what was underneath...

By the time they were back in her room Andrew was quite ready to rape her as with a laugh the girl pulled him down so he could put into practice what he'd been thinking about for the past three or four hours. They would spend the rest of the evening in passionate love-making. It was only after a particularly climactic session that Andrew remembered he had quite forgotten to take any form of precautions... At least he had the honesty to mention this to Helen.

'It's a good thing I'm a bit more practical than you are, sweetheart,' said the girl, stroking his forehead with a sensual finger tip. 'I'm on the pill and have been ever since I met you last at the Green Parrot....'

'Oh!' gasped Andrew now understanding.

'You may recall I visited the loo on the way to my room...' Andrew hadn't. 'I killed two birds with one stone by taking a pill before I came upstairs.... So – as I have acted similarly this evening,' she said putting herself once more in position. 'If you have anything left in reserve, darling, I'm all yours...'

Andrew had!

This was by no means the last of Andrew's close encounters, but of course the idyllic state of affairs couldn't last for ever and Diane was the *primum mobile* behind the complete turn around in events soon to take place.

It was the first Saturday morning in August at the beginning of the summer holiday after five weeks during which Andrew had spent all his time with Helen – and seen nothing of Diane. Andrew was still in bed about 10 o'clock, having arrived back at his flat late last night after a very active evening in Helen's room.

The doorbell rang and Andrew groaned; he couldn't imagine who that might be – someone asking for money, no doubt. Cursing silently, he opened the door to see Diane standing there, more beautiful than ever, but far from happy. Andrew blushed uncomfortably and asked her in.

'Had a late night!' he mumbled. 'Sit down, I'll go and dress, I won't be a minute.'

'Don't bother,' said Diane quietly. 'I've seen you in your pyjama before – and less! I won't be long, I just want you to tell me something...'

'What?' Andrew asked, pretending ineffectively to be unaware of the situation.

'Just this, darling, why have you left me?' There was a silence as Andrew tried desperately to think of some way to answer her without telling the whole story; it was too complicated at 10 o'clcok in the morning, too complicated and messy!

'Why have you left me?' Diane repeated, still quiet as Andrew didn't answer. 'What have I done? Please tell me!'

'Nothing, nothing!' Andrew said at last. 'I'm sorry, Diane, but I've been very busy recently...'

'Busy? Too busy even to speak to me for weeks last term? Come on, you must tell me; what have I done? There must be something that has made you change...'

'No, no!' Andrew gasped. 'Of course there isn't! It's just...'

'Just what?'

Slowly, incoherently, he tried to explain it was still the same old problem that had bugged him before; his discomfort at feeling under so much obligation to Diane and her father. She listened intently, then when he had finished, she answered gently, almost sweetly.

'I love you,' she said. 'I'm sure you love me. It's foolish to let all these things you talk about come between us – and I don't think you're right even. Your position at the school for instance, you're your own man now, the kids respect you for yourself, you owe nothing to my father any more. To go on feeling guilty about that is plain foolishness...'

'Listen!' said Andrew huskily. 'If your father withdrew his support from me, do you think the kids would carry on behaving?'

'I think they would – in fact I'm certain! You can stand up now without support from anyone, you must believe that!'

Andrew shook his head unconvinced. 'I don't think so. And anyhow there's more to it than that. I've changed, my whole attitude to life's different now and I could never feel happy in the luxury you'd give me while so many people in Passworth for a start can hardly get by...'

Diane gazed at him in astonishment. How innocent and naïve he was! Was there no way she could convince him his whole attitude was ridiculous?

'Andrew,' she said at last. 'I respect and sympathise with your beliefs, but can't you see they're just not practical? All they can do in the end, is to make you no better off than the people you pity. You should know that from your kids' behaviour before.' Silence, and Diane had to go on. 'Is there nothing I can say to convince you?'

Andrew shook his head. 'Or do?'

Her hand had been resting on his thigh, she caressed him gently, and he stirred gradually becoming aroused at her sensual touch. But he shook his head as a gesture of refusal.

'No, not now,' he muttered. 'Sex is too easy, this is more complicated than sex. If sex solved everything, there'd be a good number less divorces and separations, I'm certain.'

'Well, all right,' said Diane abandoning her play. 'I agree with you about that. But sex *is* important. I mean, don't you find me sexually attractive?'

'Of course I do!' groaned Andrew getting up and moving up and down restlessly.

'If I didn't find you attractive, there'd be no problem. But I do, you're beautiful,' he ended looking at her admiringly.

'Well then," smiled Diane opening her arms in a gesture of invitation – that Andrew stubbornly resisted.

'Can't you see,' he went on, still walking up and down in restless agitation. 'It would be so easy for me to abandon myself to you. I could love you, I probably do. But there is your family, the Seymour empire! Even you get sick of it, why else would you have arranged a bedroom that's not much better than a cell?'

'But surely,' cried Diane now getting excited, 'that must mean we are alike. We both felt the need to sacrifice which is what drove us to teach at this school in the first place...'

'I suppose you are right,' accepted Andrew sitting down, his head in his hands as he desperately tried to find a solution to the problem that tormented him. 'But the fact is you still are your father's daughter, you can't get away from that. I mean,' he cried out in sudden excitement. 'Would you be prepared to leave this place and move into an ordinary flat like mine?'

'I don't know,' said Diane after a long reflective silence. 'I have often thought of it. But when it comes to the point, I just don't know. The trouble is, I love my father, I love both my parents. I wouldn't like to hurt them. And to move out just like that would hurt them, I know that...'

'But when you married, you'd have to move out, wouldn't you?'

'To be honest,' said Diane. 'I've never thought of it. It always seemed natural that my husband would live at Carnforth Grange. God, it's big enough. There's even a separate lodge on the estate we could easily use..'.

'So we're back to square one!' Andrew exclaimed in angry frustration. 'That very fact makes your bedroom just a show, and even your teaching at Passworth. Because you know when it comes to the crunch, you have your father – and his millions!'

That really stung Diane, and her face went pale with anger. She clenched her fists, controlling an urgent wish to slap this impudent creature, for telling her what she knew was the truth. She shut her eyes, breathed hard, and managed to smile. It was quite an effort – and she could not have succeeded if she hadn't loved Andrew – loved him even though she had hated him at that moment...

'Well, so do you have your family!' she replied. 'And in the end you could go back to them, you said that yourself once...'

'But I haven't and I wouldn't,' said Andrew with angry obstinacy. 'Even when things were at their worst last term I wouldn't go back home – I couldn't admit defeat, never..'

'You're an obstinate bastard!' said Diane with slow smiling admiration. 'I knew there was more to you than my father saw... Maybe I realised that right from the first when you were suffering at the hands of 4H.' She moved towards him. 'Can't we make love now?' she asked. 'I do love you, Andrew, you know that, but don't ask too much of me – like moving out.

Anything but that,' she sighed.

They were in each other's arms, and Andrew felt at last he could make love to Diane, their talk had at least relieved him of some of his anxiety. Passionately they kissed, clinging together and without even thinking they were one flesh, one body, just as Andrew and Helen had been such a short time before.

Afterwards, she smiled with renewed confidence in her hold on him, misplaced as it was to turn out...

'That was wonderful, darling,' she said. 'You're a fine lover, I'd never have guessed it.'

She wasn't to know, Andrew thought cynically as he lay on his back staring fixedly at the ceiling, she had Helen to thank for that... Diane meantime got up and put on her discarded clothes, still smiling but now half embarrassed as she thought of her passion. She really must love that idiot, she thought to herself.

'I'm sure that made things – different, darling,' she smiled. 'I mean – we can't be just friends now, can we? Not after that...'

Andrew remained silent still staring at the ceiling, his face expressionless. Diane slowly made for the door, knowing it was pointless to expect any immediate response from him. She as always had to be patient, but he *would* respond, she knew he would – in his own time...

'Telephone me later, won't you?' she said still smiling. 'We can't separate, I'm sure now, we're too close.' Quietly she shut the door behind her and Andrew could hear her shoes tapping as she went down the uncarpeted staircase. He felt almost numb, but there was still one thing he was certain of, in spite of their lovemaking and everything they had said to each other.

He would never see Diane again, he couldn't bear to. He'd go and find Helen as soon as possible and arrange to do a bunk with her that weekend; he had no doubt she'd come with him, wherever he went. He was uncertain of where they'd go but he knew one thing; he wasn't going back to that school next term, and he couldn't stay in Passworth any longer than was absolutely necessary.

To Paradise

Chapter Nine

'What's *cocido*?'

'Stew, Bob.'

'And these white beans?'

'*Garbanzos*.'

'Very tasty, Margarita. Listen, Emma, you really must get together with Margarita some time, and pick up a few tips on Spanish *cuisine,* if you'll pardon my French.'

'Thanks, Bob, I'll bear your advice in mind.'

Don smiled at the interchange; from the expression on Emma's face, he could see she wasn't too pleased.

'Why not come to our bar?' suggested Colin. 'Pilar will rustle up some *mariscos* and *pulpo,* I'm sure...' He grinned.

'*Pulpo's* octopus, isn't it?' Emma said. 'Long coils of grey rubber, just like the Michelin ad but without the smile!'

'And *mariscos* are shellfish, that I do know!' exclaimed Bob in triumph. 'I always get nervous about sea-food, you never know what it's been up to...'

The usual banter *chez* the Spencers, Miramar, one Saturday evening in May; the chat went on to times past.

'Ten years you've been here, Don, if I've got it right,' Bob remarked.

'Ten years November, we arrived in 1990.'

'Well, we left the States seven years ago,' said Emma. 'And glory, how this place has changed since then. Bit of a wasteland, wasn't it, when you arrived?'

'This ridge here,' said Don. 'It was just a God-forsaken quarry. My first instinct when we saw it was to go straight back to José and tell him where to put it!'

'Good thing you didn't,' Emma said. 'It'll fetch a tidy sum now if you ever sell it, that's for sure... And the Almería flat you lived in, what happened to that?'

'The block's scheduled for demolition,' Don grinned. 'We got out in the nick of time.'

'Well, don't start counting your blessings too soon,' said Colin. 'With these apartments coming up like bloody mushrooms, Miramar could just conceivably go the same way.'

'Rubbish,' said Don mildly. 'For a start, hotels are banned, nothing's allowed above three storeys ...'

'That three storey rule's so much eye wash,' Colin retorted bluntly. 'It hasn't stopped Antonio building like crazy, has it?'

What Colin said was true. Since Margarita and Don drank their good luck coñacs and went to make a definite offer for the plot, Miramar had undergone a revolution. It was now a spectacular utopia, and a vast international force, Americans, British, and even Germans and Dutch, had descended on the village. Plots – at first – had been up for grabs at a quarter of the price of anywhere else, and it was quickly discovered there *was* plenty of water under the rock, which was definitely the green light to go ahead. And people did.

The result was, as Colin put it, 'bloody mushroom colonies' of buildings, following right in the wake of the houses that had been constructed first behind the village on surrounding hills, later on the high *meseta* overlooking the bay. The first to build on the *meseta* was a retired English couple, quite happy to sink their well a thousand feet deeper than those in the village in order to maintain their privacy and enjoy the magnificent sea views. So were Bob and Emma Raeburn who came pretty soon afterwards, and a considerable Anglo-American community was quickly established up above. From then onwards, Miramar was a builder's bonanza. Although – so far – no hotel or building higher than three storeys had been constructed, there was no shortage of every other kind of edifice.

But strangely enough, in spite of all this frenzied activity as far as building was concerned, Miramar village was not greatly affected in other respects. The roads still remained innocent of tar, there was only one phone, and although the supermarket was vastly more prosperous now than ten years ago, Miramar still had only the one. Incredibly too the population of the village remained obstinately three hundred, this strange fact only explained by the transitory nature of nearly everyone who crowded the village during six months of the year. None of these people actually lived in the village, they were all technically visitors.

And notwithstanding the continual building, Don Spencer still felt Miramar had not altered in any fundamental way. He and Margarita could continue enjoying the view from their verandah, the unexpected bonus they only discovered after they'd bought the plot. The view was breathtaking. From the top of the ridge on which their house seemed to balance precariously, they could see the whole of Miramar bay, which especially on summer mornings when the sun rose from the sea, shone like a dazzling mirror of silver.

Neither did the building, so furiously opposed by Colin Harding, actually damage the landscape; on the contrary the landscape was improved, for surely it was preferable to be surrounded by inhabited dwellings rather than bare and sterile rock.

But in fact Don had a pretty shrewd suspicion Colin's hostility was based on something a little less altruistic than environmental concern; namely the problems of competition from a larger community.

He'd come with Pilar the previous summer, one simple aim in mind, to enjoy the sun, the wine, and the life-style he was certain were there for the taking in Miramar. He was tired of the rat-race of London, and when on holiday near Mojácar two years ago he came across the beauty of Miramar bay, he fell in love with it instantly. He ran a pub in east London and had long detested having to deal with Saturday night drunks and the ceaseless effort of pleasing not only his customers but the owners of the pub to whom he was completely accountable.

So he handed in his notice, used the nest-egg he'd managed to save for just such a chance as this and sank the lot in a little place in Miramar, going "dirt cheap" as he put it. And Pilar, the Spanish waitress he'd married a few years before after a holiday in Lloret de Mar, was quite happy to go along with his ideas, especially as that meant a return to her homeland.

But dreams they were soon to discover are different from reality. Life was cheaper in Miramar, much cheaper, than in Hackney; but incomes were also much lower. And whereas in the *Crown and Thistle*, Colin had enjoyed the advantages of a regular fixed income, he had to depend in *La Bodega Marítima* on the uncertain whims of his customers. During the summer, life was fine with plenty of visitors and generous tips, but in the winter the custom dropped to zero. Then Colin realised that next summer it'd be to his advantage to accumulate as much money as possible to be used during the lean months. But to do this he was faced with the choice of putting up the prices of his drinks, or opening longer hours. He tried the price-rise and soon regretted it – immediately the number of customers visibly reduced. He saw he had to open longer hours – and what was worse employ two staff to enable him to do it. Quckly he saw his dreams of enjoyment and leisure vanish like the dew at sunrise; he had to work harder than he'd ever done in London. More than once he asked himself if all this was worth it. The sea where he'd fondly imagined he could swim daily remained like a mirage inaccessible to him.

And Colin also envied bitterly people like Bob and Emma. Bob had been a real estate manager in California, and a good one. He and Emma lived well on the *meseta*, entertained often, and had only themselves to please. Much of the year they travelled, either in Spain or Europe, and their conversation was of the usual sophisticated kind, relating mainly to food, drink, and the latest scandal in Miramar – or anywhere else. Bob was well aware of Colin's shoulder-chip, and he took malicious delight in teasing him, bringing into the conversation topics he knew Colin would object to; like the new restaurant...

'Talking of building,' Bob remarked nonchalantly. 'You know Antonio's busy refurbishing that restaurant – the one that folded up last summer?'

Colin groaned in anguish. 'Oh no! That'll be the final straw! I thought that bleeding take-away was well and truly extinct.'

'It was,' said Don. 'A rift between the Frenchies who ran it, I believe... But Antonio's decided to try and resurrect it so he's looking for a couple to run the place.'

'What about you and Pilar?' Bob asked Colin with a grin. 'You keep saying your bar's not making enough money.'

Colin glared, not liking Bob's little joke. 'No thanks,' he snapped. 'I'm happy where I am; we prefer to run our own show not someone else's.'

'Just an idea,' Bob replied. 'By the way, Don mentioning "rifts" reminded me, how are Kristina and Bernardo getting along? There always seems to be some human drama surrounding that couple...'

'Kristinas's too attractive,' said Pilar drily. 'It was a mistake to employ her – I advised Colin not to at the start – but he insisted...'

'How did you get her to stay in Miramar?' Emma asked. 'She's Swedish, isn't she? Hasn't she a home to go to?'

'It was Bernardo I took on,' Colin retorted. 'He had bar experience. Kristina was his girl friend so I took her as well. Why you all seem to think I chose Kristina first I can't imagine.'

'Can't you?' asked Pilar, at which there was a chuckle; Colin was well known for his attentiveness to nubile young *demoiselles*.

Only Don stayed quiet but he didn't consider Colin entirely to blame; Kristina was the kind of girl who attracted men like a flame attracts moths. She was svelte, blonde and twenty, and a man had only to come within range for her to switch on immediately. The number of relationships she'd had in Miramar since she arrived must have topped double figures; and that in spite of her known friendship wth Bernardo.

But Bernardo's attitude was strange. He was a morose, dark little Spaniard, pushing thirty, who'd travelled around Europe as a coach driver among other things. His family lived in Almería province – which was why he'd returned there with the result of one of his tours to Sweden, young Kristina, bored and anxious for adventures.

Kristina and Bernardo looked incompatible from the start – but somehow they still kept together even now for whatever the girl did, Bernardo appeared not to notice. Colin was Kristina's latest interest, and again the Spaniard behaved like the wise monkeys who saw no evil... Miramar had to wonder at his forbearance, only Bob having the effrontery to say out loud what was in everybody's mind.

'Kristina's little short of a nymphomaniac,' he grinned. 'She made a play for me last week and I'm near-on seventy.'

'Now don't you pretend you didn't like it!' chided Emma. 'Men are so vain, a girl's only got to smile for them to think they've scored.'

'Not at all,' grinned Bob. 'But can I help it if women find me attractive? Anyhow, to change the subject, Don, I've been looking at that lovely picture by your mantelshelf. Who's the artist, may I ask?'

'Grete Müller,' Don replied.

'Grete? I don't believe it. Isn't she into all this surrealism now?'

'She is but this is from two years ago.'

The portrait was of a beautiful young girl, tall and dark, with Miramar bay as the romantic backcloth.

'Who is she?' asked Emma.

'Our oldest daugher Stephany,' said Margarita not without pride. 'She was staying with us that summer.'

'She's beautiful.'

'I wish to God Grete hadn't changed her painting style,' Bob complained. 'I mean that's a great picture, decorative, you know. But the stuff she produces these days, I can't understand it at all, no way...'

'They call it abstract art,' Don smiled. 'Grete measures her canvas before she starts.'

'But is a dollop of paint slapped on canvas art, even if it has been measured?' Emma exclaimed.

'I'm no expert,' said Don. 'All I know is some of these dollops fetch a whole mint of money.'

'That's more like it!' said Bob enthusiastically. 'I must get Grete to do me a few; you never know they may fetch some well needed cash when the Raeburn fortunes are at a low ebb.'

'Bob's always into speculation,' Emma smiled. 'He's thrown more money down the drain on so-called investments than Miramar has sunny days...'

'I think I've earned more than I've spent, honey,' Bob said complacently.

'So you'd have me believe! But how *is* Grete these days? She's not so young now, is she, to have to fend for herself in that shack in them thar hills...'

'Well she did go there so she could paint undisturbed,' Margarita said to an accompanying chuckle.

'*I* sure wouldn't want to disturb her!' said Bob. 'That steep track up to her place is no joke, with or without a jeep! Your road is bad enough, Don, but at least it's short. Hers, it goes on twisting and turning like a flaming corkscrew for at least a couple of miles. And one slip off the road and you could find yourself a-tumbling down into the never-never land. No, sir, if she wants to see yours truly, it's she'll have to make the first move not me!' There followed a titter.

'It's amazing,' Colin remarked in the silence of anticlimax. 'The people who treat Miramar like some sort of Shangri-La...'

'Well, there's you and Pilar for a start,' said Don with a smile.

'It wouldn't be quite so bad if it *was* just us,' Colin went on. 'I mean, it's all the hangers-on who are beginning to materialise.'

'What d'you mean "hangers-on"?' asked Margarita.

'All these beach-tramps for a start. They've been coming in hordes, haven't you seen them the last few summers?'

'I must confess I had to speak to a pair the other day,' said Bob. 'Sleeping on the beach they were, and not just sleeping.'

'It's getting on my nerves,' Colin grumbled. 'Our bar's right next to the beach, and the first thing you see in the morning is a whole crowd of them out there, waking to the light of day.'

'They don't do any harm, do they?' Don said.

'I suppose not, but they're untidy, leave a hell of a lot of litter near my bar, and I have to clear it up.'

'I feel sorry for them,' said Margarita. 'Usually they're homeless, trying to get some kind of living out here, because there's nothing back in cardboard city London.'

'They're no better than gypsies!' Bob exclaimed. 'You just watch out, Colin, or they'll have your property, and not just the inanimate sort either!' He chuckled.

'Are there any on the beach now?' Don asked.

'Can't say I noticed,' said Colin. 'There were three or four this morning but they drifted off towards Almería. There's more for them there, bar jobs and that ...'

'It's high time someone complained to the *Guardia Civil,* the beach isn't a free hotel,' said Emma. 'And a lot of them are junkies too – I don't like it!'

'Now, now,' said Margarita soothingly. 'It's a free country, let them enjoy our climate if that's all they can afford.'

The conversation switched tracks and became more mellow; noone liked to think of Miramar as anything but a serpentless paradise. They were only too happy to forget about young beach-bums, and they carried on talking on more agreeable topics for another hour or so until the party gradually broke up.

But once at last in bed, Don found it hard to sleep – though Margarita had no such problems; her snore continued rhythmically to fill the room with sound, while Don lay in bed beside her wide awake.

What a motley collection was Miramar, he thought, as shown by their gathering just over. Its denizens had just one thing in common, an urgent desire to escape from their particular status quo; the Raeburns through retirement, Colin and Pilar Harding in search of a more independent existence, and he and Margarita through some kind of sentimental wish fulfillment.

Otherwise they were all completely incompatible. What had American Bob, retired, tough, successful, physically fit though grizzled, have in common with Cockney Colin, middle-aged and struggling, using his libido partly to compensate for feelings of failure.

And the women: Emma, the ash-grey socialite, enjoying the material advantages of her husband's success but no way submissive, elderly now but still attractive and all the more anxious therefore to keep up appearances.

Pilar: worlds distant from the Raeburn dynasty. In spite of maintaining a cynical reserve that curdled on the tongue like very dry sack, she still commanded respect. Handsome too in a dark, moody fashion, and willing to tolerate Colin's flirtations as long as he provided her with a roof. ... It was here Don pictured clearly Pilar shrugging an elegant and dismissive shoulder.

And what of Margarita and himself? Don reflected sleepily. His position was probably a sort of village pater-familias. Speaking Spanish he was useful, being English he provided reassurance. Margarita? Quite simply the harmonious Spanish hostess, giving the authentic flavour to an expatriate society, with the inestimable advantage of speaking perfect English.

And while Don's thoughts were getting increasingly confused, just as he was finally dropping into sleep, a young couple were retiring for the night – on the beach. They were two of those "beach-bums" so much objected to and maligned. They'd arrived at Miramar an hour before without a *peseta* for the beds they were supposed to require. Even so you could hardly call them unfortunate, for they could still enjoy the unequalled pleasure of freedom – and each other.

'Are you comfortable?' asked the lad.

'Yes,' the girl replied. 'Are you?'

'This sand's the perfect mattress.'

'Warm?'

'Yes, but I'd like to be warmer...'

The girl stretched open her arms and allowed the boy into her embrace. They kissed, softly at first and then more passionately. They were naked. Their clothes covered them like primitive blankets to protect them from the breezes they knew would come before dawn. The boy kissed the girl's lips, her face, her breasts. He felt himself ready to make love to her, and she knew it for she could feel him pressing hard against her lower belly. She moved away a little, allowing the boy to cover her, her thighs opened, and quickly but softly, the boy was sliding into her warm wetness, so smoothly she hardly noticed, not until much later she felt her crisis cause her to break with low cries the silence of the night.

Chapter Ten

THE time was 7 A.M. The sun had risen not long ago and was already shining on the still Mediterranean waters of Miramar bay. A few sailing boats were anchored close to the shore, and paddling in the breakers that in spite of the calm still beat regularly on the white sand, a man with his dog walked southwards towards the low cliff. The usual atmosphere of Sunday morning, quieter than during the week as the fishermen hadn't gone out; their boats were pulled up close to the white houses. The weekend visitors in the apartments were still asleep, having stayed up late last night, chatting and drinking. The atmosphere was quite idyllic.

An elderly still lithe figure appeared at the southern side of the bay. He waved to the man with the dog who waved back. Noone said a word, words were not needed now, to break the peace would have been almost sacrilege. The elderly figure walked carefully towards the rocks at the foot of the cliff. Don Spencer enjoyed a morning dip, especially on Sunday, and he wore trunks under his khaki trousers, and a towel was draped over his shoulder. He liked this spot. It was a distance from the village and so more private, and above him loomed the white cliff, pitted with intriguing caves that Don liked to investigate.

He stopped near the sea, dropped the towel as a marker onto the sand, and removed his trousers, prepared for the dip. He knew the sea wouldn't be too warm just now, partly as it was still early in the year and the Mediterranean gets quite cold in winter, partly because the weather was still fresh and the sun hadn't yet had time even to warm the beach. In spite of all this, Don enjoyed his morning swim. It toned him up, gave him a better appetite for the breakfast that would be waiting for him. Margarita didn't like to swim but still rose early, enjoying the morning quiet, and putting things to rights that hadn't been done the evening before. This morning there was quite a lot to do, clearing the aftermath of the party. She and Don had felt too tired last night to do any clearing then.

But as he moved slowly towards the sea, bracing himself mentally for the shock of entry into water that would be far from warm, he saw a shape behind some rocks; the shape looked human. In fact as Don turned in his tracks, he could see not only that it was human, but there were two of the species. A boy and a girl lay close together under their clothes, fast asleep, quite unaware anyone was watching them. The clothes didn't do a great deal to cover them, and slightly embarrassed to see they were naked, Don turned away and decided to proceed with his swim, and ignore them at least for the time being.

He plunged as noisily as possible into the sea, and once in splashed hard, hoping the disturbance would wake the couple, so that by the time he re-emerged, they'd be dressed. Don wished to speak to them – but had no desire to address them while they were naked.

He swam a distance out and was glad to see the figures move and sit up. Now they noticed him, floating in the calm sea, and quickly they put on their clothes. This didn't take long as their outfits consisted solely of T-shirts and jeans. Don wasn't forced to stay in the water any longer than he wanted.

He came out and went to his towel, drying himself thoroughly. He smiled at the pair and they smiled back, now standing together, not looking in the least disturbed.

'Hullo,' said Don. 'Sleep well?'

'Yes,' said the lad. 'Nice spot!' He gestured round the bay. 'The first time I've seen it. We arrived here late last night in the dark. What's it called?'

'Miramar.'

'Miramar. I like it. We don't know this area at all.'

'Where are you going?'

'Oh, probably Almería, we're just wandering...'

Don looked more closely at the couple. He rather liked this fresh-faced boy, he seemed intelligent. He couldn't have been more than twenty two. His cut-glass accent betrayed some privileged background, and Don wondered how that sort of lad could end up sleeping rough on the beach.

Though as Don looked at the girl, he wasn't quite so puzzled, for in her own style she was quite a stunner. She had long black hair combed straight so it hung down her shoulders and back; melancholy dark eyes;

and her face was the more haunting through her full red lips that contrasted vividly with the extreme pallor of her skin.

So far the lad had done the talking, but the girl was clearly not missing a thing, and Don felt at once that of the two she was the stronger character. She met his searching glance with equal force but still remained silent, standing just behind the boy, not for protection, simply as a reserve aid – to be used if necessary.

Don didn't wish to talk to them much longer, they were obviously anxious for him to go away. But he had to tell them about the ban on sleeping on the beach; he decided to grasp the nettle and tell them straight out.

'A ban?' said the boy. 'We didn't know...'

'I'm afraid there is. You'll have to find somewhere else to sleep tonight – or move on ...'

'We've no money,' said the girl suddenly in a Northern accent. 'We can't afford a place to stay ...'

Again Don looked at her, liking the determination of her chin and mouth, that belied her negative words.

'How long do you want to stay here?' he asked.

'We don't know ...' began the boy.

'Look here,' Don said. 'I'm sorry to harrass you but there's a strong feeling in the village against – wanderers... I've nothing against them, why shouldn't they enjoy themselves in their own fashion? But there are some people here less kindly disposed...'

'You mean you want us to – push off,' said the girl with an ironic smile. 'Don't worry, we're going, come on, Andy,' she said, pulling him away.

'No, no! I'm sorry! I can see you're hungry, and you won't get a lot to eat without cash. Will you come to my place? I live just up that hill.' He pointed to his house that could be seen on the ridge.

'We know what you lot think of us,' snapped the girl. '"Beach-bums", ain't we? We'd rather not trouble you. Come on!' she repeated to the lad.

'I want to talk to you,' said Don. 'And we can't talk here. I'm going back for breakfast so it'll suit everyone if you come and eat with us. Then we can talk – in comfort...'

The word "comfort" produced a reaction; Don wondered when they'd last had a night in a bed. But the girl was still unwilling.

'What d'you want to talk to us about?' she said suspiciously. 'Can't we talk here?'

'Just an idea I've got,' said Don. 'And it's best discussed over breakfast. Okay?'

'It's very kind of you,' said the boy. 'And we *are* a bit hungry...'

'Starving more likely,' thought Don. Aloud he said: 'Coming?'

'Coming,' muttered the girl after a pause, then, 'Thanks,' but her face still remained sceptical.

'When did you last eat?' Don asked as they trudged up the steep path.

'Yesterday. We had some money then,' the boy replied.

'I see.'

A silence, that lasted until the group arrived at the cottage; Margarita was standing at the door.

'I saw you talking on the beach,' she smiled. 'I guessed you might be coming up for breakfast. Do you like orange juice?'

They went into the dining room to be greeted not just by orange juice, but *croissants, mermelada,* and a large jug of aromatic coffee. The youngsters were soon tucking in as if their last meal had been last month. Don and Margarita ate theirs at a more leisurely pace.

'More coffee?' Margarita asked, seeing the mugs of their guests were already empty, and soon she was realising she'd have to get more coffee and *croissants* at the earliest opportunity. Even so, she was greatly consoled that more barriers had been removed in ten minutes by a square meal than one hour of Don's persuading...

'Thanks a lot,' sighed the girl, leaning back in her chair, a not unsensual sight.

'You've eaten enough?' Margarita asked. 'No more coffee?'

'No, thanks,' said the lad. 'That was the best breakfast we've had since leaving England.'

'And when was that?' asked Don quickly.

'Nine months ago – last August,' the lad replied, in spite of the girl's meaningful look.

'You don't need to tell us anything,' Don smiled. 'But we're interested if you want to. You might tell us your names for a start... Mine is Don Spencer, and this is my wife Margarita.'

They looked at each other questioningly, they decided, then it came out, or at least some of it. Andrew Makepeace and Helen Curtis, they were called, he was a languages teacher, she a student, both from near Manchester. Last August Andrew had chucked in his job and taken off. He and Helen since then had been "bumming" round Europe, stopping in places when they ran out of cash, working till they'd stocked up once more, then carrying on again. Mostly the jobs were in bars but they turned down nothing; cash was always the priority.

Now – after nine months, they'd reached the furthest point south they were likely to go; they drew the line at Africa. Though maybe, Helen smiled, there was still Portugal ...

'What'll you do now?' Don asked. 'There are no bar jobs here. You'd be better off in Almería...'

'That's where we planned to get to yesterday,' Helen said. 'But the dark caught us out. Anyhow we'd better push on now.' They got up. 'Thanks for a fantastic breakfast, it'll see us through the day...'

'Stop a minute,' said Don. 'You haven't heard what I asked you up here for ...'

A look of slight impatience came over Helen's face; she'd hoped Don wouldn't bother with that for she could see no way that it could be of any interest to them. However she had just eaten an excellent breakfast, and decided it would be best to humour the old guy at least for the moment ...

'Yes?' she asked politely but she couldn't resist a glance at the clock.

'There's no hurry,' smiled Don. 'At least there needn't be ...'

'What do you mean?' Andrew asked, also puzzled; he was as much in the dark as Helen ...

'D'you fancy staying on here?' asked Don blandly.

'Here?' Helen repeated. 'What on earth do you mean? We can't stay with you.'

'I don't know why not. We've a spare room. But no, I didn't mean that. You wouldn't like it with us old stagers...'

'You speak for yourself,' said Margarita.

'What *did* you mean?' Andrew asked mystified. 'You just said there are no bar jobs in Miramar ...'

'There aren't – but I was thinking of something else.'

'What?' Helen asked. 'A shop?'

'A restaurant...'

'A restaurant? Is there a restaurant?' Andrew said.

'Not just now; but there will be. One's being refurbished right now – and it's due to open next month. Antonio, the owner, is looking for a couple to run it ...'

Helen sat down. This was too much, far too much first thing on a Sunday morning. She and Andrew stared at Don, completely dumb; their powers of comprehension had for the moment been switched off completely.

'Listen,' said Helen at last. 'Have I got it right? You *were* asking if we wanted to run a – restaurant?'

'That was the general idea,' Don smiled.

'Look, it's really kind of you,' Helen said slowly. 'But you can't do a thing like that.'

'Why not?'

'You don't know us! I mean, we could be anybody!'

'But I do know you,' Don replied. 'I know you very well. You've told us about yourselves, not the whole story I am aware of that, but I believe what you have told us; you couldn't have made up a story as unlikely as the one we've just heard. If you'd been lying, you'd have told us something just little more – plausible?'

They all laughed. 'I suppose so,' grinned Andrew. 'But even so, you must think we're mad, well, not reliable anyhow ...'

'Oh you're reliable enough, or you could be if you had something to be reliable about. Thus my offer. But you've not answered yet, what do you say?'

'It sounds marvellous,' said Andrew. 'Obviously we'd love to run a restaurant, especially in Miramar. I mean, Miramar's just perfect, we couldn't have a better place to live in ...'

'So you'd like to stay more than a week?' Margarita asked with a smile. 'That's how long you've stayed in places before...'

'At the moment I want to stay here for ever,' Helen sighed, her earlier doubts now completely vanished. 'And it's really great of you to make us this offer... Even so, I still don't see how we can accept it ...'

'Why not?'

'Well, we've no restaurant experience.'

'Can you cook?' asked Margarita.

'Well, yes, not bad ...'

'Can you read a recipe book?'

'Not in Spanish.'

'I'll help you,' said Andrew. 'I know Spanish.'

'You do?' cried Don. 'You must look at some of our Spanish novels.' He gestured to the large bookcase at the back of the room.

'So where's the problem, Helen?' cried Margarita, ignoring Don's interruption. 'Unless you don't like work ...'

'Oh, we'll work!' exclaimed Helen. 'Won't we, darling?' she said pointedly to Andrew.

'It'll have to be a conditional contract,' Don said. 'Or else Antonio may refuse to have you; a reasonable profit for the restaurant after a month. How does that strike you?'

'Okay!' said Helen enthusiastically. 'You can tell Antonio we are pleased to accept those conditions. We'll make a profit, all right.'

She was smiling as she spoke but suddenly her expression changed completely.

'I'm sorry, Don,' she said. 'There *is* another problem, and it's serious...'

'What?'

'You said this restaurant wouldn't be ready till next month; that's still ten days from now. How do we manage till then? We're skint ... Look we're off to Almería!' she said moving to the door. 'We can get some money there and then come back...'

She was passing through, Andrew following, but Don called out with unexpected authority.

'Come back, you little fools, I haven't finished!'

In spite of herself but furious Helen turned; with Andrew quite lost just standing there. Now what was going to happen?

'There's no way you can go,' Don went on. 'Where will you sleep in Almeria?

'Where we've slept the last nine months,' said Helen sulkily. 'Out in the open or if we've a job the pay will get us a bed. We'll manage. Come on, Andy!' Again she turned to go. 'Thanks again, Don – and Margarita,' she said more gently. 'We *will* be back – if you want us – at the end of the month.'

'Please stay,' said Don, rising to his feet. 'I told you I haven't finished.

I knew this would be hard for your pride, and I like you for it. Now sit down, the two of you and *listen...*'

Don's continuing authority worked, the two youngsters came back into the room and sat down – silent and in Helen's case sulky. What did the old geezer want now?

'I am quite happy to lend you some money until the restaurant is ready,' Don explained.

'Lend?' cried Helen. 'We can't take your money... That's out of the question!'

'Why not?' said Don. 'You can repay us once that restaurant's making a profit – as I know it will.'

'Look here!' interceded Andrew uncomfortably. 'I really don't like this! You're taking a hell of a chance with us. For all you know, we could be just a couple of....'

'Beach bums?' said Don with a smile.

'Beach bums! And there's no way we can afford to pay you back if things go wrong...'

'I'm prepared to risk that,' said Don easily. 'It's not as if we were hard up. We would never lend what we couldn't afford to lose...'

Again the pair looked at each other, trying to make up their minds. At last they sighed for they knew they had to accept Don's offer absolutely – in spite of their reservations.

'Shake hands?' Andrew asked.

'Shake hands,' Don replied. 'Now leave your bags here and go and have a swim, you need a holiday...'

'And you will come back for lunch,' called Margarita from the kitchen where she had diplomatically retired...

Chapter Eleven

DURING the fortnight the restaurant was being refurbished, Andrew and Helen relaxed and enjoyed themselves. Don found them an *apartamento* in the village, which though no larger than Mrs Reynold's room and on the first floor, had a feel about it that made it seem another world entirely. For a start it looked out onto the sea, and it was delightful for the couple to be able to sit on the balcony in the morning and gaze across the bay dotted with its multitude of small craft. But best of all, at least in Andrew's opinion, was that there was no Mrs Reynolds downstairs, and Helen and he could entertain who they liked, when they liked, and how they liked.

The room had two single beds but that didn't matter. The first night they moved them close together and when that still wasn't right, they simply shared the same bed. They made love before they fell asleep but were too exhausted to do it with conviction; their European safari had taken its toll on their energy.

When Andrew awoke, he wasn't sure at first where he was, then he remembered. He was with Helen in their new flat and they were about to enjoy their first morning in Miramar. She was still asleep and Andrew half sat up to look at her. The girl's face in repose was quite different from how it looked when she was awake. It had none of the sulkiness which Andrew was the first to admit had its attraction, but also showed her basic unease. Now she was content, her face had a new serene beauty. Her long black hair, framing her heart-shaped face with its anaemic, charismatic pallor, draped modestly over her breasts, for she – like Andrew – was naked. A smile played on her usual pouting lips. Andrew lowered his face and kissed them and she stirred.

'What's the time?' she whispered, still half asleep.

Andrew looked at his watch. 'Nearly eight; old Don will have had his swim by now.'

'Rather him than me,' said the girl, opening her eyes. 'How long have

108

you been awake?'

'A few minutes. But I'm quite happy to lie here a bit longer...'

He snuggled close to Helen under the sheet and put his arms around her, enjoying against him the touch of her breasts; he played with them softly with his finger tips and the nipples went immediately erect. He himself was stirring pleasurably and he drew the girl even closer to him so she could feel him pressing between her thighs. Again they kissed and Helen slipped her tongue into his mouth and with her finger tips stroked his lower back and bottom, tickling very gently between the cleft. Now Andrew wanted urgently to possess her but she stopped him by turning over.

'What's the matter?' he asked disappointed.

'Not too quickly! Let's have some fun first.'

She turned to him again, and removing the sheet completely, climbed on top of him, her legs wide apart. She started to kiss his face with long wet kisses, licking his lips and cheeks. While the fingers of one hand were stroking gently the back of his neck, with the other she was tickling his stomach and inside thighs. Soon all this was too much for Andrew as he writhed in ecstasy, almost forcing Helen off him. At that she laughed a little, and stopped teasing the lad, instead she pressed him down with the weight of her body and put her arms around him.

'You can have me now if you like,' she whispered in his ear. 'But I want to stay on top.'

Gasping Andrew nodded, unable to speak, and moments later, flat on his back with Helen rising and falling with a steadily accelerating rhythm, he was convulsed with exquisite sensation.

'I enjoyed that,' she said afterwards. 'Come on, let's go and have breakfast, I'm hungry.'

They went to *La Bodega Marítima* just along the beach. They were the only customers, and noticed it was quite small, not up to a full meal really although meals were on the menu.

'A proper restaurant's definitely needed,' Helen thought.

Kristina, the Swedish waitress, came forward with a smile. Colin was in the kitchen, staring like a lynx at the newcomers through the half open door; Pilar was too busy to spy.

'Yes?' said Kristina, her smile aimed especially at Andrew.

'Two milk coffees,' Andrew said, trying not to notice too much the girl's low cut blouse and her very short skirt.

All in all she was even more sexy than Bob Raeburn had implied. She was tall and blonde with an urchin cut that would have made her look quite boyish if the rest of her wasn't so alluringly feminine. Her skin was very fair too, not the snow-white paleness of Helen's but with a sheen the colour of butter milk.

'Anything to eat?' she asked, with very little accent.

'What have you got?' Helen asked, noticing without much pleasure Andrew's hypnotised expression.

'Rolls and marmalade.'

'With butter, please,' said Helen briefly, having no wish to engage this girl in conversation; she knew a man eater when she saw one.

The two enjoyed their breakfast, though they weren't unaware of two pairs of eyes watching them off-stage. Colin liked to know about visitors – especially English ones, and Kristina was interested in any man. Helen however was not at all anxious to satisfy their curiosity any longer than necessary. As soon as they'd finished, she got up and led the way out, Andrew following with a backward look towards where Kristina might be.

'Let's have a swim,' said Helen meaningfully to Andrew. 'I think you need to cool off a little.' She laughed at Andrew's blush.

The couple spent the rest of the day swimming, relaxing, and eating. They managed to avoid further meals at *La Bodega Marítima* by visiting the supermarket and getting picnic food; Don had lent them enough money for a fortnight. For the next week this was their programme, with occasional visits and meals with the Spencers who were always pleased to entertain them. They loved sitting on the verandah overlooking the bay and exchanging gossip for hours. Andrew was pleased to read some of Don and Margarita's Spanish novels, and there were English ones too for Helen.

At last Don had definite news of the restaurant's opening date; he came down one Sunday morning to their flat to tell the couple personally. It was lucky they'd got up early for once and had not dallied love making. When Don called up to them, they were able to come down promptly and look efficient.

'Good news,' said Don. 'Antonio has more or less given you the jobs, but he wants to see you to explain a few details, and I'm afraid he doesn't speak a lot of English – or at least often he refuses to.

'No problem,' said Andrew. 'And thanks a million for everything.'

'The same goes for me,' echoed Helen. 'You, Margarita – and Antonio – must come and have our first meal – and it will be on the house. Just name the day!'

'Well, to start with you can come over for lunch with us, and then we will go down to see Antonio at the restaurant. He *is* expecting you...'

They enjoyed a delicious lunch – very Spanish with *tortilla (Spanish omelette)* followed by salad and sword fish caught that morning in Miramar bay. They then went down to see Antonio. He turned out to be a slim efficient young man with a tooth brush moustache and a brisk manner. Don introduced Helen and Andrew to him.

'You speak Spanish?' he said looking at them doubtfully.

'*Sí, hablo,*' said Andrew, trying to hide his acute nervousness. 'I speak quite well.'

'*¡Muy bien!*' said Antonio continuing in Spanish. 'Come and have a beer and we'll talk.' He led the way into his restaurant – and got some from the fridge.

'I knew we'd be here before the restaurant opens, so I got some supplies,' he said with a smile. Helen didn't quite get the drift of this, but it didn't matter as her face was usually impassive anyway. Not that Antonio hadn't given her soon a look of approval, for smiling or otherwise Helen always attracted notice.

The restaurant was nearly finished – and pretty impressive already. It was on the beach, a little in front of the flats skirting the bay, and so had a view of the sea from three sides. The dining room was beautiful with a marble floor and neat varnished tables all hand-made from local wood. On the walls were paintings, mostly pictures of mountains and lakes, the *décor* was in perfect taste. Helen and Andrew had to gasp at the thought they might soon be in charge of such a place.

'Well,' said Antonio, still looking a bit doubtful – and Helen for one had a definite qualm. 'What do you know about running restaurants?' he asked in English. 'Don tells me you have had experience...'

'My mother owns a restaurant and I helped her,' she said to Andrew's utter amazement; he knew well she had no knowledge at all of restaurants, other than that they were places to eat at.

'Ah!' said Antonio approvingly. '¡*Mucho mejor!* That makes *all* the difference! Don,' he said, 'You didn't tell me the *señorita* was an expert on restaurants, only she could run one, which can mean anything...'

'I am sorry,' said Don blandly. 'I assumed she would tell you herself...'

Andrew was amazed at Helen's sheer effrontery, and Don's, but decided in for a *peseta*, he'd better put in his chip and support her.

'And I,' he said in Spanish. 'I am an expert on Spanish cooking, especially fish.'

'And French?'

'I know something, but my specialty is Spanish..'

He felt wisely if he expressed expertise in every type of food, Antonio might doubt his veracity – and therefore Helen's. The Spaniard nodded approval.

'That is all right,' he said turning to English. 'Okay, you have the job; you can start as soon the restaurant is completed in three days time.'

'Thank you,' chorused the young couple, filled by their success with a mixture of delight – and dread...

'But remember,' Antonio continued. 'If you lose money after a month, you go. Fair?'

'Fair!' cried Helen. 'You need have no worries; we'll make you a fortune. And I *will* learn Spanish,' she added smiling widely much to Antonio's approval.

In fact as he looked at her attractive face and figure, he decided he'd have given her the job anyway, Spanish or no Spanish. This girl would draw in the customers without any doubt.

But as well as food, he added, there was another problem; they would have to find staff to assist them.

'You are the bosses,' Antonio stated. 'So it is better you choose who you want, but they must be Spaniards if possible from the village...'

They nodded smiling agreement, Andrew feeling quite terrified, for engaging staff just had not occurred to him....

They were then given the key, and told to order whatever was required. Price was no object, the Spaniard said magnanimously, and feeling pretty happy he and Don got up to go.

'Good luck,' smiled Don. 'I look forward to the grand opening...'

'You and partners are invited,' said Helen. 'It will be your best way of testing our cooking skills...'

'Wonderful!' exclaimed Antonio. 'We will be there...'

'I need another drink, a stiff one!' sighed Andrew when they were alone. 'I think we may have bitten off a bit more than we anticipated with this restaurant lark. Think we can cope?'

'We've got to, darling!' said Helen sweetly. 'It's either that or back to sleeping on the beach!'

'What a lot of lies we told too! I hope none of them come home to roost!'

"We mustn't let them! Don't worry, Antonio can't check my little story; and it was the only way of making sure he gave us the job. I saw the doubtful looks he was giving us."

'I saw how he was looking at you, and his look wasn't that doubtful!' grinned Andrew.

'Pig! Now then, let's decide how many we have to take on. It'll be quite a few, this is no *Bodega Marítima*...'

In the end they decided they'd need one for the bar, at least two waiters, and a couple of girls for the kitchen, one of whom had to cook. The pair were over an hour deciding all this, and what food they'd order; after which they were quite ready for a swim.

'No point in overdoing it on the first day,' said Helen. 'We'll lock up and go and have a swim. Come on, I'll beat you to the flat!'

From then on, Andrew and Helen were up to their necks in work. The restaurant was ready in three days, but that didn't mean it could open – far from it! There were a thousand things to do in preparation for the grand opening, which in the end they decided had to be delayed a fortnight.

Apart from ordering food and appointing staff, there was advertising of the new restaurant which they decided to call *El Periquillo Verde* after the Green Parrot where they had made their first meeting. The advert duly appeared in the local paper in Ferroviaria the nearest town – causing an immediate sensation in the village – and around. From then on people were constantly calling in and asking questions, the main one being when was the opening date. It was clear they were fed up of *La Bodega Marítima* in spite of the attractions of Queen Kristina...

It was clear from the outset that Helen adored the whole restaurant business – in spite of her lack of practical experience; but Andrew found himself less keen. He disliked interviewing people, at least having to turn the majority away; for once the news spread around there were jobs going, they were inundated with people only too anxious to offer their services. Also both he and Helen had to learn as they went; night after night they found themselves working and planning, and they were lucky ever to finish before midnight.

Helen bloomed on it all – and it was soon clear who was in charge. She picked up Spanish remarkably quickly, even if it was of the pidgin variety – and had a way with people without offending them. Soon the staff were chosen exactly as anticipated, five in all.

'Marvellous!' sighed Helen after they'd picked the last recruit.

'Think we've got the right team?' Andrew asked feeling slightly dazed.

'Yes, they all know each other and they'll get on fine. Look who we've come up with, Rodrigo a trained waiter and Carmen a proper cook. Not bad for a couple of greenhorns, eh?'

'Will we be ready on time?'

'Don't see why not. We've got the staff; the food comes tomorrow, and it's just a question of sorting out the menus. I've written something out (can you please vet it?) and we'll go into Ferroviaria to have it photocopied.'

Helen's confidence was amply justified, for the restaurant was a cracking success from its opening night a really special occasion. Don and Margarita were there together with Antonio and his wife Mari Luz, dark haired slim and beautiful. Even the press was there and Antonio got up to make a speech wishing the new managers the very best of luck. The staff all worked together perfectly, there were no hiccups and Helen in the kitchen gave Carmen a kiss as she had to take a fair amount of the responsibility for the food. Helen's job was mainly to supervise and control – which she did admirably.

During the first days of the restaurant, she and Andrew made a good team. He was an excellent front man in spite of his initial uneasiness, and Helen had a practical approach that got things done. She handled their staff firmly but tactfully and they soon liked and respected her for she was ready to work as hard and harder than they did. She got Andrew to give her Spanish lessons so she could speak even better.

'I know they all understand English,' she said. 'But it's not right to expect them to speak it when we're in their country. I wish I could speak like you...'

Andrew was proud of his Spanish. It made a vast difference when he was trying to explain things, because although their team did speak some English, it was pretty basic, and quite often they floundered if something tricky turned up.

And he'd practically told the truth about his knowledge of Spanish food. He discovered he knew far more than he thought when talking to Antonio, and made a point of finding extra Spanish cookery books in Ferroviaria. He explained the recipes to Helen and she wrote them all down in English for future use.

'Try this *gazpacho*,' Andrew suggested. 'Ice cold with extra tomato and onions...'

He also worked on *tortillas* and managed to make the egg taste different, a not inconsiderable feat.

'You could be a great cook!' Helen cried admiringly. 'I think I'd better get out of the kitchen and let you take over...

'No, no! You're better at handling our team – anyhow they're used to you – and your Spanish!' said Andrew with a grin.

'Now then, now then, Andy!' cried Helen. 'Don't show off! We can't all be bloody linguists!' She gave him a playful pinch.

On the following Saturday – a full house – Don and Margarita came again to dine.

'Since you opened, we've been hearing plenty of reports about this place,' Don smiled. 'We came to hear *your* story! Well done, both of you; your experience is standing you in good stead,' he added with a twinkle.

'It's been damned hard work,' Helen confessed. 'No time for lying on the beach, never mind sleeping there. Still, it's worth it, I'm really enjoying this job.'

'Me too,' said Andrew, but with a shade less enthusiasm. He was finding the pressure a little too nerve-racking for complete comfort.

'You look as if you're thriving on it anyway,' Margarita remarked. 'I've never seen you fitter. And your complexion, Helen, am I right in thinking it's got more colour?'

'It has,' Helen admitted. 'I'm usually pretty anæmic but the work, good food, and sea air, seem to be doing the trick...'

'I'm glad,' Margarita smiled. 'I was a little worried about you before, to tell the truth ... Now then, talking about food, is there anything you can recommend specially?'

Andrew picked out two of the best dishes, *chuletas de cordero,* lamb cutlets, and grilled trout. He'd really gone to town in preparing for tonight, knowing the Spencers were coming. But the best was in store for the couple. Antonio dropped in, ostensibly for a chat, but in fact to see how the *ingleses* were faring. He was delighted.

'¡*Magnífico!*' he exclaimed. 'And the place is packed too. ¡ I *Estoy contentísimo!*'

He joined Don and Margarita – somehow they found a space for him: meantime Andrew remained in the dining room to see all was well while Helen returned to the kitchen.

'Well, you were right,' said Antonio sipping his *café con coñac.* 'Those two have made it – already!'

'I thought they would, just talking to them,' said Don with a smile. 'They are both obviously intelligent, and the girl especially has what it takes.'

'Yes,' said Antonio thoughtfully. 'I noticed that. An attractive girl – and tough; quite a combination.'

So with the success of *El Periquillo Verde* established. it looked as if Andrew and Helen were about to live happily ever after. But that would have been too easy. There is no paradise without a snake of some kind and in this Mediterranean paradise of Miramar, the snake was called Colin Harding, who was far from happy at the restaurant's good fortune.

He and Pilar found business at *La Bodega Marítima* was shrinking to an all time low. People only came for drinks and snacks, and Colin was forced to lower his prices in order to try and undercut their rival.

'The bastards!' Colin moaned to Pilar. 'We'll have to keep open longer; what a life!'

They soon found themselves working eighteen hours a day, and trying to devise methods of attracting back some of the customers they'd lost. They began by increasing the size of the *tapas* and offered "business style" lunches at fixed economic prices.

'We are winning,' Pilar reassured him. 'People are beginning to return. Once the novelty of this restaurant has worn off, we'll be back to normal.'

'We may be winning,' Colin grumbled. 'But I've lost thirty pounds in weight in a fortnight, and that can't be good.'

And there was yet another cloud on the horizon. In spite of the restaurant's phenomenal success, Andrew wasn't as happy as he should have been. After the first month, Helen was beginning gradually to take complete control of *El Periquillo Verde*. Her Spanish was pretty good now and she didn't need Andrew's help in that direction; and she had the food taped absolutely. In fact she was able to read and understand the Spanish cook books unaided, so again Andrew was more or less redundant.

Helen had always been in charge of the kitchen and the staff; now with her expertise spreading to cover the other demands of the restaurant, Andrew was unhappily aware he was not much more than a figure-head in the place.

Romantically they seemed to be drifting apart too, for their love making had become almost a thing of the past. By the time they were in bed, Helen was so tired she fell asleep at once, leaving Andrew tossing and turning, restlessly awake.

He tried to voice his grievances but Helen was impatient.

'I don't know what you're fussing about, Andy,' she snapped. 'The place is doing bloody well.'

'Yes, but it's entirely your show now; I hardly get a look-in any more!'

'I can't help that! What do you want me to do, give you my job in the kitchen?'

'Just stop monopolising the place, that's all; it *is* supposed to be a partnership.'

'Oh, stop moaning, Andy, especially for no reason! Now, if you'll excuse me, I've got to get on...'

And she picked up the menu to see what had to be prepared for that night.

Andrew drifted off very unsettled. The truth was he'd never really taken to the restaurant, even though in the beginning he'd done well; he'd found it too much like hard work. Now ironically there was not enough work for him to do so it had become boring.

To make things even worse, he also suffered from guilt; was he doomed to go through life, forever dissatisfied? Having managed to escape from the frying pan of Passworth Community College, here he was up to his neck in the fire of *El Periquillo Verde*.

'You can't win!' he reflected bitterly.

But when his depression was at its most acute, a diversion took place which was to alter things considerably.

One Saturday in early August, with both Andrew and Helen relaxing for once after a pretty hectic lunch, a young English girl stepped into the restaurant. It was Diane Seymour, looking more beautiful and elegant than ever.

Chapter Twelve

.

ANDREW could hardly believe his eyes. Diane was the last person he would have expected to see in *El Periquillo Verde*. She smiled at him with every appearance of pleasure and lack of surprise. As usual she was immaculate, her long fair hair loose about her shoulders, and her complexion a rich honey colour. She was wearing a white dress whose simplicity disguised its expensiveness. What a contrast she presented to Helen, Andrew was thinking, who looked almost lifeless in comparison.

Just then, her face dead-pan, she was staring at this visitor, trying to work out who she was. In a moment the penny dropped and she couldn't resist whispering to Andrew:

'So your posh lady friend has tracked you down at last!'

Quickly Andrew got up.

'Diane!' he exclaimed. 'How on earth ...?'

'You're a very bad letter writer!' she said with mock severity. 'Your parents asked me to look you up while I was round here ...'

So that was it! Andrew flushed as he saw what must have happened. Diane had dug out his address from his parents in Camberford – even though he'd asked them not to tell anyone where he was. As he looked at Diane he didn't know if he was pleased or sorry.

'Where are you staying?' he asked.

'San José,' she said, now looking towards Helen who had come forward reluctantly. Andrew introduced her, aware of the mocking smile as he attempted to give the impression Helen was of no real significance to him. In this he knew he'd failed utterly, but Diane gave no obvious signs of disbelief.

'Who are you with?' Andrew asked.

'Mother and Father are in the village, shopping.' She looked at her watch. 'In fact I said I'd be meeting them in five minutes time ...' She turned in the doorway, but Helen spoke up before she could go.

'Please stay,' she said, stressing her Manchester accent deliberately. 'Seems a bit daft to come all this way and go straight off!'

119

Diane paused at that, her face showing momentary indecision.

'Well, thanks,' she said smiling again. 'That's nice of you – but I must go very soon anyway so I won't sit down.'

'Do you teach at Andrew's school?' Helen remarked.

'That's it, I'm just a colleague. We got pretty worried when he vanished into thin air last year – and then he's hardly contacted anyone since – not even his parents...'

'They know I never write letters,' Andrew protested. 'And I said I was okay anyhow...'

'That wasn't the impression I got,' smiled Diane. 'Still never mind, you're obviously managing fine, I can see that, I mean this *is* your restaurant, isn't it?'

'We run it,' Helen said. 'Why not stop for a meal – and bring your parents?'

'I'd love to! I'll see what they say – but we've got a big programme so I can't promise.' She turned again to go. 'Well, Andrew, it's been nice to see you – and so successful! That's good news for your family – I promised to ring them as soon as I got back home.'

'Nice to see you too,' Andrew muttered. 'How long are you here for?'

'A week, we go back on Saturday ...'

With a smile and a wave, she was gone, leaving a noticeable silence in the dining room of *El Periquillo Verde*.

'Nice girl!' said Helen. 'Why did you leave her?'

She looked at Andrew with genuine curiosity; this lad was still as much a mystery to her as the first time they met in the Green Parrot.

'I didn't love her, I loved you!' Andrew exclaimed with a stress that brought a flattered smile to Helen's melancholy face.

'And do you love me now?' she asked teasingly.

'Yes!'

'Well, go on, prove it to me!' she cried lifting up her skirt.

And they made love there and then on the floor, with a passion and intensity that Andrew hadn't experienced since their encounter way back in Helen's little bedroom in Passworth... Even so he still found himself as uncertain of his feelings afterwards as before.

The truth was that thanks to Diane's dramatic apperance in *El Periquillo Verde*, his mind was irresistibly drawn to their last encounter in Passworth. Up till now he'd willed himself to forget that occasion, it was a part of his life he would never return to even if he wanted. But now he knew Diane was close at hand – and concerned about him, things were altered completely. She must still love him, he was certain, the letter writing was an excuse employed for Helen's benefit.

Thus reassured, he allowed his thoughts to return to Passworth and his last meeting with Diane; it was intoxicating! Immediately he could feel the girl's sweet lips on his, and he felt immediately aroused. Somehow the fact that for the past year he'd forced himself to forget that morning made it all the more exciting now he was allowing his memory full play. He couldn't wait to see Diane for further delights, whatever the consequences might be!

But when? He couldn't tell Helen his plans and it wasn't easy to slip away without her knowledge as she was nearly always around. In fact no opportunity presented itself until the following week; somehow things got in the way all the time. But just before eleven on Wednesday, Andrew saw the chance he'd been looking for; Helen had gone to the supermarket, the restaurant was quiet, and he – for once – was free.

Like lightning Andrew made for his car, one of his choicest perks; ('A car is *essential* in Miramar,' Don Spencer had smilingly explained. 'How else can you get even to Ferroviaria?'); and minutes later he'd left the village, heaving immense sighs of relief he'd escaped unnoticed! His joy would have been marred considerably if he'd known Helen had been a witness to his whole departure, discretely positioned in the next side street along from their flat.

It was halfway to San José that Andrew realised he had no idea where Diane was staying. San José is quite a bit larger than Miramar with at least half a dozen hotels and a good many *apartamentos.*

'Oh well,' he said to himself. 'I'll just have to ask around.'

After that he had the nagging anxiety the Seymours might have gone out for the day, and he became convinced his journey was going to be no better than a wild goose chase. Even so he kept on, but he had become very depressed by the time he approached the village.

'I'll hunt for half an hour and then I'll go back,' he decided, as the first houses were appearing on the sky-line.

But now he'd completed the journey he felt a bit more cheerful, for San

José is indeed attractive, and it was the first time he'd visited it. Being close to Almería it is quite prosperous and developed, with smart white villas, nice hotels, plenty of shops, and an enclosed beach. It was the height of the tourist season now so crowds were everywhere, all over the streets and spreading onto the beach which was a mass of golden sun-tanned bodies, most of them only wearing suggestions of swimming gear.

Andrew drove with care through the main street, attempting to avoid the dozens of jay-walkers who'd clearly decided cars had no business there. He wondered where he could park and was nearly resigned to driving to the edge of the village and walking back. But suddenly he saw a space, only just big enough, and as he was attempting to reverse into it for the third time, out popped Diane, loaded with food-stuffs, from the nearby supermarket. It was her turn to be astonished!

'I never expected to see you again!' she exclaimed, looking far from pleased at the experience. 'Where's your girl friend?' she demanded.

'At Miramar. Can I give you a lift?'

'No, thanks, our hotel's just across the road. Why have you come here?'

'I had to speak to you – to explain...' Andrew got out of the car as Diane started crossing the road. Quickly he followed her.

'Explain what?' she said coldly. 'I can't see you've anything to explain. It's all perfectly clear!' They were now in front of the *Hotel Real*, and she was starting to go in. 'Don't follow me! Can't you see I don't want you?'

'Please!' Andrew begged. 'I know you think I'm a two-timer and a bastard ...'

'I do!'

'But you *must* give me a chance! It's not how you think it is at all ...'

Diane looked at Andrew over her food-stuffs, long and hard. She was sure he was lying, probably he'd been lying all the time in Passworth, but when it came to it, she didn't really care. She loved him and was prepared to put up with anything to win him to her. The fact he'd come to see her alone meant she had a chance and pride wasn't going to to prevent her from taking it.

'All right!' she said at last. 'We'll talk. But not in the hotel. We'll go to a bar. Just wait while I get rid of this shopping.'

Five minutes later they were sitting at the *Bar Playa* and Andrew had ordered two beers. He looked at Diane, and saw deep lines of strain on her face, it must have really upset her to learn so abruptly he had another girl friend. How well she'd carried it off though in *El Periquillo Verde,* she'd given no sign of being upset at all.

'Let's have this "explanation",' she said ironically. 'Who is that girl for a start?'

So Andrew gave her a version of the facts, a fairly imaginative version. He admitted he'd known Helen in Passworth but their relationship had been non-sexual. He liked her and got on well with her because she came from a different class from his own, and she opened his eyes to things he'd never known about before. Diane listened as he told his story with an appearance of sincerity. She wondered if there was any truth at all in what he was saying; she wanted there to be!

'And what about her now?' she asked. 'Why did you bring her to Spain with you?'

'She wanted to come! It would be an education for her. Now she helps me run the restaurant, she's very good...'

'And she had nothing to do with you leaving me?' Diane said with great scepticism.

'She hadn't, Diane, I promise! I told you everything in my flat, you remember – and that *was* the truth!'

Diane was inclined to believe that if nothing else, for she knew her position had been a problem for Andrew. As for Helen, she didn't really care, the important thing was that he'd left her today and come to see her. She smiled and relaxed.

'Do you love me?' she asked.

'I – think I do,' said Andrew slowly. 'I haven't been able to forget you anyway.'

'I'm sorry you left, it really broke me up, especially at first.'

They chatted more happily now, and Diane was able to ask the question she'd been longing to ask all the time; what was Andrew going to do now?

'I'm not sure,' he said. 'There's this restaurant – it makes plenty of money, and Helen needs me – at the moment anyhow.'

'Do you want to come back to me?'

'There's still the problem of your family; they're so overwhelming ...'

A pause while Diane thought things over.

'I could leave them,' she said quietly at last, hating to suggest this but feeling she had to. 'I'm not tied to them, you know ...'

But Andrew read her mind like a book and said at once:

'You'd not be happy leaving your family, you'd be like a fish out of water. Look, Diane, I promise to decide things soon. If I possibly can, I *will* come back to you and we'll get married. Things are different now from last year. But I need just a bit more time to make up my mind once and for all ...'

'Fair enough,' Diane said. 'I'll not force you, that's where I went wrong before.' She paused. 'Would you like to come up to my room?' she asked with a smile.

'Your parents, are they there?'

'No, they've gone to Almería. I didn't feel like going with them today.'

She didn't tell him she'd not left San José at all that holiday, except to visit Miramar, hoping Andrew might come to see her.

But in her room, a beautiful light one looking onto the sea, they were suddenly overwhelmed by shyness. They were uneasily aware of the long months that had passed since they were last together alone, and they were not quite at ease with each other. Diane quickly tried to smooth things over and rushed into speech.

'I'm glad you came to see me, Andrew, I missed you a lot, you know. That note, I just couldn't believe you were really going.'

'I had to, at least I thought I did, it wasn't your fault, if anybody's it was mine, I just couldn't take the pressure...'

'That – last time in your flat, you did love me, didn't you?' Diane sighed.

'Of course I did,' said Andrew. 'I couldn't have had sex with you otherwise. It was marvellous. But even so, I fought against my feelings; I was frightened... I – didn't want to be trapped. Before you came I had decided in my own mind I was going no matter what! I'd already written the note.'

"Do you want to make love now?' asked Diane softly moving towards him. 'You can come into my bedroom if you like, it's a bit more private than this one...'

'Yes, here *is* a little too public,' grinned Andrew. 'We might get arrested for indecent exposure...'

So they retired to Diane's bedroom where behind drawn curtains in a beautifully sensual light, they spent the next hour in amorous dalliance, Diane provoking the lad in every way she could devise, and Andrew responding in a fashion she found eminently satisfactory. This must make a difference, she was saying to herself as she watched Andrew writhing in rapture while her fingers paddled up and down his most sensitive areas. They made love in the end, but not till both were at the edge of an abyss that was almost unbearable.

'I loved that,' sighed Diane afterwards, putting on fresh lipstick and trying to assume some kind of decorum; a difficult task just then as she was completely naked. 'Did you?'

'Smashing!' gasped Andrew enthusiastically, spread eagled under her on the bed.

'Have you ever had that sort of sex before? With Helen for instance?'

'Oh no!' Andrew exclaimed. 'I told you, our relationship's never been physical...'

But his voice lacked conviction, and he had to turn away to avoid Diane's searching stare. He needn't have worried too much though, for she was laughing.

'Come off it, Andrew!' she cried. 'Do you expect me to believe you've never had sex with Helen? I can't believe that for a moment!'

Andrew decided after thought the truth here might be the best policy, even if it was presented in a modified form. He said at last:

'All right, I admit it, I have had sex with Helen. But,' he went on. 'I don't love her, not really!'

'I think you do – or did. But I don't care. I love you, Andrew, and I'll do anything you want – and that includes sitting on your face.'

'Do!' Andrew invited.

And she did.

His thoughts were in chaos as he drove back to Miramar some time later. He'd never have dreamed Diane, pure, virginal Diane, could behave like that. He'd thought that sort of playful lust was characteristic only of Helen – it was what had drawn him to her at the start. How things had changed! He thought of his life with her now – he'd had passionate sex with her last Saturday but it was the first time in months. Did she love him? He didn't really know. She never expressed herself in the way Diane did, openly and frankly. She still teased him, mocked him, it was her way, but in terms of open endearment, she'd never gone in for that at all.

Now he longed to go back to Diane, but he didn't know how Helen would react if he came out and stated this. He felt he owed her a lot too, it was thanks to her the restaurant was so successful, she was its driving force. Realistically Andrew knew he could leave her to manage it without affecting the restaurant adversely at all. Well, why not do just that? It was in channels such as these that Andrew's thoughts were moving as he drove back from San José to Miramar.

He was also debating how he could explain his absence to Helen. To lie or not to lie, that was the question! He didn't know lies would be quite unnecessary, as she'd been expecting him to go off at the first opportunity. In fact she'd gained a lot of fun out of making his escape as difficult as possible. Now she was waiting for him, filled with sardonic amusement as she calculated what tale he would present to explain his departure.

She was at their flat for once, having left Rodrigo in charge of the restaurant.

'Hullo,' she said with a smile as he came into the living room. 'Where've you been? I noticed the car had gone ...'

Andrew had still not decided on a suitable story. He blushed and mumbled he'd not gone anywhere really, he just felt restless and drove around....

Helen was disappointed at this tame performance.

'So you haven't been to San José?' she asked provocatively.

'Why should I go there?' asked Andrew, trying to sound surprised at the suggestion.

'Isn't that where Diane is staying?'

"Yes, but I told you I'm not interested in her ...'

'I see,' said Helen.

She was smiling but said no more. She liked Andrew really, and saw no point in teasing him unmercifully; but her thoughts remained deep.

So did Andrew's as he wondered furiously how much Helen knew, and whether she minded about Diane.

But she carefully kept her thoughts to herself, and continued after that day to treat Andrew the same as usual. As time went past, Andrew soon couldn't help thinking that Diane had never really walked that Saturday into *El Periquillo Verde.* The whole episode and the succeeding events had been just a dream!

So for the time being, he decided to make the best of things and remain with Helen. He wouldn't forget Diane but he'd push her – as before – into the back of his mind. He felt he owed a lot to Helen anyway, and having deserted one girl in the last year, his fine scruples made him unwilling at this stage to do the same again. He was not completely satisfied with his life in the restaurant business, but he still thought it was infinitely preferable to Passworth Community College. For these reasons he was determined to accept the status quo; at least for the moment Diane would have to continue managing without him.

Chapter Thirteen

J UST as every cloud has a silver lining, there is no paradise without its serpent; in Miramar the serpent was Colin Harding, owner of the rival restaurant *la Bodega Marítima*. While Andrew was making up his mind about his future, Colin was busy hatching plots to try and make certain he had none, at least not in the restaurant business.

Even when Andrew and Helen first arrived at Miramar, *La Bodega* was only moderately successful. Now its fortunes had plummeted to an all-time low, and Colin knew he had to do something – and *pronto*, as Pilar was telling him in no uncertain fashion.

'There's no point in staying open any more hours,' he moaned at her suggestion. 'We're open twenty hours a day as it is – and empty for at least sixteen. It's that damned restaurant, everyone goes there now!'

'A pity we weren't better established before they opened,' said Pilar drily. 'We'd have more regular customers now...'

'All right, no need to rub it in! When I came here, it wasn't to work my guts out, and that intention hasn't changed. There are other methods, and I think I'll have to use 'em!' he ended quietly with a cunning gleam in his eye. Pilar looked at him sharply, suspecting something crooked but unwilling to know too much. Even so she felt a warning might be in order.

'Just you be careful with your "methods", or you'll get yourself – and me into trouble!'

'No danger of that!' grinned Colin, opening himself a beer. 'My ideas are always strictly legal.'

'You just watch it! If you get copped, I won't be round to bail you out, I can promise you that!'

'You won't need to bail me out, so stop nagging, will you?'

'I'll stop nagging – permanently one day!' snapped Pilar; it was as well Ed and Connie Atwood came into the restaurant just then or there might have been some blood spilt, metaphorical or otherwise...

They were two of *la Bodega's* regular customers, coming from Hackney,

Colin's neck of the woods, and so they had friends in common. Ed was a slim little chap with short hair, dark but greying, and very shrewd brown eyes. Connie equalled him for smartness, just, but in other respects was his foil, being large, plump, and fair. They were retired shopkeepers, familiar with most of Spain's *Costas* except for this one, and debating now whether it could be their retirement home.

'Cor, it's 'ot!' groaned Ed, fanning himself with a *Mirror* he'd picked up in Ferroviaria. 'Let's 'ave two beers and quick!'

'Still quiet?' asked Connie with a grin, looking round at the empty tables.

'Quiet as a tomb!' Colin moaned, pouring three beers, one for himself, and bringing them to their table. He took a seat, Pilar meantime shrugging an eloquent shoulder from behind the bar. This was his idea of running a restaurant, she reflected cynically: drinking his own beer and chatting! She retired to the kitchen with a double purpose, to get away, and to think about lunch in the unlikely event of people coming in for it.

'Any *tapas?*' asked Connie. 'Ferroviaria always makes me hungry.'

''Fraid not,' mumbled Colin. 'Our stocks are a bit low ...'

'Not surprising with no customers!' grinned Ed, taking a sip of beer. 'Crickey this beer's bin sunbathing! 'Aven't you got a fridge?'

'We had a power cut this morning,' lied Colin, not liking to confess he'd forgotten to cool the beer.

'Seems to me,' said Connie, not in the least taken in by Colin's explanations. 'It's not surprising you've no customers, you take no trouble at all.'

Colin flushed at the home-truth but said nothing. He was sick of this situation. How could he be keen if he knew it'd all be a waste of effort; he could never compete with *El Periquillo Verde,* not on equal terms anyway. Sulkily he took a swig of beer and thought about his "method", which would be put into effect as soon as possible...

'Now you've offended him!' Ed grinned. 'Not such a bright idea when we're about to ask him a favour...'

'Don't worry about my feelings!' Colin grunted. 'Pilar taught me long ago the value of a thick skin.'

'So you'll let us have the benefit of your advice?'

'Why not? It's the only thing I can afford...'

'Okay then,' began Ed slowly. 'When Con and me retired last year, we'd managed to save up a fair amount over the years – and now we've got quite a sizable lump sum! How should we invest it, that's what we're trying to decide...'

'Surely that's up to you!' protested Colin. 'All right, I could advise you, but at the end of the day I'm certain you'll be better off following your own judgement...'

'It's not as simple as that,' Ed replied. 'I mean we don't speak the lingo and know damn all about Spanish property laws...'

'Now *you* speak Spanish – well, Pilar does, and you know the people here. You could help us if we find something that looks okay...'

Colin was feeling right fed up by now. He was sick of expats coming up to him and trying to pick his brains, even if they were his personal friends... He had enough problems of his own without being expected to solve someone else's. This couple had nothing to worry about anyway, they had plenty of money, their only bother was what to spend it on! Christ, if he was in their shoes he wouldn't be sprinting after people, asking their advice, he'd be busy spending! It didn't occur to him, of course, this attitude was the reason he had no money to spend ...

But in spite of his annoyance, Colin was too downy a bird to show it, not now anyway, Ed and Connie were not only expats but customers – and customers with tongues! He couldn't – definitely – afford to offend anyone just now; if things got any worse, not even his precious 'method' would save him.

But how to answer Ed and Connie – without offending them, and at the same time avoiding any kind of trouble? Colin cudgelled his brains to find some method – and he did! Don Spencer, who somehow seemed to come to everybody's aid!

'I'm not the best person to help you, not expert enough at the end of the day,' he said slowly. 'And Pilar speaks Spanish, but the ball stops there... What I'd advise you to do is go and see Don Spencer. Do you know him?'

'We've heard of him. Bit of a local patriarch, isn't he?'

'You've said it! He practically started this village in its present form, ten years ago, he and his Spanish wife, Margarita. When they arrived, there was nothing here at all, just bare rock. That and a few cottages by the beach, belonging to the villagers, mostly fishermen.'

'I see,' Ed remarked. 'Do you think Don Spencer might be able to help us?'

'I'm sure of it! Just find a place you're interested in, then go and see him, he'll advise you whether it's a good buy or not! In fact, if you mention his name when you're haggling over the price, I bet they'll bring it down at least 10%, you'll see!'

'I'd like to meet Mr Spencer,' said Connie. 'I mean, it's not as if we was presuming , but if we did settle here, we'd meet him anyhow, him and his wife! So better sooner than later, I always say. Could you fix an invitation?'

'No need,' said Colin magnanimously. 'They live in that house above the bay.' He pointed to it. 'Just call in, they're always pleased to see visitors. And their house is worth a visit, it's got the best view in Miramar by a long chalk!'

'Well, thanks a lot!' said Connie as she and Ed got up to go. 'It makes a great difference, having your help. It's very kind of you and Colin! Especially after my rude remarks just now ...'

'Oh, don't worry about that,' Colin said. 'This place'll pick up soon anyway, we've had a similar problem before – and got out of it!'

'Hope you're lucky this time,' Ed replied as he and Connie went out. Pilar came in at once from the kitchen where she'd been listening avidly to the whole conversation.

'I'm not sure it's such a good idea bothering Don and Margarita with other people's problems,' she said drily.

'Oh, they don't mind, I'm certain!' Colin opened another beer. 'They like being useful; it makes them feel important!'

'You'll be an idle perisher to your dying day!' said Pilar and went back to the kitchen. She'd long given up trying to make Colin see any point of view but his own. So having expressed her disapproval, she left it at that.

But she was really fed of him in every respect, and what made matters even worse was she felt she should have seen through him right at the start. Instead she was taken in just as everyone else was – at first; his easy charm and appearance of helpfulness deceived her completely.

The final blow was *La Bodega Marítima*. Colin had been certain this would make, if not a fortune for them both, at least a comfortable living, and look how that had turned out! They were broke, and he still refused to shift himself more than the essential. He kept the place open long hours, but that was all, he did nothing else to improve the services he provided, which was the reason the place lost custom in the first place. Colin's main handicap from beginning to end was his fundamental idleness.

Kristina and Bernardo weren't much use either. Kristina was so notorious as the sex-bomb of Miramar, she actually put off most people, especially the wives; while Bernardo's continual moroseness was hardly an asset in a waiter. If Pilar had had her way, they would have departed long ago, and there was only one reason why they stayed, Colin and Kristina enjoyed a relationship that contravened his marriage contract.

Pilar knew all about this but did nothing; she'd long ceased to care for Colin physically and felt in a way it was fair enough he should get his pleasure elsewhere for he got none from her. All she was concerned about was that he should make their bar pay, and as long as he did that she didn't care who he went after. She at least had a roof over her head – which to a girl brought up in the slums of Barcelona and forced aged eighteen to go to England in search of work, was definitely enough.

But now she could see the situation had changed. *El Periquillo Verde* having undermined completely what profits they'd enjoyed before, Colin was hardly even providing her with a roof. Soon she knew she'd have to decide; would this be the last straw that would split them irrevocably, or would she stoically soldier on, continuing to endure her conjugal yoke?

In the end she decided to postpone any decision. Her future as a lone woman with no children and nothing in the way of qualifications might not be so much better than life with Colin, who in spite of his idleness and philandering, was still company of a sort, and even reasonable company at times.

He certainly had a way with girls, and it was this talent that had bowled her over when they met four years ago in Barcelona They were both on holiday, she visiting her parents, he already planning to set up a bar somewhere in Spain. She fell at once for his good looks and his charm, which she cynically recognised he could even now deploy with her to some effect, and though she knew it was just a hollow sham, it made her hesitate to be shut of him completely.

Also, she reflected with a wry grin, his "method" might work; it had before when the restaurant in the hand of the Frenchies presented a similar problem. Let him have this as his last chance, Pilar decided, and after that she'd know what to do ...

So Colin went ahead with his scheme – which not surprisingly involved Kristina. On his instigation, it had been she who caused the rift between the French couple. She'd made up to François, young, impressionable and only just married, and effectively seduced him; worse still Michelle caught the pair in *flagrante delicto*. This last was of course a basic part of the plot, for Kristina had deliberately picked a time for the seduction when Michelle's absence was unlikely to be very long; the unfortunate François was caught with his pants literally down.

They didn't divorce, no thanks to Colin or Kristina, but their restaurant enterprise was entirely kaput, and shortly after that *La Bodega Marítima* had recovered its former monopoly; Colin's bacon was saved, at least for the moment.

Now however, he realised, that with the element of competition reintroduced thanks to the success of *El Peroquillo Verde*, he was once more back to square one; and if his restaurant was to survive into the autumn, now was the time to enlist Kristina's services. He immediately therefore acquainted her fully with the situation – and the remedy.

'There is no problem,' she smiled. 'I like the boy, he's sweet! I will enjoy making love with him.'

'Just make sure the girl gets to know about it,' Colin reminded her.

'Of course! It will be like last time,' she laughed. 'Oh, it was so funny, I can still see the expression on Michelle's face.'

Colin looked at Kristina appreciatively for at that moment she was sexier than ever. She wore a loose white T-shirt over bare breasts, and her shorts revealed considerably more than they hid. She was also in the pink of health, with sparkling blue eyes, her urchin cut like golden stubble, and lips sensually generous in their fullness. She looked good enough to eat, and Colin as he eyed her scantily clad body was anxious, if not to eat her, certainly to enjoy her to the full.

Kristina meantime was not unaware of the effect her person was having. She preened herself, put out her tongue, and moistened her lips, moving towards Colin, her hands lightly brushing her thighs. A slow grin spread over his face, as he too approached her.

'I dare say you could do with some payment in advance,' he drawled, taking her in his arms. 'I'm rather short of cash, but here's something in kind...'

Their faces met in a long, slow, kiss, while Kristina pressed her body against his, her breasts providing a delicious cushion against Colin's damp sweat shirt.

'Kind?' she gasped when their mouths separated at last.

'Don't worry. sweetheart, you've got the message,' Colin breathed, as his hands went to work on her shorts. If they'd been intended to provide any protection at all, this was soon rendered null and void, as they together with her knickers slipped all too easily off, to be quickly pushed aside and forgotten. The nearby couch provided the couple with a suitable base for their subsequent activities, which for once were orthodox as they didn't have a lot of time to think of original positions. Even so their passion was quite sufficient to reduce Kristina to threshing ecstasy and Colin to exhaustion, his face sandwiched between her raised thighs. It took him a good ten minutes to recover.

'You've got to put our scheme into practice – and quickly,' he at last managed to tell her. 'Can I leave it to you to find the best moment?'

'Of course, darling,' she smiled, her fingers gently caressing his cheek. 'I'll have it all done by tomorrow, you'll see ...'

The following morning about ten o'clock, Kristina went into the village, ostensibly shopping. In fact she was looking for Helen, whose movements she knew very well. She was aware, for example, that she went into the supermarket regularly at this time, and also that Andrew would almost certainly be at home. Even *El Periquillo Verde* had its quieter moments, early morning being one of them, and then Rodrigo or Carmen would look after the restaurant.

Kristina went into the dim coolness of the supermarket, which was pretty full, a large proportion of the customers being non-Spaniards. But there was no sign of Helen, and Kristina wondered annoyed if today of all days she was going to give the supermarket a miss. Fuming silently, Kristina went round, going through the motions of shopping, and at last joined the queue at the till. No luck! she thought. I'll have to try again tomorrow; Colin won't be too pleased.

But as she was going out of the exit door, she suddenly started, for there was Helen going in by the other; and better still, she hadn't noticed Kristina. Brilliant! Quickly she made her way to their flat, which was just a three minute walk away. Only one thing bothered her as she went, she hoped Helen wouldn't be back too quickly. Fast worker through Kristina was, she required at least a quarter of an hour to get Andrew where she wanted him. But never mind, she consoled herself, even if Helen did come back early, she had a perfectly good reason for being there, at least she hoped Helen would think it good, the reason she'd present to Andrew in a few minutes time.

Quickly she climbed the steps leading to the flat, enjoying the slight breeze that came in from the sea. She tapped on the door and waited, no reply! She cursed to herself in Swedish! Don't say Andrew's in the restaurant! she whispered, but still she tapped again, hoping intensely he was in. And at last just as she was giving it up as a bad job, there was a faint movement inside. Great! He *was* in, he must have been in the loo! The door opened slowly to reveal Andrew's faintly dishevelled self, his face looking quite astonished to see Kristina standing there in front of him.

'Hullo!' he said. 'What's the matter?'

'I've got a bit of a problem, may I come in a moment?

Chapter Fourteen

IN FACT Andrew wasn't in the loo when Kristina tapped on his door, he was still in bed. He and Helen had been up even later than usual last night, chatting to some friends till two, an hour after closing time. Helen had got up early as usual this morning, but Andrew just turned over and went back to sleep.

This wasn't unusual for him. In spite of his virtuous resolve to stay with Helen, it hadn't extended to keeping up with her rigorous day that stretched from seven in the morning until whenever they got to bed at night. His heart wasn't in the restaurant business at all now, and though during the day he followed her instructions conscientiously it was without conviction.

On the surface Helen disregarded this, realising she would be wasting her time in grumbling, but the rift between the two that had been very obvious prior to Diane's appearance had now recurred and was deeper than ever even though it was unspoken.

Kristina's first tap on his door was just a distant echo to Andrew, still barely out of the land of Nod, and he was almost returning there when she tapped again, more loudly.

That did it, he really awoke now, jumping quickly out of bed at the urgency of the summons. Hurriedly he threw on his trousers and a shirt, and went to the door, where seeing Kristina standing there, he stared at her fixedly an expression of extreme astonishment on his face.

'Hullo!' he said. 'What's the matter?'

'I've got a bit of a problem,' she replied. 'May I come in a moment?'

'Why yes, do!' Andrew exclaimed, after a short pause when a thousand thoughts shot through his mind. Kristina entered the living room, he following. 'Have a seat,' he invited with a smile, indicating the settee. 'Would you like some coffee? I'm just about to make some.'

'Oh yes, thank you!' she gasped as she sat down, turning away from him until she was almost in profile, and as he looked at her he couldn't help

136

wondering if this visit was connected with *La Bodega Marítima's* financial problems in some way. If so, from her appearance he couldn't imagine any sexual shenanigans, for the girl was dressed far too modestly for that. Her grey flared skirt came down to well below the knee, and she wore a white short-sleeved blouse with only the top button undone. But most astonishing of all, Andrew was thinking, her face instead of wearing its usual pert expression was quite serious and subdued.

'So what's the matter?' he asked at last, feeling someone had to make the first move.

'It's difficult to say,' Kristina replied after more hesitation. 'Colin's restaurant...'

Andrew nodded; – so he *had* been right about that, at least. Even so, why should she come in this way? Had she known Helen was out? His mind went back to an incident that happened some time ago...

'We knew you were having a hard time,' he answered slowly.

'It's more than a "hard time"!' Kristina exclaimed. 'Colin's completely broke!'

'I'm sorry but what...?'

'I know it must seem strange me coming to you like this, but you're our only hope...'

'Does Colin know you've come here? Did he send you?'

'No, no! He has no idea! He wouldn't have dreamed of asking any favour ...'

Andrew looked closely at the girl and wondered if her visit really was her own idea. He doubted it and shook his head perplexed.

'I'd be pleased to help you,' he said in the end. 'But I don't see how ...'

'Surely it's possible to come to an agreement!' Kristina cried. 'At the moment you have almost all the people who used to come to our restaurant. They don't come to us at all now. If you could for instance agree not to open at midday or close one day a week, it would make such a difference to us, and you could afford it I'm sure.'

Andrew stared at the girl, even more amazed than before. What naïve effrontery to make such a request! And so unrealistic too! Even if *El Periquillo Verde* closed two days a week, it'd make no difference at all to the other, people would simply not eat out on those days. He decided to stall.

'I'm not really the person to speak to about this,' he said. 'Helen's the boss of this outfit, and she's shopping at the moment. And to be honest, I don't think she'd agree to your idea anyway.'

'But, Andrew,' the girl cried, suddenly agitated and swaying from side to side on the settee. 'You don't know our real situation! Colin will have to close the restaurant completely if things don't improve soon. Can't you persuade Helen?' she demanded.

Her hands clutched convulsively at her skirt, pulling it up over her knees which in her distress had swung apart, presenting Andrew with an unrestricted view of her white knickers and golden thighs; he was instantaneously aroused. Neither were things improved when the girl leapt to her feet and knelt by him, her hand resting on his knee.

'Is there nothing you can do?' she sighed.

'You don't know Helen,' Andrew muttered, guiltily enjoying the gentle caress of Kristina's fingers on his leg. 'She's as obstinate as a mule in matters of business.'

'There must be some way of helping Colin,' Kristina replied, now sitting on the arm of his chair, her body very close to his as she leaned against him. He couldn't help becoming only too aware of her breasts near his face, beneath the white cotton of her blouse; he stared at their shape in fascination.

'Would you like to see my breasts, would you like to kiss them?' asked Kristina roguishly, seeing with crystal clarity what was passing through Andrew's frenzied imagination.

No sooner invited than done! In next to no time her blouse was wide open with Andrew busy sucking her nipples, erect and throbbing under his tongue's administrations. She started swaying again, but this time with sensuous pleasure, her hands under her skirt and between her open thighs.

"Shall we make love?' sighed the girl after a while. 'Do you want?'

Andrew definitely wanted. He was pretty sure of her ultimate intentions but was too far gone to refuse this wanton nymphet anything. He allowed himself to be led to the settee and lay down on it, Kristina kneeling on the floor beside him. He gasped as she pulled his zip down and eased his trousers off, which casually she discarded on the floor behind her next to her knickers she had also just removed. Then she was sitting on the lad's lap, rocking back and forth, causing him to writhe and groan; and she lifted herself in readiness for the final consummation which for Andrew was devoutly to be wished.

'There's just one thing I feel you ought to know,' said Andrew afterwards.

'Yes, darling?'

' Helen went to Ferroviaria after the supermarket...'

'What?'

'So I'm afraid she won't be coming in shortly to catch us at it...'

If Andrew had wished to make an impression, he certainly succeeded. Kristina leapt clear of the bed in her astonishment.

'So you know!' she breathed, staring at him with half frightened eyes.

'I guessed!'

'I still don't understand. You weren't here when this restaurant was open before, and the French people went so quickly away...'

'You can't scotch rumour in a tiny village like this. Don Spencer told us the restaurant closed very suddenly, we know your place is having a hard time, it seemed very probable there was a link between their collapse and *La Bodega Marítima.*'

A silence followed of the pin-drop variety while Kristina digested this not very appetising information.

'So,' she said at last still quietly. 'You were just leading me on, you, you *bastard!* Well, I hope you enjoyed it...'

'I did, it was great!' smiled Andrew.

'Are you going to tell your girl friend?'

'I don't know.'

'I'll deny everything if you do! Or say you attacked me. Yes,' Kristina went on thoughtfully. 'That *would* be better. You attacked me, darling, when I was trying to defend myself. I can always produce some bruises as evidence.'

'I'm sure you can,' said Andrew looking at her in amusement. 'Inherited from former boy friends, no doubt. But listen, Kristina,' he went on. 'I think you misunderstood me. I'm sorry about your restaurant, really! If there was something we could do, believe me we'd do it.'

Kristina's face changed at that from annoyance to contrition.

'I'm sorry I – made after you,' she said. 'But if it makes it any better, I did like you. I never go with people I don't like.'

' Your trouble is you like everybody,' grinned Andrew.

'Well, almost everybody,' said Kristina, grinning back as she got to her feet. 'I suppose I must go. As you say in England, you can't win them all.'

'But surely,' smiled Andrew. 'There is no reason for you to go. Helen won't be back for quite a time still – and I won't tell her, I promise. After all you did say you liked me...'

'You *are* a bastard – and unfaithful too.' said Kristina with unwilling admiration.

'I'm not tied to Helen, you know. We have an open relationship, she can sleep with whoever she likes...'

'Has she said that? asked the girl sitting once more on the bed.

'Not in so many words. But I may be leaving anyway.'

'Both of you?' asked Kristina her arms around the lad and her lips caresssing his face...'

'No, just me. I am not happy here and Helen doesn't need me...'

'I see.' Kristina whispered in his ear. 'But she will carry on the restaurant.'

'Yes, she enjoys doing it... But I still have to make up my mind. It's possible I cannot be happy anywhere...'

'And do you have a girl back home.'

'Yes,' said Andrew unwillingly.

'And does she love you?'

'Unfortunately yes. She even came out to find me ..'

'You really *are* a faithless bastard. And you look so innocent. I thought it was only I who was that way inclined...'

She gave a silvery giggle and continued to caress Andrew with feathery fingers on all his most sensitive areas. Neither was Andrew idle and soon they had reached the stage they had been at fifteen minutes ago.

'Can you do it again?' asked the girl.

'I think so, I am young and at least fairly fit... Which is more than I will be when you've finished with me, you little tease...'

'Yes,' sighed Kristina continuing her fondling. 'Men are bastards and women bitches. That's what makes the world go round – somehow...'

Finally she rose to her feet, and looked back at Andrew, all the time smiling provocatively, her blue eyes sensual slits; the lad was very quickly completely overcome by all this.

'It's quite obvious you enjoy watching me in this position,' she remarked.

'I like you in any position but the one you have at the moment is extremely satisfactory.'

'Then you won't object to taking advantage of your state in order to satisfy mine?'

'Certainly not,' said Andrew rising to his feet, ready, willing, and very able to give a practical demonstration of his promise. Shortly afterwards, to judge by Kristina's frenzied cries and the convulsive rocking of her pelvis, it was clear that Andrew's demonstration was competely successful.

'That was wonderful!' Kristina sighed later when both had calmed down to some extent.

'Helen's a good teacher,' Andrew sighed modestly. 'I knew nothing before I met her.'

'But now you are expert, really! I must come and see you again.'

Andrew muttered something evasive; he wasn't too sure if he could keep up with this Scandinavian chick on more than rare occasions. He wouldn't have admitted it but at that moment he was completely shattered; this was very evident when Helen returned, Kristina having vanished some time before.

'What's the matter with you?' she asked suspiciously. 'You look as if you've just had a ten mile run.'

Immediately he told her of Kristina's visit and its purpose, Helen listening, her face expressionless, always a sure sign a lot was happening behind it. When he'd finished a censored version of his part in the encounter, there was an ominous silence.

'I've been expecting this scenario,' she said at last quietly. 'I don't like it one scrap.'

Her Manchester accent had broadened which always happened when she wanted to show someone up or she was angry; and for the first time since she'd left England she lit a cigarette. Andrew recalled how he'd seen her smoking in the Green Parrot, and explained it was just a public pose; she was really no smoker.

'It makes you look sophisticated,' she grinned. 'Boys are more likely to be interested if you have a cigarette hanging like a phallic symbol.'

But now she was smoking for an additional reason, and Andrew knew the girl meant business as she inhaled deeply, her face as pale as it had ever been, her eyes jet pools of fury, and her mouth a sensual trap. At last she smiled a slow malevolent smile, and the expression on her face became a combination of concupiscence and enjoyment.

'It's not Kristina I'm going for,' she said viciously. 'It's Colin, the bastard! He thinks he's God's gift to women, and he's going to find there's at least one who's not impressed!'

Andrew made no comment but with a thrill of excitement he was imagining what Colin was going to be in for; he had no envy for him at all.

Chapter Fifteen

E*L Periquillo Verde* was in full swing. It was Friday night, always very busy, and even though the tourist season was past its peak, there wasn't a free place in the room. Helen and Carmen were in the kitchen, coping with unceasing demands, while Andrew and Rodrigo rushed from table to table, with never a spare moment. Rodrigo was really expert, Andrew was glad about that, and his memory was phenomenal. Often he was able to help and reassure his boss on professional detail; he made a vast difference.

Don and Margarita were at their regular table with a small party of friends; Bob and Emma Raeburn of course, and Grete Müller had joined them for once, although she was generally unwilling to forsake her inland fastness.

'My work is my preferred company,' she would say if she was pressed to join some social. 'If I had wanted to be among people, I would not have bought my little *casita* in the country.'

The conversation this evening was as usual about the inhabitants of Miramar except for those within earshot, there being rules even for gossip.

'Say,' drawled Bob, helping himself to more *trucha con jamón*. 'There's sure been some rare birds round here this summer...'

'Anyone in mind?' Don asked with mild curiosity.

'That couple from London, I was thinking of, Laurel and Hardy.'

'Oh you mean the large and the small,' Emma grinned. 'Atwood, they're called. Retired shopkeepers.'

'That's them,' Bob replied. 'The lady looks as if she could eat her hubby for breakfast – and still have room for a second helping.' He laughed.

'Watch it!' Maagarita warned. 'They've just come in...'

Automatically the whole party turned as Ed and Connie entered the restaurant, and with broad smiles made their way towards them; they looked like an ocean liner escorted by a tug.

'Good evening,' said Connie. 'You don't know us, I think. I hope you don't mind us speaking to you for a moment.'

'But of course we know you, no one can escape being known in Miramar,' said Margarita warmly. 'You're Connie and Ed from London. Just fetch yourselves chairs, will you, there's plenty of room!' Quickly she reeled off the names of those present as with difficulty the Atwoods wedged themselves at the corner of the table.

'Strangely enough, we were talking about you just before you came in,' said Bob mischievously.

'Oh? Bob smiled. 'And what were you saying? Something slanderous, I expect.'

'Quite slanderous!' agreed Grete. 'In a small place like this, slander's the main occupation; in fact for some it's the only occupation.' She shook her iron gey head and stared in Bob's direction; he affected not to notice.

'Maybe we'd be wise to change the subject,' said Connie cheerfully. 'Colin Harding told us the other day, Don might be able to help us with a problem...'

'Ah, Colin,' Don replied as if had heard that sort of remark from Colin before. 'Is he a friend of yours?'

'That's them,' Bob replied. 'The lady looks as if she could eat her hubby for breakfast – and still have room for a second helping,' he laughed.

'Watch it,' Margarita warned. 'They've just come in.'

Automatically the whole party turned as Ed and Connie entered the restaurant, and with broad smiles made their way towards them; they looked like an ocean liner escorted by a tug.

'Good evening,' said Connie. 'You don't know us, I think. I hope you don't mind us speaking to you for a moment.'

'But of course we know you, no one can escape being known in Miramar,' said Margarita warmly. 'You're Connie and Ed from London. Just fetch yourselves chairs, will you, there's plenty of room!' Quickly she reeled off the names of those present as with difficulty the Atwoods wedged themselves at the corner of the table.

'Strangely enough, we were talking about you just before you came in,' said Bob mischievously.

'Oh,' Ed smiled. 'And what were you saying? Something slanderous, I expect.'

'Quite slanderous!' agreed Grete. 'In a small place like this, slander's the main occupation; in fact for some it's the only occupation.' She shook her iron grey head and stared in Bob's direction; he affected not to notice.

'Maybe we'd be wise to change the subject,' said Connie cheerfully. 'Colin Harding told us the other day, Don might be able to help us with a problem ...'

'Ah, Colin,' Don replied as if he had heard that sort of remark about Colin before. 'Is he a friend of yours?

'We are from east London,' Ed remarked. 'So we've some friends in common. Colin said you're quite an expert on Spanish real estate.'

'Hardly an expert!' Don demurred.

'I bet you know enough to advise us; that is, if you don't mind ...'

'Not at all,' said Don urbanely. 'Though here isn't quite the best place perhaps. Why not call in at our home on Monday morning? We're always up about ten.'

Ed and Connie nodded their happy acceptance of Don's invitation, and the talk went on to other things, the Atwoods' first impression of Miramar for example.

'It's great!' Connie enthused. 'Pity about the *Bodega Marítima* though; it's having a hard time.'

'Maybe if Colin wasn't such an idle so and so ...,' Bob began.

'Agreed,' said Grete. 'But Miramar has never needed two restaurants, that I've always thought.'

'How *is* Colin managing just now?' asked Don.

'Well, I don't know,' Ed admitted. 'He claims he'll get by, but God knows how! Hardly a soul goes into *La Bodega* now. I'd have thought it's just a matter of time before he has to throw in the towel and close down...'

'They come and they go,' Bob remarked cynically. 'Glad this place at least is keeping up. May it long continue!' he grinned holding up his glass. 'Though it's Helen we have to thank for that, not Andrew; the lad seems half lost these days, especially when he's dashing about...'

'Shh! He's just coming!' Emma hissed. 'Hi, Andrew, how goes it?' she asked with the exaggerated friendliness of someone with a guilty conscience; the lad came up to them for once without a tray.

'It's not so bad,' he smiled. 'The main pressure's off, I think, with people served. As long we don't get another batch later ...'

'Are you still enjoying your work, if you don't mind me asking?' Don said sympathetically. 'You look a bit hard pressed just now ...'

'I do enjoy it! Although ...'

'Though what?' Bob asked with a grin, but his eyes were unmistakably curious.

'This job's massive!' Andrew exclaimed. 'People don't know what's involved until they tackle it themselves. Helen's wonderful and she loves the work, and Rodrigo's a great help; otherwise no way could I survive. As it is, it's fine, really.' Andrew gave at least an attempt at a reassuring smile. 'We're a grand team, hope it shows...'

'Our evening's been A1 as always!' said Bob solemnly for once. 'But I take your point about the work. Why don't you recruit more staff? Your main problem would be fending off would-be recruits, not finding them ...'

'We're thinking of it, at least Helen is. But it's not so easy getting good staff even if there are plenty of takers. They've got to fit in with our team for a start, and be reliable, and of course they need to be paid. Not, I suppose, that there's such a problem these days,' Andrew said wistfully. 'But I never did like interviewing people, especially when you are going to have to turn them down.'

'You're doing a grand job anyway,' smiled Don. 'Have you seen Antonio lately?'

'The owner? Oh, he hardly ever comes in these days, just once a month to audit his accounts..'

'He knows all is well!' Bob remarked. 'You can bet your bottom dollar he'd be round like a shot if he suspected things weren't apple pie.'

'I've got to go,' said Andrew with an apologetic smile. 'Enjoy the rest of the evening, folks. I've been chatting too much, as usual; bet Helen's got something I ought to be doing...' He dashed off towards the kitchen without a backward glance.

'No, he's not happy,' said Margarita looking after him. 'Now, Helen *is*. Strange, eh? Do they get on all right?'

'As far as one can tell,' Emma remarked. 'Even so I think he may leave; the job's too much for him.'

'As long as the hotel survives, I don't care a monkey's what happens!' said Bob with ruthless indifference.

And while the assembled company continued their pleasurable speculations, things were happening in the kitchen not one of them could have dreamed of. Helen and Andrew were busy discussing her strategy for dealing with Colin's machinations.

'You won't be too tough with him, will you?' Andrew gasped.

'I won't!' Helen answered grimly. 'But he needs a lesson badly."

'Are you sure it's necessary? I mean the *Bodega*'s falling apart, Colin's plot didn't work, so what else can he do?'

'You never know with a type like that, he's cunning enough to think of some other ruse – that works!'

'All right – I suppose. But what are you going to do? Are you off now?'

'Yes, now's the best moment! He'll be at home as it's fairly late, and I know on Fridays after eight, he leaves Pilar and Barnardo in *la Bodega* just in case anyone turns up.'

Andrew nodded his head in agreement with all this; he wasn't entirely happy revenge was necessary, but he half felt Colin had it coming, and so was willing to go along with Helen. Anyway, he cynically told himself, even if he'd gone against her, she'd not have taken any notice, so he might as well agree... He was relatively sincere as he stood by the door, watching her go out into the night and said: 'Well, good luck!'

'He's going to need it,' Helen answered with a grin.

Meantime in the restaurant, the chat continued; now it was Grete's turn to be put under Bob's sardonic spotlight.

'How's your painting coming on?' he asked, half serious, half provocative.

'Okay,' Grete answered briefly, refusing to be drawn; she knew very well Bob's arrant philistinism. But her very brevity served to goad him into a more direct attack.

'I hope you've moved on from your '*abstract*' phase,' he grinned.

'I have , though I don't suppose *you'd* notice.'

'Bob'll never understand any picture that doesn't look like a photograph – and a coloured photograph at that!' Emma smiled.

'You're darned right, m'dear! What the hell's the point of discovering perspective, if afterwards you completely ignore it?'

'We don't ignore it,' said Grete patiently. 'We use it and develop from it, looking at perspective from a new dimension.'

'All I know is this,' Bob retorted. 'I want a picture that's pleasant to look at on my wall not like the back of some more than usually ugly elephant.'

'Elephants are beautiful,' said Grete. 'But you wouldn't understand that...'

'What Bob said about beauty reminds me of an anecdote that might interest you,' put in Don. 'Some time back, this was in England, a number of us were looking at two paintings in my house. One was a beautiful woodland scene, all trees and sunlight and content, the other was wild and stormy, grey and disturbing, a desolate windswept town under a turbulent sky. Most of us preferred the first picture of course.'

'And who was the painter?' asked Grete.

'Nobody famous, a local artist quite well off and successful, I believe. The other was El Greco, the painting, his view of Toledo under a storm.'

'Which goes to prove,' said Bob. 'You needn't be a great painter to make money, and that to me is the only thing that is important!'

'So speaks our great philistine,' said Grete.

'Maybe at this point, a change of topic is called for,' said Don trying not to smile. 'No topic in civilised company should last more than two minutes, and this one has gone on for nearly five...'

'I'll go along with that,' grinned Ed. 'This talk is way above me, let's get down to earth a little, shall we?'

'By that, I suppose you mean sex,' Bob remarked.

'His favourite subject,' sighed Emma. 'When he's not talking about it, he's got it on his mind.'

'Well, sex is kind of important, isn't it? Far more than art, anyhow. Without sex, man would not have developed even as far as the Altamira caves.'

There was a general titter and the atmosphere was immediately relieved. In fact Bob had been getting just a little tetchy as his taste was questioned; it was his one weak spot. From now on, the conversation passed to other things, and the newcomers of course came in for attention.

'We've seen most of the Mediterranean,' said Connie. 'But this is quite different.'

'Better?' asked Margarita.

'Oh, definitely! For a start it's that amount quieter, I've heard there *is* a drug problem round Almería and a fair amount of casual sex all over, but compared with the Costa Blanca or Ibiza, it's a little paradise in my opinion.'

'Well it's more Spanish than most other places.' said Margarita. 'A lot of the high power resorts have become international ghettos which the Spaniards avoid except to pick up what cash they can.'

'All I can say is this,' Ed remarked. 'I hope with its growing prosperity, Miramar can keep its special identity.'

'It has – and that should continue,' said Don. 'It still has the great advantage that – so far – it is little known outside Spain, and is quite difficult to get to.'

Meantime as Andrew worked with Carmen in the kitchen, he was relieved the main pressure of the evening had now eased. He debated whether to go and renew his conversation with Don's party but decided against it. Maybe it was because he was anxious about what was happening in Colin's domain; he had a suspicion the result of his encounter with Helen was going to be far-reaching.

'¿Has terminado ya?' he asked Carmen, ready to let her go.

'Sí. sí,' she said. 'I have nearly finished, only some clearing away to do.'

Andrew looked at the girl with a more speculative eye than usual, as a person not as an employee. She was rather sweet, he thought, small with thick dark hair and large flashing eyes. A bit of passion too, Andrew was sure, when she cared to show it. But he didn't fancy risking a slapped face by going beyond his role as boss, he knew she came from a good Catholic family with its still powerful taboos.

Rodrigo, quietly on duty in the restaurant, was different. Not just a Spaniard but an Andaluz with all the insularity and ironic charm of that region. Usually he was rerserved but a few glasses of vino tinto would soon break all that down, and a flood of eloquence would pour forth that was almost impossible to control. He and Bernardo, even though from rival restaurants, often got together in their free time, and then the sparks well and truly flew. Bernardo would still remain the melancholy type he was, small and hunched and cynical, but there was humour too and observation. A Spanish speaker who could join in their talk could get a whole lot of entertainment from that duo; and Andrew, being able to do just that, obtained on a good few occasions a pleasure that compensated for the many problems he felt burdened him.

But at last the enthusiasm of Don's party died down, and they prepared to leave. Carmen had gone some time ago, so had Rodrigo. Andrew somehow had no wish to go back into the restaurant. He was happy with his own thoughts, mainly about the past, present, and the future. Of the future he was stiill as uncertain as he had ever been. The only thing he was sure of was that he wanted to know what Helen was doing at that particular moment.; and he had a strong suspicion he'd have until next morning to find out.

Smilingly he went into the restaurant, once he was quite sure Don's party was going.

'Thanks, lad,' Bob said affably. 'A very pleasant evening. Is Helen there?'

'No, she went a few minutes ago, she had some things to settle...'

'Well, give her our thanks too,' Don smiled. 'We'll see you both again soon. Why not come up to our house one afternoon? You haven't been for quite a while.'

'We're always so busy.' Andrew sighed.

'Don't let work present you relaxing. Come yourself if Helen can't drag herself away...'

'Thanks, I may,' agreed Andrew. 'Goodnight, sleep well ...'

The silence was devastating when the last of the last of the party had disappeared. Andrew locked up and slowly made his way to his empty flat; he couldn't remember feeling more depressed.

Chapter Sixteen

HELEN had gone purposefully towards Colin's bungalow some distance away on the other side of the village and inland. It had a sea view but was not nearly as attractive as the chalets nearer the bay. Helen wished she felt the confidence she was assuming. When it came to it, she wasn't at all sure she'd be able to deal with Colin. He'd be on his guard and if there was any physical exchange, he'd have a great advantage.

'Still,' she said to herself. 'He's probably pretty soft, these lazy bastards usually are; I'll manage him!'

She crossed the square, enjoying the casual democratic atmosphere. Children as young as five years old played together under the bright street lights while the Spanish locals sat and chatted on the low wall round the square. Helen could see *La Bodega Marítima* in the distance; it actually had a few customers for once, and Pilar and Bernardo were busy. She wished she could just sit down and relax, enjoying the serene beauty of a starry Spanish night, instead of going on her rather distasteful errand.

She turned away from the square and marched along darker streets without much lighting and unpaved towards the Hardings' residence. When she got there, she saw its shape just off the road was completely dark, there seemed to be no lights at all. She went to the front door and listened; an absolute silence reigned within, so much so she only knocked as a matter of form, with no expectation of a reply...

'Blast!' Helen muttered. 'He's not in!'

Immediately she thought he could be with Kristina; she hadn't been in La Bodega. Again Helen cursed, this time more luridly. She should have realised Casanova Colin was unlikely to be at home when he had free time; he was almost certainly having it off with Kristina or failing that with the latest talent available.

She decided to go back home. There was no point in returning to El Periquillo, Andrew could easily wait for the news of the non-event, which wouldn't upset him unduly anyway. Ten minutes later Helen was climbing the stairs to their flat.

'Excuse me!' she cried out as the burly figure of a man came charging down, apparently about to knock her over. He managed to stop short with amazing speed however, and she saw who it was in the half light. 'Colin!' she exclaimed.

'I was looking for you!' he said with a leer. 'Can I come in a moment?'

Helen was still staring at him in amazement. This was incredible; both parties looking for each other at the same time. But could it be for the same reason? She decided to postpone her plan of campaign, at least for the moment, and hear what Colin had to say.

'All right.' she said quietly, bottling up her conflicting thoughts. She led the way up the stairs and into her flat. 'Have a seat!' she said, pointing to the settee where quite recently Kristina had been invited. Colin dropped into it with considerably more force than the girl; Helen sat on a chair, feeling she might get some advantage from her superior position. That way, she reflected, she'd have plenty of room for manoeuvre, whatever happened.

'What do you want?' she asked, still quiet, and her expression completely neutral.

'Can't you guess?' Colin said with open hostility.

'Is it about your restaurant?'

'Of course! You know, I suppose, you're forcing me out of business...?'

'I didn't as a matter of fact,' Helen said calmly. 'I knew you were having a hard time ...'

'It's more than hard, it's bloody impossible! I sent Kristina here to try and get some kind of compromise.'

'You sent her?' Helen repeated. 'But Andrew told me you had nothing to do with it...'

'That was Kristina's story, she's a good kid, she was trying to protect me!'

'Well, anyhow,' said Helen, taking a deep breath as she prepared for action. 'Now we're on the subject of Kristina, and I'm glad *you* mentioned her, saving me from having to, you sent her expressly not to make some kind of deal with Andrew, but to seduce him, as she seduced François on *your* instructions!'

'That's a bleeding lie!' Colin roared. 'She told me she put the deal to him quite clearly; to close your place for a spell so as to give us half a chance...'

'I know she said that,' Helen agreed, once again with a deadly calm. 'But that wasn't the only thing she was doing; while she was talking, she brazenly flaunted herself in front of him, like this!' Helen exclaimed, suddenly lifting her skirt and exposing her knickers; the move had an immediate effect on Colin who went brick red. 'Want me to go further?' she sneered. 'Take them down? Play with myself? Because that's what Kristina did in front of Andrew, I had the whole story from him personally...'

She hadn't in fact, she'd only guessed what happened from Kristina's well known reputation, but her message struck home because Colin was staring at her as though pole-axed.

'The young bastard!' he gasped when he was able to give his anger some kind of expression. 'I never thought he'd have the nerve to tell you. You're fuckin' permissive, ain't you, Miss?' he said, getting up and standing menacingly over her. Not one jot did she flinch, all her face showed was absolute contempt for this Mediterranean Lothario.

'Fuckin' permissive,' Colin repeated, liking the sound of the words. 'I mean, you don't mind what your boy friend gets up to, do you? You'll let him try anything, won't you, you slut!'

'Yes, I'm a slut! But you're just a randy old bastard!' Helen scoffed, she too standing up, her face pale, insolent, and provocative. Violently she tore open her dress, exposing her breasts, the nipples crimsonly erect, and forced her face right close up to him. 'You can never get enough of it, can you? Well come on then, sex maniac, what are you waiting for? Let's have the only thing you can give a woman, *screw me!*'

She was deliberately goading him to rape her – and in her flat; the story she'd tell would therefore be completely convincing. In Colin's place, she might have found it difficult to persuade people she hadn't asked for it.

That was her plan, thought out in every detail; but when it came to its practical application, somehow, incredibly, it wasn't going to work. For the simple reason Helen had overlooked one vital factor, her own sexuality.

This wasn't clear at first, and Colin was rising to the bait of her last taunts; what man could fail to before that provocative siren? He caught hold of her and kissed her passionately on the lips, his arms around her, crushing her smaller body to his, and with a sudden thrill of fear she realised she was quite helpless, she could hardly move, never mind struggle free. Colin was continuing to kiss her everywhere, on her mouth, her face, her neck, and then her breasts, sucking the nipples till she was lost in a mist of ecstasy. She hadn't felt this way with a lover for years, and all she knew was she found it marvellous. Her resistance, her aggression, her dislike of Colin, were dissolving in her passion, the only thing she wanted was to be overcome, seduced, raped by this fantastic man!

'Take your pants off, I want you to screw me, now!'

'You little whore!' groaned Colin. 'You bloody marvellous little whore! I love you!'

'Don't love me, you bastard, just fuck me!' Helen snapped.

Seconds later, flat on the floor and her thighs wide apart, she got what she'd been begging for, she was well and truly fucked as she'd never been fucked in her life before.

'That was wonderful!' she sighed when the room stopped spinning round above her. 'You really are a demon lover, Colin.'

'And you're the best lay I've had since I've been in Miramar, no kidding!' Colin gasped. 'And that includes Kristina.'

'You say that to all your whores, I bet,' said Helen, softly caressing him with feather finger tips; Colin wriggled with pleasure.

'All right I do!' he admitted. 'But for once it's true, you're wonderful!'

'And you're a mature man!' Helen said flatteringly, still caressing and teasing him and enjoying the way he continued to writhe under her touch. 'But tell me, Colin,' she said suddenly changing her tone. 'Can you tell me, how such a great lover as you are, definitely! can be such an idle bugger! And such a cheap crook! Because the way you screwed up those Frenchies was pretty crooked, go on, admit it!'

'No one's perfect!' Colin grinned. 'And look at you, no fucking morals at all, as I said before...'

'But you don't know what was at the back of my mind when I came here.'

'What then?' he asked a little less cheerful now. What *was* at the back of this hell cat's little mind?

'After seducing you, which admit it, I did, I was going to spread a report round the village that you came here and raped me in revenge for spoiling your business...'

That struck him!

'You bitch!' he gasped in fear, sitting up, and moving away from the caressing fingers. 'You fucking bitch!'

'It's no more than you got Kristina to do to Andrew and others...'

Worse and worse! Especially as he knew this girl was speaking the simple truth; all Colin could think of now was how to get away from this place! But before he left, something told him he had to put his case – such as it was... He turned to Helen in abject supplication.

'Look at it, from my angle,' he said, trying to think straight, now well away from her hand. 'What else could I do? I'll admit as well as being a good lay, you run a great restaurant, I know for sure I could never compete with you. I'm just a pub manager, that's all, not a restaurateur, and let's face it, I'm not so bright either. The only way I could have beaten you was playing dirty, and even that didn't work.'

A pause while Helen digested Colin's confession. The truth was that while she'd been half won over by Colin's love making, this little speech, spontaneous and unprepared, had conquered her completely; at least it was honest. She'd thought of him before as just an immoral idler, but now she could see that if this was the case, he was also a realist, and she respected that.

So now she was ready to present to him what had been at the back of her mind.

'I haven't finished. I am not going to spread any report on you, but there is a solution.' she said at last, wondering how he would take it

'What?' said Colin suspiciously.

'You must come in with me...'

'How d'you mean?'

'There won't be any change – at least not on the surface,' Helen said quickly. 'You and Pilar will still be in charge of La Bodega; but as part of a – management committee....; you two, Andrew, and me. We'd work together to run both restaurants, I see no other way of saving yours.'

A long, long pause while Colin chewed this over. Instinctively he revolted against the idea which would make him sacrifice the independence he'd left London to find. And to a woman! But in the end he had sense enough to see it was either that or going bust completely; and the sensitivity to recognise this woman was doing him a hell of favour. Which was maybe the most bitter pill to swallow of the lot.

'Tell me,' he muttered at last. 'Why are you offering this – partnership? I mean, what's in it for you? You don't need no more money, your restaurant's getting you plenty. You can't have changed just because I'm a first class stud...'

'But, sweetheart, you are, and that matters to me!' Helen whispered. 'Didn't I say just now you would have to keep me satisfied? You may not be the world's best restaurant manager, but as a lover, you are without a par, I promise!'

She didn't like to admit she loved this bluff macho Londoner, who at least had the guts to admit his limitations, and this had gone a long way towards making her want to help him.

Meantime a flattered smile was spreading over Colin's pudgy face; she couldn't have said anything to please him better. Even so he wasn't going to give in too easily.

'It would be a committee?' he said at last..

'Of course, a committee of partners...'

'I mean, you wouldn't have all the say?'

'Not at all. Four heads are better than one, surely...'

'Not if one of them's yours, my darling,' Colin was thinking. 'You'll be able to run rings around the lot of us.'.. Aloud he muttered: 'Okay, it's a deal,' still hardly able to believe he could be saying this. Solemnly the two shook hands, perhaps it was a little incongruous what they'd been doing not long before.

Helen was in bed when Andrew returned, astonished to find her at home.

'Quick work!' he said, coming into the bedroom. 'I take it you emasculated him...'

'Not quite,' she replied, in a somewhat strange tone. 'I think he deflowered me – that is if I'm physically capable of being deflowered ...'

'What a confession!' gasped Andrew, sitting on the bed. 'I never thought I'd hear you of all people saying that.'

'You can't win them all,' Helen grinned.

'So what's happening? Is Colin moving out? Are you going to spread it around he attacked you?'

'Neither! We're going into partnership.'

'Partnership?' Now Andrew really was amazed. 'What on earth...?'

'It's the only way,' said Helen calmly. 'He hasn't the faintest idea how to run a restaurant, and he admitted it. We're forming a management committee, he and Pilar and us two; that way I am sure we can get his show properly on the road.'

'But I thought you disliked him!' Andrew exclaimed. 'I mean, you're doing him a real favour. Why?'

'He's not such a bad bastard!' smiled Helen. 'And he sure can fuck; it was the best rogering I can remember, with all due respect to you, sweetheart.'

'Any skill I have, you taught me, I know,' Andrew admitted ruefully. 'So it was that which – converted you,' he went on, still slightly puzzled at Helen's complete change of tack.

'Well, not entirely; I'm probably just soft!' said Helen restlessly. 'I couldn't really kick someone in the balls when he was down – though I intended to, I promise. But Colin was down, desperate, he came after me, I didn't have to beard him in his lair, all the action took place *chez nous.!'* she grinned.

There was a silence, while Andrew tried to undersrtand this strange magnetic girl.

'Do you know?' he said at last, feeling there was only one conclusion he could come to.

'What?'

'I think you're bloody marvellous, Helen!'

'I think I'm a piece of shit,' she answered, stretching out her arms. 'Come here, my darling, and fuck me, why should *you* be left out? You may not be a cock-man like Colin, but you'll do, you're all right!'

Pilar was still in *La Bodega Marítima* when Colin looked in; she was alone. Bernardo had gone some time ago and there were no customers. She was about to lock up.

'Colin!' she said, surprised to see him. 'What are you doing here? I thought you were at home.' She looked at him suspiciously. 'Where have you been? With Kristina?' She had no illusions – or expectations – of any kind of marital fidelity on his part.

'No, with Helen.'

'Oh!' That surprised her. 'And what happened? Anything?'

Could this be part of his famous 'scheme'? she wondered, not at all sure how any encounter with Helen would turn out; she was to her an unknown quantity of still waters that almost certainly ran pretty deep.

'What happened?' Colin repeated in irrepressible triumph. 'Why, everything, everything's happened, and we're saved, saved, saved!' he shouted.

'Don't talk rubbish! How can we be saved?' said Pilar, sceptically. 'We're broke, and that's not going to change overnight, no way.'

'Even so, we're saved!' repeated Colin. 'We're going into *partnership* with *El Periquillo Verde* ...'

That really staggered Pilar; she swayed on her feet, and Colin had to hold her before she fell, and lead her to a chair.

'I need a drink, a brandy!' she said faintly, sitting down. 'Get me one will you?' Colin obliged, helping himself to a beer. 'Now then, repeat what you just said!' she ordered.

'We're going into partnership with *El Periquillo verde,*' Colin said, his face split open by a huge grin.

'But how?' Pilar demanded incredulously. 'Why should Helen do such a thing? She has no need ... And you! You said you'd *never* work with someone else. What changed you? I can't understand any of this....'

It was here it got difficult for Colin. He knew Pilar was aware of his extra-marital activities, but they'd never discussed them, she let him go his own way, cynically accepting his behaviour in return for the home he used to provide. It was as well for him he didn't know Pilar was almost at breaking point; that very evening she'd made up her mind to tell him bluntly she'd had enough and was leaving; she could take the situation no longer.

Now the irony was almost entertaining that Colin's illicit behaviour – that had largely saved the restaurant and his marriage – was a taboo subject he could hardly refer to. In the end with a lot of stone-walling and circumlocution, he gave some version of what had taken place between him and Helen. And Pilar nodded when he'd done, having a pretty clear idea of the scenario, even if she couldn't fully understand how Helen could be so generous. At last she decided within herself, people were unaccountable, shrugged an elegant shoulder, and said to herself it must be – at least partly – Colin's charisma that had rescued them; for which blessing she was indeed grateful.

'So you were able to – persuade her!' Pilar smiled. 'Well done, Colin! Even so, this Helen, she must be some girl; I'd like to know her...'

'You will, we'll be working together – as partners!'

'Partners!' Pilar repeated. 'It's wonderful!' Tears suddenly came to her eyes. 'You know, Colin,' she said. 'I think I could love you, if you let me, just now ...'

'You could?' Colin exclaimed, amazed this austere impregnable fortress might be accessible for the first time in years.

'Yes, I think so...'

'Here?'

'Why not – here?' Pilar suddenly giggled. 'We're not likely to be disturbed now...'

Colin wasn't at his best with Pilar that night – for obvious reasons, but judging by her cries, it was unlikely she noticed. When eventually they returned home, she was completely happy, and Colin very satisfied he'd done a good day's work – in every respect.

Chapter Seventeen

THE revival of *La Bodega Marítima* took place almost immediately. Helen sprang into action the next day and things started changing with alarming speed. First she told Kristina to lower her skirt hem by at least six inches.

'You're scaring the customers away,' she smiled. 'You're a waitress not a prostitute!'

Kristina didn't know whether to slap Helen's face or walk out; in the end she did neither. She had a strong suspicion if she started any slapping, she'd get the same back – with interest; and she knew that to walk out would delight Helen too much for it to be a serious option. So finally she had to swallow her pride, nod her head, and say, 'Yes, Helen', with at least an appearance of obedience. But she was secretly swearing revenge on that interfering bitch; she hated and envied her and her bitterness would have been even greater without the alloy of respect.

But Helen guessed pretty accurately what was going on in Kristina's mind, having been born much earlier than yesterday. She said nothing, neither did she allow her thoughts to be in any way apparent, but she was already preparing for trouble from that quarter. She wished she could have taken the initiative and fired Kristina at once, only refraining because this would upset Colin, who still availed himself of her services on a regular basis.

Bernardo was easier to deal with, being a man, for Helen could always charm a man whatever his temperament or persuasion.

'Listen, *querido*,' she said putting a soft hand on his arm. 'We are a restaurant where people come to enjoy themselves, we are not a funeral parlour. Would a smile – at least occasionally – be possible?'

'I am not one for smiling when there is no reason,' said the gloomy Bernardo.

'But there *is reason!*' Helen insisted. 'Look, I am gloomy too, haven't you noticed?'

Bernardo admitted he had noticed the girl's habitual melancholy; in fact he'd long been secretly attracted to her because of it.

'My face is naturally glum,' Helen went on. 'But I can look happy, see?' And her face suddenly lit up like the sun emerging from behind a black cloud; Bernardo couldn't avoid smiling in return. 'I smile to make others smile!' she exclaimed. 'And that is part of the job of working with people in a restaurant, they have to be cheered up!'

'All right,' agreed Bernardo. 'I will smile, sometimes. But not the continual smile of a few I could mention, please!'

'Not the continual smile, *querido*,' Helen reassured him. 'Just the professional, *¿bien?*'

'*¡Muy bien!*' Bernardo exclaimed, and his smile at that moment was definitely genuine.

'Two problems dealt with, I hope,' Helen was thinking. 'Now for the big one – with Colin!'

But in the event he was no trouble at all; he was only too anxious to co-operate, if by so doing, this would lead to better prospects, Kristina was his only weak spot.

'Just go ahead, darling,' he said cheerfully. 'You're the boss, and we're your obedient servants...'

As he'd anticipated, the committee meetings were a formality, with Helen in complete charge. Colin wasn't going to argue, neither was Andrew, and Pilar's regard for her was soon tantamount to infatuation. Helen felt a little uneasy at this development, and hope it wasn't going to become a problem. She had enough on her plate, coping with the two restaurants as well as the sexual requirements of Andrew and occasionally Andrew, without having Pilar as well. Even so, her almost besotted expression as she stared across the committee table was quite flattering. Maybe when things were a little more under control, they might get together; it'd at least be a change from men...

Within just over a week, business for *La Bodega Marítima* was booming. Every evening it was packed, its patrons travelling from as far afield as Ferroviaria and Mojácar, as rumour magically spread of the restaurant's amazing improvement. Kristina and Bernardo were perfect. Kristina took out her long grey skirt she'd last worn to seduce Andrew; and managed to seduce instead the whole restaurant. She preserved successfully the right veneer of professional decorum, while her modesty hinted at untold possibilities. The result: delight for both sexes, the men bowled over by her coquettish charm, the women, seeing in the girl's immaculate appearance a model they might themselves copy.

Bernardo took to heart Helen's advice to smile – and even managed not to overdo it, he also became far more sensitive to customers' needs. Success breeding success, he soon developed enough confidence actually to enjoy his job, which he'd found previously the height of boredom. By main training a coach driver, he'd only become a waiter at *La Bodega* because – to start with at least – he was captivated by Kristina; he thought Miramar would be a suitable place for them to settle. But soon her unfaithfulness undermined his feeling for her until at last he could only take refuge in apathy and depression. That he didn't leave her or tell her to go to hell was only because she was cunning enough to give him her delights sufficiently often to convince him that aeons of emptiness were worth those moments of sublime pleasure.

Helen however changed that. Her interest in Bernardo drew him out of his shell and it wasn't long before the distant attraction he'd felt for her became something a lot more positive. Meanwhile all who patronised *la Bodega Marítima* wondered at the remarkable change that had come over him; he was definitely a new and improved Bernardo. Only Helen was aware of the cause of the metamorphosis, and she wasn't going to say anything.

Andrew meanwhile remained quite unaffected by all this. Ever since Helen's confrontation with Colin, he'd felt more out of place than ever; she ran everything now, not only was she the star of the show itself, the cynosure of everyone's eyes, she had become the show itself, while Andrew was less than nowhere. And this had at last reached the stage where not only was the situation difficult, he was beginning to think it was impossible.

He started looking back at his life in Passworth almost with affection. Earlier he'd been certain it would be a form of betrayal to succumb to the fleshpots the Seymours offered. Helen had then seemed the pure idealist, the working class heroine, fighting against injustice; now Andrew was beginning to see her as something less than perfect. She was beautiful, charming, attractive, agreed, but she was also capable of being quite ruthless if it suited her, and amoral if she felt that was the best way to get what she wanted.

As Andrew reached that last conclusion, he realised he didn't love

Helen at all, he wondered if he ever had. She'd interested and fascinated him, but that wasn't love, it was a form of mesmerism. Equally he'd only intrigued her, she considered him an *'odd ball'*, an academic eccentric with no real grasp of the realities of life. She was fond of him in a fashion but fondness is an immeasurable distance from love.

Now Diane, Andrew knew she loved him, and maybe her background wasn't as terrible as he'd persuaded himself. It could hardly be worse than his situation now, a nobody overshadowed by a brilliant partner; at least with Diane he would have his own identity, and did it matter that this identity was assumed?

Suddenly light dawned on the lad and he realised what a fool he'd been to push Diane aside and all she had to give him. Talk about wresting failure from the jaws of success, that would be his epitaph, definitely! If only it wasn't too late! As this possibility occurred to him, he was seized by a terrible fear that Diane had found someone else, better, more suitable, than him. And the more he dwelt on that possibility, the more certain he became it must have happened. He even reached the stage when he didn't think it was worth going back to Passworth, it would just be a waste of time, a failure, like everything he put his hand to...

The only thing he wasn't bothered about was leaving Helen; he knew she could easily manage without him, he was quite unnecessary to her. And as he thought again of his role as a Mr Nobody, he was certain anything was better than that, even finding himself back in England without Diane....

But now he was clear as to his course of action, he had to tell Helen; somehow this wasn't at all easy – at least to Andrew. In the end as usual it was Helen who grasped the nettle on his behalf, for she'd been aware all the the time of what was on his mind.

'When are you leaving, Andy?' she asked with her usual mocking grin. Andrew jumped thinking she must be clairvoyant.

'Leaving?' he repeated, trying to appear surprised. 'What do you mean?'

'D'you think I'm blind? For the past few days, you've been like a cat on a hot tin roof. You're not happy either, so putting these two states of mind together, you must be thinking of leaving, it couldn't be anything else...'

'You're right, as usual,' Andrew sighed. 'I've decided at last, I do want to go! I don't fit in here at all. I might not fit in anywhere, but here's become impossible.'

'I'm too much in charge?'

'Yes, I'm nobody here ...'

'And you'd be somebody in Passworth ...'

'I suppose that's about it,' Andrew admitted. 'Pure vanity in the end.'

'Not at all. I like being somebody – who doesn't? I said you were a fool to turn Diane down and I meant it. But now you've at last come to your senses, it could be too late; How d'you know she hasn't found someone else?'

Andrew was stabbed to the quick.

'D'you think so really?' he gasped.

Helen hadn't the heart to torment him more.

'Not really,' she smiled. 'But you have to face the possibility...'

'It's all right, I have, and I'm prepared to risk it, I'm going back to England whatever happens...'

'Good boy!' Helen's smile was no longer mocking. 'The first wise move you've made since I met you; lucky I anticipated it by a week.'

'A week? What do you mean?' Andrew was completely mystified.

Still smiling she explained she'd written to her mother in Passworth, asking if she and Tom would like to come and help with the restaurant.

'I said nothing about you going!' she reassured him. 'And you don't need to, not unless you want. We could still do with their help with all the extra customers.'

'You're incredible, Helen!' Andrew exclaimed. 'You're too good for any man, never mind me!'

'Listen, Andy!' she cried, with an unusual sincerity; for the first time since she'd known him, she was going to say what was really in her mind. 'Why do you always idealise others – and undervalue yourself? You are, you've always been, your own worst enemy! First you run away from a brilliant future, and now you don't even realise the fantastic debt I owe you! I know I'm a bloody success here, but who was responsible for it in the first place? You! You brought me here from that hell-hole, Passworth, you presented me with the chance to build a new future. But far from expecting any thanks for this, you've forgotten I owe you a bloody thing! Andy, you stupid bastard!' she exclaimed. 'It's you who's the fucking miracle worker, not me! Come here, I *want* you!'

And there and then they came together on the kitchen table, with a passionate intensity neither had experienced with the other, not even in Passworth. There were tears in Helen's eyes when they parted, Andrew was quite shocked, he could never remember her in such a state before.

'I'm sorry, Andy,' she sighed, holding him to her. 'I wish I loved you, you're such a *good* person, far, far better than me ....'

'Oh, I'm not good, I'm too indecisive to be good ...'

'You're sweet,' said Helen kissing him on the lips. 'And I'm just a bitch; I sometimes think I can't love anybody at all ...'

'You can and you will!' Andrew exclaimed. 'Someone more like you than I could ever be! We were never meant for each other, not really, even though we had something to give each other. I gave you the chance to make a fresh start; and you gave me time so I could look back at my life and see what I wanted from it.'

'Go to Diane!' Helen kissed him again. 'I know she'll take you back, she'd be a fool not to, and I'm a fool to let you go.'

Soon after that, Andrew went to tell Don Spencer of his decision. He felt he ought to, for it was he who had set him and Helen up in the first place, and to go without saying a word to him and Margarita would be probably rude and certainly disturbing.

He walked along the beach in order to enjoy the beauty of the scene, looking towards the south cliff to see if Don was still there, but he had gone and the cove was deserted; Miramar visitors tended to lie in until later The sea was completely still that morning, and the atmosphere so quiet Andrew was certain he was as near to Paradise as was possible on this earth. A tear came to his eyes as he realised that in leaving *El Periquillo Verde* he was also leaving this.

'I'm just an idiot!' he thought angrily. 'How can I give up this for – Passworth? I must be mad!'

Still he went on, for he was determined to leave. He remembered a friend of his in England who, obliged to forsake a beautiful area for somewhere considerably less salubrious, said, 'You can't live on scenery.' Andrew wasn't quite in the same situation for he did have a living in Miramar of a sort, but completely overshadowed by Helen, he'd grown to detest his position. To be a Seymour satellite would be a pleasure in comparison.

Andrew now climbed the path to the Spencers' cottage. On the horizon he could just glimpse the long flat shape of an oil tanker, while close to the shore the dozens of small craft, from yachts and dinghies to cabin cruisers, seemed suspended on the surface of the still blue calm. The whole panorama was idyllic.

With a sigh, Andrew turned away and looked towards the Spencers' cottage. Now he was so close he felt in his chest an almost painful tenseness. How would they react to his news? Would they be sympathetic or impatient with his U-turn? He felt strongly tempted to go back, or better still just invest some other reason for his visit.

Margarita was at the door as he approached, his head a morass of confused intentions; her welcoming smile went a long way to allay them.

'Nice to see you, Andrew,' she said. 'Do come in, I'm glad you've taken up Don's invitation.'

'Thank you,' said the lad. 'Sorry Helen's not with me, she's busy – as usual.'

'I'm sure,' Margarita led him into the living room. 'Don,' she called. 'It's Andrew.'

'Good,' came Don's voice from the next room. 'Won't be a moment, I only just got back from my bathe.'

'I thought you wouldn't have missed it, even though I didn't see you on the beach...'

'Coffee?' Margarita invited. 'We've not had breakfast; we're a bit late this morning. I take it you've had yours?'

'Yes, thank you. But I will have a coffee, that'll be nice. Though I hope I'm not in the way ...'

'No, no! It's nice having a young face, makes a change from two old ones!' She laughed, Andrew joining in. 'You remember your first breakfast with us – when Don found you and Helen on the beach?' She handed him his coffee.

'Oh yes! It seems a – long time ago ...'

'Only four months, but I suppose a lot has happened in that time.'

'Masses! Almost too much.'

'Well, hello, young man!' Don's cheerful voice broke into Andrew's somewhat sad reflections. 'How are you?'

'Fine, thanks! I just thought...'

'You'd like to pay us a call...' Don helped himself to coffee and a croissant. 'You're not – bothered about something, are you?'

'Well...'

'Because if you are, just spill it. We'll be only too pleased to help you if we humanly can.'

'It's not advice I want,' Andrew began.

'No?'

'It's more a decision I've come to – and I thought I'd better tell you about it; it's rather crucial.'

'We noticed you've had something on your mind,' Margarita said. 'I'm glad you're settled about it.'

'Yes. It wasn't easy, everyone's been so kind here, I've been happier in Miramar than anywhere else before ...'

'But you're still leaving us,' Don smiled.

'How did you know?' Andrew's face was a picture of astonishment. First Helen and now Don seemed to know everything; were his intentions that obvious?

'You've looked – unsettled for a long time ; it was clear something was on your mind.'

'It's difficult to explain it,' Andrew sighed. 'I've been unsettled, it's true, and I've also been happy, Miramar's so lovely. But...'

'It's the restaurant, isn't it?' prompted Margarita gently.

'Yes, it's the restaurant. I'm not really suited to that kind of work. Whereas Helen ...'

'Took to it like a duck to water,' Don remarked with a smile.

'She loves it! Dealing with customers, ordering food, planning menus! And her energy is fantastic, I can't keep up with her, she's wonderful!'

'Yes, Helen *is* rather wonderful,' said Margarita. 'What does she think of you going? Is – she upset?'

'Strangely no! She thinks I ought to go; that made it so much easier. She's inviting her mother and brother to come and help her when I go.'

'I'm glad,' Don smiled. 'And I think you're making the right decision too. It's pointless doing something if your heart isn't in it.'

'I'll miss Helen of course,' said Andrew, amazed he could be talking on such intimate matters without any embarrassment. 'But one thing my time with her has taught me – I don't love her. Once I thought I did.'

'It always seemed to me you weren't quite suited,' Margarita observed. 'Nothing obviously wrong, but something slightly amiss. Like you and the restaurant perhaps.' She smiled.

'Exactly! The problem of Helen and me was we're just too different –

different background, temperament, everything really. At first the difference attracted us together; she said she couldn't make me out at all when we first met. I suppose I presented her with a challenge,' Andrew said wrily.

'Yes, Helen likes challenges,' Don remarked. 'But the attraction of opposites is a bit of an illusion, you know. Even if two people *seem* very different, they always have a strong bond that unites them, if only experience.'

'We didn't have even that,' Andrew sighed. 'But really I thought we did.'

'So, what will you do now?'

'Go back to teach, I expect. I was quite good at it – in the end. It wasn't because I couldn't do it it that I left.'

'Why *did* you leave?' Don asked with mild curiosity. 'You never told us, and it seemed rude to question you when you arrived, if you didn't want to talk.'

'I was a damned fool, I suppose that's the true answer. I had a brilliant future for the taking – and I turned my back on it!'

'Why?' Don asked.

'Oh, I don't know.' Andrew wriggled uncomfortably. 'I just felt I had to disapprove of all the corruption going on at my school. Too sensitive and innocent, I suppose.'

'So you decided to search for paradise,' Margarita smiled. 'You are not alone in Miramar, the place is full of people like you – us for example. But there is always the serpent!' she ended cheerfully.

'The serpent has been the problem all along, here is no better than Passworth so I might just as well go back there where at least I *was* wanted.'

'You mean – someone loves you?' asked Don.

'Yes.'

'Was this the young lady who came here some time ago, and asked for the *Periquillo Verde?*'

'Yes,' muttered Andrew blushing with embarrassment.

'My dear young man, I *saw* her!' Don exclaimed, astonished out of his calm. 'She was quite beautiful! How could you leave a girl like that? And is she rich?'

'Yes!'

'With all due respect, young Andrew, you are a fool! Go back to her – if she'll have you – and quickly!'

'I intend to!'

'That's settled then, dear boy,' smiled Don, quickly recovering and once more his urbane self. 'Go back, without regrets. I think a toast now would be admirable – to recall a famous toast my wife and I had ten years ago. I hope your fortune turns out to be as happy as ours. A *coñac?*'

'A *coñac* would be perfect,' said Andrew.

'*¡Salud!*' said Margarita. 'Your very good health!'

Chapter Eighteen

DIANE Seymour and Terry Parsons were in bed together, they were both naked as they'd just made love. Parsons put a hand on Diane's breast and caressed a nipple.

'Good, eh?' he gloated, but whether about what he was doing, or their earlier activities was unclear. Diane remained silent, she lay on her back, a blanket round her waist, and stared at the ceiling; her mind was very far from her present situation in her bedroom at Camberford Grange.

She was thinking, not of what Parsons was doing to her nipple, but of that Saturday morning over a year ago in Andrew's flat, the day before he slipped his leash and vanished from her life.

His disappearance created a sensation in the Seymour household. Diane's mother tried to treat the matter as unimportant – without any success; George reacted in every way possible. First he was amazed, then furious, and in the end cynically wise.

'I told you from the start he was a poor bet,' he told Diane, rubbing salt into the wound. 'Your big mistake was to love the bugger ...'

'Don't *call* him that!' Diane exploded in one of her rare rages. 'If it hadn't been for you, he *would* have married me ...'

'If it hadn't been for me, he'd have been sacked! But listen, lass,' George went on more gently. 'It's pointless us going on at each other, it's the fault of neither in the end. What we've got to decide is what we do now. I'll have to tell Jones for a start.'

'Andrew wrote to him before he went,' Diane sighed. 'Said he wouldn't be coming back, apologised for all the trouble ...'

'Typical! To act like a fool and then apologise! I've no patience with that sort of fellow. No backbone, can't you see?'

'He'd *plenty* of backbone! He may have been misguided but he was no chicken! He *chose* to go to our school, don't forget that, and he didn't run when the going got tough either. Not until he was established and had all to lose ...'

'More fool him!' George sneered. 'All right; he had backbone – of a kind. But he's definitely a screwball and you're well rid of him. Get yourself someone normal next time, without those weird idealistic fantasies.'

But Diane had no desire to do this, not yet anyway; her first move was to telephone Andrew's home and find out if he was there. He wasn't, they'd received a brief note saying he'd gone abroad to 'try and decide about his future.'

'Abroad?' repeated Diane, almost stunned at the news. 'But where abroad?'

'I don't know,' said Andrew's mother calmly. 'He's probably just travelling around; he's done it before. Don't worry, Diane, he'll be all right, he's quite good at looking after himself.'

Diane could hardly make any coherent response. Abroad! He might be anywhere! If he'd stayed in this country, she could have informed the police, advertised for him to come back , at least she could have *tried* to find him. But abroad meant she could do nothing; it was awful!

'Listen, my dear,' Catherine Makepeace was saying. 'Why not come and see us? You're obviously very upset, it might help reassure you. Are you very fond of Andrew?'

'I love him.'

'I see. Well, I'm sorry he should have gone off like this, it's not like him usually. When will you come?'

They agreed the next day would be convenient, and Diane lost no time in getting herself ready for a couple of days in Camberford so that, as Catherine put it, they could get to know each other properly.

Camberford is five miles south of Woking, and therefore not so close to London as to be oppressed by it, or too far for easy access. Catherine was waiting at the station with her car.

'A pleasure to meet you,' she smiled, shaking hands. 'I can't say I've heard a lot about you because Andrew never talks about his friends. But I can see already he was very lucky to find you, and even more foolish to leave.'

She sighed and Diane wondered whether this was born of experience. She'd taken immediately to Catherine, and felt they had a lot in common, appearance for a start. Both were fair, elegant, and sophisticated, both were intelligent, and both were at their wits' end how to deal with

Andrew...

Five minutes' later they arrived at the Makeapeaces' villa. Deborah was naturally waiting for them in the hall, anxious to get all the news as soon as possible. Catherine introduced her to Diane, and then advised her not to ask too many questions, knowingher natural propensities.

'I wan't going to,' she said slightly nettled. 'I'm glad to meet you,' she went on, visibly impressed with her new acquaintance. 'Why on earth did Andrew run off? He must have been even madder than usual...'

Diane smiled and said something polite, she already felt she was going to enjoy herself with this family; she did. Even so, when she was about to depart, she wasn't a great deal wiser about Andrew than before. She'd met Peter, his father briefly, but he was not exactly communicative, although she was satisfied she'd made a fair impression on him. But his main concern, she could see, was to have as little to do with Andrew's dilemmas as possible. Maybe he was right! At all events Catherine promised that as soon as they obtained some kind of news from him, she'd let her know, and Diane had to be satisfied with that.

She returned to Carnforth Grange, glad she'd met the Makepeaces but no more decided about the future; it was extremely frustrating! Even so she decided in her own mind that for the time being she'd keep Andrew on ice. What happened after that was anyone's guess...

By the beginning of the next term, Jones had found someone to replace him, the woman who'd been turned down at the original interview. Jones had the somewhat sardonic satisfaction of seeing she coped a lot better than Andrew at first. She knew very little and her method of teaching was to get the kids to copy vast tracts from the various textbooks to hand; her main asset to the school was her classes were silent.

Diane kept going, encouraged intermittently by Catherine who was receiving cards saying Andrew was travelling across France. At least, Diane thought, he's not in the States or Australia, maybe he'll settle shortly. But it wasn't till six months had passed that Catherine told her he'd found an attractive village, Miramar, in the south of Spain, and had decided to stay there. Diane was over the moon, and at once made plans to go out and see him that summer.

Meantime at the school, life around her hadn't been standing still. She noticed that with Andrew off the scene, Terry Parsons, the deputy head, suddenly seemed to have developed a strong interest in her. In fact ever since she arrived at Passworth Community College, he'd always been very polite and helpful; it was to a considerable extent thanks to his support she'd been so successful right from the start. The kids realised at once that as well as a powerful father, she had the favour of a school boss, and it being established she was one of "them", she was virtually unassailable. She therefore managed without any difficulty at all to lead a charmed life, and for her, discipline problems were non-existent.

Diane was very well aware of Parson's extra attentions but didn't attach any importance to them. She knew her own attractiveness to the opposite sex with its accompanying advantages, but not for the moment did she consider Parsons a possible suitor. To begin with he was her chief, more so than Jones whom she rarely saw, and she was young enough to consider his position put him beyond such human things as romance. Anyway he was married, and no girl will look seriously at a married man, especially with a young family, – unless he is extremely rich – until she has considered all the available alternatives – and rejected them.

She wasn't unattracted to Parsons even so, though she hoped she'd never shown this. He was in his mid-thirties, short and stocky, a little like her father, and with a strong no-nonsense personality that impressed both staff and kids. To Diane he was completely the boss, to be respected and obeyed, it wasn't until much later when Andrew had vanished from the scene, that she discovered the truth about him and his desires, especially where she was concerned.

He'd married young, soon after graduating from Birmingham University with an indifferent degree in maths. He knew he was no academic, more the practical, sporting type, having played rugby at school and college. He had the additional bonus of a powerful personality that attracted women, which in the end proved his undoing, for he married over-hastily the first girl who fell seriously in love with him. Molly was a dark, passionate art student of no great intellect but tremendous sensuality, who adored Parson with a vehemence he could no way return. This unequal feeling had the effect of driving them apart until eventually his fires were completely quenched. By the time Diane arrived at the school like a breath of fresh air, he and his wife shared the same house but little else, not even their bed.

All this Diane discovered after Andrew's amazing departure; she knew she had two admirers and the no less remarkable fact that Parsons had been fancying her for the past two years. As she realised this, she couldn't help feeling, in spite of her emotional ties to Andrew, that Parsons' determination deserved recognition of some kind. Consequently, although she was delighted to receive news about Andrew, especially that he'd at last decided to settle in a place she could visit, she didn't see why this should debar her from all contact with other members of the opposite sex – the one she preferred having proved so unreliable. She therefore in due course allowed Parsons access to her friendship, which in the nature of things didn't remain platonic for long.

'Does your wife know about us?' Diane asked after they'd made love together for the first time on the settee in Parsons' office one day after school.

'I don't know and I don't care,' he replied. 'I've told you many times, our marriage is dead. I only love you, Diane; you do believe that, don't you? I've loved you ever since you arrived at this place...'

'So you told me; I could hardly believe it! Parsons, the deputy head, in love with a young teacher straight from college. Very flattering! Did you know about my father when you fell for me?'

'Of course I did!' Parsons admitted. 'The whole school knew you were a rich man's daughter, but that doesn't mean I didn't love you, and still do!'

'A fortune can be quite a powerful aphrodisiac,' murmured Diane, her head resting on Parsons' chest.

'Would that matter so very much?' he asked, caressing gently her long blond hair.

'Not in itself perhaps, but aphrodisiacs have the habit of wearing out after a while leaving the partner at a considerable disadvantage.'

'That wouldn't happen to us, I promise.'

'I'm not so sure about that, you've already sworn a life-time's fidelity to one person at least. You might tell me in honesty too,' Diane went on sweetly. 'When you were lusting after me last year, did you vent your spleen on Andrew? I've been often wondering about that just recently. I mean, it was you, wasn't it, who helped Jones with his report and finally shopped him on catastrophe day...'

She felt a thrill of triumph after that speech, for Parsons had stiffened most uncomfortably, and she was pretty sure she'd hit the target. Even so, he reacted fast and said smoothly:

'What are you talking about, sweetheart? You know Makepeace was exonerated after that incident; and the report, Jones told me, was perfectly normal. What's driven you suddenly to pitch into me for all that?'

Diane gave a cynical laugh. 'Come off it, Terry,' she chuckled. 'Tell that to one of your other girl friends. You know perfectly well it was only my father who saved Andrew from the chop. You and Jones together had been preparing his crucifixion for months.'

This time she really had hit the mark for Parsons suddenly removed from her almost roughly, and got up from the settee.

'That's offensive rubbish, and quite uncalled for,' he snapped. 'Makepeace was a professional matter, and nothing to do with us. You've no right to imply personal feelings would make me act improperly to another member of staff.'

Diane sat quite still and looked sideways at him; for a moment she wondered if her suspicions of malpractice had been mistaken. Something obstinate made her continue.

'I thought you loved me,' she said in honeyed accents.

'I do! What's that got to do with it?'

'It seems to me,' Diane said carefully. 'If you really loved me, it'd be quite natural, without going as far as improper conduct, at least to hope Andrew would come a cropper...'

Parsons paused, thinking over what Diane had said. 'I suppose that's true,' he admitted at last. 'But to hope for something is a far cry from behaving unprofessionally; that accusation would be slander and I'd prove it if anyone levelled it against me!' he ended defiantly.

'I'm sure you would, darling,' Diane smiled. 'That's what makes you so successful, you go as near the line as humanly possible – without actually going over.'

'You mean you still think...?'

'It doesn't matter what I – or anyone – thinks; nothing can be proved! Come here, I want to kiss you, properly!'

'You're a bitch and I love you,' said Parsons, returning to the settee. 'All right, I'll admit it, but only to you and in private; Jones and me we did do the dirty on Makepeace. He had his reasons and I had mine, they just coincided. He felt uncertain about him right from the start, I traded on that for all it was worth. The result you know! Anyhow it made not a ha'p'orth of difference, the fool deliberately threw everything away when he had you in his hand and a bright and certain future before him. I can still hardly believe it,' he said shaking his head.

'Me neither,' Diane sighed. 'All right, Terry, I'm glad you told me the truth.' She put her arms around him. 'I know you're a bastard, darling, but I can't talk, I'm not much better than a bitch myself; after all,' she went on, kissing him on the lips. 'I am my father's daughter and it's possible I've decided Andrew's brand of idealism was just a little too futile ... I'm willing to give you a chance.'

'I won't let you down,' Parson promised.

But in spite of Diane's earnest assurances, she wasn't so easily able to push Andrew to the back of her mind, she still had her visit planned for August , and once she'd spoken to him there and found out how he was placed, she was sure she'd be in a better position to decide her future, with Andrew, Parsons, or neither if that seemed best.

In the meantime she went to her father, to tell him about her new relationship so she could freely invite Parsons to her room. She had no desire to repeat any future liaisons in his office, the settee there being a lot less comfortable than her bed. George's reaction wasn't as sympathetic as she would have wished.

'The man's married!' he spluttered. 'And he's got three kids, plus a wife who's devoted to him ...'

'Too devoted,' Diane answered calmly. 'Terry's sick of her, he's been anxious to leave her for years.'

'You're amazing!' George seemed completely nonplussed; which was somewhat ironic, considering he'd been all for his daughter taking up with someone less idealistic than Andrew. 'Couldn't you find someone *without* all these complications? I know Andrew wasn't perfect, but at least he was single...'

'I'm glad you admit he had one thing to recommend him,' said Diane drily. 'But as it seems very uncertain he'll marry me, why shouldn't I at least consider Terry?'

'Are there no other single men interested in you?'

'Lots, but I'm not interested in them. Look, Father, we've been over this before, I may not love Terry, but I am attracted to him, and he is a good lover, that to me at the moment is quite important.'

'So that's why you've come to me, is it? To give you permission to bring him here and have a little nest in your room ...'

'In a word, yes. My room's a lot better than a hotel – or his office.'

'His wife doesn't know about you then?'

'No, not yet,'

'That's something! It's when the wife discovers what's going on the cat's among the pigeons. There's still a chance, I suppose, you may come to your senses *before* she finds out. All right, lass, tell Parsons he can come here, but discretely, that means only when we're NOT entertaining, he gets no social invitations, clear?'

'Clear, Father,' said Diane with unusual humilty. 'It's very good of you to be so tolerant.'

'Does the man love you?' George asked uncomfortably.

'I doubt it, but neither did Andrew – in the end ...'

George shrugged his shoulders, quite baffled; there was really nothing else he could do.

So Parsons had access to Carnforth Grange and Diane's favours, but theirs was a very different relationship from hers with Andrew. Whereas she'd been constantly obliged to coax the lad into action, with Parsons she had a full time job cooling down his ardour which was constantly ready to boil over. She limited their assignations to once a week – or less, and the latest she permitted him in her room was midnight, never was he allowed to sample breakfast at Carnforth Grange.

All this time Diane was counting the days to when she was going to Miramar to see if her true affections lay there. Parsons couldn't help being aware of this but his patience was amazing, never did he show anything but an absolute willingness to humour her every whim and fancy. The truth was he'd already waited nearly three years for her, and so, he reasoned, just a few more weeks were neither here nor there; in addition he felt he had nothing to fear from Andrew...

At last August approached and Diane began to make more practical arrangements. She contacted Andrew's mother who told her he hadn't written for weeks; that Diane decided to use as a rather feeble pretext for visiting him, it would at least be more presentable than the truth. Both her parents were going to accompany her, thanks mainly to George's urgent persuasion, two rooms had therefore been booked for them all at the *Hotel Real* in San José. Mary had been fully informed about Diane's two main interests but as usual she kept her own counsel; she was firmly resolved to maintain her role of sympathetic observer – and hoped there wouldn't be too many pieces to pick up later.

But after the week at San José, in spite of Diane's unbridled love making with Andrew at the *Hotel Real*, and his qualified wish to marry her 'some time', she returned to Carnforth Grange more dissatisfied than ever. He really was a hopeless case, she had to confess even though it was just to herself in the privacy of her room, where she shed a good few tears her first night home. And his indecisiveness wasn't the worst part of it either, if it had only been that, she would have been prepared to accept his good intentions and continue to wait for him if not indefinitely at least for a considerable period.

But there was Helen! How much did this girl mean to him, even though he insisted she was just a friend? Was there such a thing between the sexes as a "friend"? Diane doubted it, such friendships either tended to dwindle away to something completely negative, or became – all too quickly in some cases – a sexual relationship – as with Parsons for example. The more Diane thought about Helen, her overt attractiveness and sexuality, the more certain she was that Andrew was physically and emotionally committed to her. And as Diane reached this certainty, she became equally sure she now had no future with Andrew, Helen was the deciding factor, a girl who clearly had a lot more to offer him physically and as a partner than she did.

She hardened rapidly in her attitude towards Andrew; she almost hated him now for having strung her along, not just now, but all last year, when he'd obviously known this girl. He was a two-timing bastard! she told herself in impotent fury. If he'd thought at all of how she was likely to feel, he could never have behaved the way he did. He should have told her to go, plainly, not placated her with soft promises of 'some time'. Now tears of hatred and frustration were flowing and she was weeping freely into her pillow; it was only when she thought at last of Terry that she was able to stop.

Terry! Why the hell should she get herself so upset over a greenhorn like Andrew when she had Terry for the taking, a proper man, a mature successful male who could satisfy her physically the way she'd grown to want, and materially in that he would be able to contribute his share to their partnership, not be completely dependent on what she – and her father – had to offer. So thinking, Diane was at last able to pull herself together, relax, and enjoy the best and serenest sleep in weeks. She knew

– clearly – her path forward, it was with Terry, and Andrew could just go to hell!

At this point Diane returned abruptly to the present and her bedroom where she lay naked except for the blanket round her waist, and Parsons was playing with her nipple.

'Penny for your thoughts,' he grinned. 'Were you thinking of we know who?'

'Yes, and you'll be pleased to hear I've reached a decision.'

'Which is?'

'I've had enough of Andrew Makepeace!'

'Christ!' breathed Parsons. 'And it's taken you two years to discover this! What was the final straw?'

'Spain, I suppose, he still couldn't make up his mind even there…'

'Kiss me, sweetheart,' Parsons sighed, snuggling up to her as he sought her lips. 'If only you knew how happy that makes me. That's to say, if I *am* the one you want, you haven't said that, you know …'

'Haven't I?' Diane smiled. 'I – must have forgotten. Make love to me, darling, that might jog my memory, and I want it as I've never had it before. Think you can manage after your previous efforts?'

'You bet! And you'd better hold tight because this is going to make the cork-screw at Blackpool seem like a run on the promenade.'

Parsons was as good as his word; though they'd made love only twenty minutes previously, he was able to drive into Diane like a battering ram, and her screams must have been heard far down the corridor.

'That was marvellous, darling!' she gasped afterwards. 'You're the best lover I've *ever* experienced, not that I've experienced a great many…'

She didn't like to confess Andrew was the only other man she'd made love to and Parsons was content not to press her on that point.. They lay together, still kissing, and soon Diane couldn't resist caressing Terry with teasing fingers. There was a small electrical response…

'You were wonderful,' she sighed. 'When can you do it again?'

'You've had it twice in half an hour,' grinned Parsons, wriggling pleasurably. 'And I am thirty five, don't expect miracles, even from me.'

'I don't expect miracles, Terry, but what I experienced just now was magic, I promise!'

Just then there was a tap at the door and Diane shook her head in irritation.

'I said I wasn't to be disturbed except for a dire emergency,' she said. 'What *is* it?' she called out impatiently..

'The phone, Miss, said it was urgent...'

'You can't win!' Diane muttered in fury. 'I deliberately refused to have a phone in here but that doesn't stop them. Who *is* it?' she asked aloud.

'Mr Makepeace.' She was almost transfixed.

'Andrew!' she breathed, turning to Parsons. 'But he's in Spain! What can he want?'

'Well, here's your chance, darling,' he said lazily, lighting a cigarette. 'Now you can tell him to piss off.'

'I will!' muttered Diane putting on some clothes. 'Bloody cheek ringing at 9.30; I'll give him what for, don't you worry about that.' Aloud: 'Tell him, I'm coming."

'Yes, Miss.' Footsteps were heard descending the stairs.

'That's my girl,' said Parsons, putting down his cigarette. 'But first you can give us a kiss.'

She stopped, brushed her lips against his, and then she was away, shutting the door quietly behind her; two minutes later she was speaking almost nervously into the phone.

'Hullo, Diane here, is that Andrew?'

'Yes,' came his voice.

'Why are you ringing like this – and late too! Are you in Spain?'

'No, I'm home – in Camberford. I've just got back. Listen, Diane, I've decided at last. I want to marry you, whenever you like... I love you, Diane, really!'

Chapter Nineteen

ANDREW had departed from Almería airport the previous morning. After his good luck toast with the Spencers, he went straight to the travel agents in Ferroviaria and booked a single flight to London via Madrid. It was for the following Monday, giving him a few days to sort himself out, buy presents for his family – and Diane, and generally acclimatise himself to a future in his home country. Helen had become very subdued, Andrew noticed, in contrast to his own increasing excitement; when it came to it she had no desire for him to go.

'I'll miss you – a lot!' she said, her eyes over bright.

'But I'll be back – regularly! I could never leave Miramar entirely – or you!'

'Don't talk nonsense – you'll have Diane!'

'I hope! I can't believe she'll still want me now I really have made up my mind.'

'She'll want you, I'm sure! I can't think why, but she will ...'

Helen and the Spencers saw Andrew off at the airport; they made a rather quiet quartet. Suddenly now the die was irrevocably cast, he felt rising within himself a distinct feeling of panic; if he could have changed his mind even at that late stage, he would have done so.

'Are your family expecting you?' Don asked.

'No, my arrival will be a complete surprise.'

'Or shock!' Helen contributed with a grin.

'The very best of luck!' Margarita gave him a kiss; Helen came deliberately forward.

'May I speak to Andrew a moment?' she asked in somewhat pointed tones.

'That means we old stagers should withdraw and give the youngsters their chance,' Don chuckled.. 'Helen, we'll see you at the car. Come, Margarita.' With a paternal wave, he escorted his smiling wife away. 'See you next summer, Andrew,' he called. 'Or before...'

Andrew sadly waved the couple goodbye.

'Marvellous, aren't they?' said Helen. 'Now you can give *me* a kiss, you fool; if Margarita can kiss you, so can I!' There were tears in her eyes as they embraced. 'I want you to listen and remember this!' she insisted. 'If anything goes wrong with your plans, and I'm sure it won't, there's always a job for you in *El Periquillo Verde* – with or without Diane.'

'Helen, you're terrific!' Andrew sighed. 'I don't *want* to go now, honestly! I'm such an idiot, you're quite right about that ...'

'You must go – you've decided! Ring Diane this evening, and tell me tomorrow what she says. Promise?'

'Promise!'

With a final kiss, Helen was gone, she didn't turn round, Andrew was very glad to get into the aircraft, surrounded by strangers and the businesslike efficiency of the cabin crew; he'd found those last few minutes almost unbearable.

The *Aviaco* flight arrived at Madrid an hour later, giving Andrew just over two hours before his British Airways afternoon flight to Heathrow. An awkward length of time, insufficient for the fairly lengthy journey from *Barajas* to *La Puerta del Sol,* but quite enough to enable him to become depressed about what he'd left behind and what he was going to. By the time he was on the Boeing 757 en route for the UK, he was absolutely convinced he had nothing to look forward to there, certainly no Diane or job at Passworth, probably no job anywhere...

Andrew reached home about 6.30 after a boring journey by tube from Heathrow to Waterloo and the commuter train to Camberford. He had had to stand most of the way as it was the middle of the rush hour. He still had the key to his front door but didn't even try it, he knew he'd get the combination wrong in his present unsteady condition. He rang the bell, waiting a long half minute for someone to answer, it was Deborah – of course, always anxious to meet visitors; he had the satisfaction of seeing utter amazement on her face.

'Andrew!' she exclaimed, letting him in. 'What are you doing here? You're supposed to be in Spain...'

'Well, I'm not!' said Andrew smartly, dumping his two bags on the floor. 'How are you?' he asked, hoping with his own question to forestall hers.

'Oh, I'm fine, as always. Mother!' she called. 'It's Andrew, he's come back...'

Confused female sounds could be heard in the living room, followed by a dry cough, unmistakeably from Andrew's father. Five seconds later Catherine Makepeace emerged, looking even more astonished than her daughter.

'Darling!' she cried. 'You never told us you were coming back. Are you all right?'

'Oh, I'm okay...'

'How long are you here for?'

'I don't know ...'

'Come and see your father,' Catherine said, ushering him into the living room. Peter for once wasn't hidden behind his paper, instead he'd lowered it and was staring at Andrew in rather cynical surprise.

'Well, well,' he said with a chuckle. 'The prodigal has returned; I'm afraid we've finished the fatted calf, it was the remains of our Sunday lunch...'

'It doesn't matter,' said Andrew. 'I'm not hungry, they feed you quite well on the plane.'

'I'll get you a snack,' said his mother, leading him to the kitchen. 'I bet you're hungry really.'

'I dare say I'll get the full story – eventually!' Peter called, returning to his paper.

'I want to know too,' said Deborah, still at hand and faithful as a shadow. 'What happened, Andrew? Did you get fed up – again?'

'Something like that,' he mumbled, tucking into a cold chicken sandwich Catherine produced apparently from nowhere.

'Now Deborah, curb your curiosity, do!' she said with patient good humour. 'Allow your brother at least a few minutes before you bombard him with questions.'

'Well, it's natural, isn't it? Don't *you* want to know?'

'I dare say: but he'll tell us in his own time, not ours!'

'Typical clams, both of you!' said Deborah sulkily, going to the door. 'I'll ask Father what's going on – when he knows, which'll probably be some time next year ...' She went out shutting the door a shade over-firmly behind her.

'What a girl!' sighed Catherine, shaking her head. 'She'll either make some earth shattering discovery some day, or just burn her fingers through being too curious.'

'Probably both,' agreed Andrew. 'Not that there's any secret about me coming back. As I said just now, I got fed up. The restaurant I was helping to run had no future – at least for me.'

'I see,' his mother answered, gazing at him not for the first time in open mystification, for she didn't see at all. 'But what will you do now?' she found herself asking, in dread of the reply. 'Have you any plans?'

'I've *plans!*' said Andrew carefully. 'Whether they'll come off's another matter, I'm gambling they will ...'

'Gambling?' Catherine felt even more at sea.

'Yes; do you remember Diane from my school in Passworth? She telephoned you recently, I think...'

'You mean the girl who went to see you in Spain earlier this month? But we *know* her! She came to see us a year ago – just after you vanished. She was very worried, we could see she was – fond of you; we thought she was splendid!'

'She is; that's why I'm going to telephone her and ask her to marry me ...'

That really made an impact; Catherine was now staring at Andrew as though he'd performed an act of levitation – or something equally impossible.

'But, darling, this is wonderful!' she exclaimed. 'We'd no idea; we'd given up hope you were interested in her, especially when she came back from seeing you without any definite news. To be honest, we thought you were quite mad to leave a girl like that in the first place. Why did you?'

'Oh, reasons!' mumbled Andrew. 'But I've sorted them out at last, thank God! Now I'm going to ring her up and put things right – completely.'

'When?'

'Well, perhaps a bit later in the evening. I think she may be eating now, they eat quite late. I'll telephone about half nine ...'

'That sounds perfect,' Catherine smiled. 'And you must tell me what she says – at once; no secrets this time ...'

'No secrets,' said Andrew, but he didn't feel nearly as cheerful as he looked. In fact the Seymours' late dinner hour was mainly an excuse for postponing his phone call because he was so nervous of the outcome. All the fears that had haunted him during his journey from Almería now returned, and when at 9.30 he picked up the receiver to ring Carnforth

Grange, he was almost certain his call was doomed. In spite of this he managed to sound normal when the maidservant answered the phone.

'Can I speak to Diane Seymour?' he said

'Miss Seymour? I'm not sure; I think she's busy ...'

'It's important, I must speak to her!'

A pause. 'Who shall I say is calling?' the woman asked.

'It's Andrew Makepeace ...'

'Mr Makepeace?' Her whole manner altered at once. 'Good evening, sir! You should have said it was you straightaway. Of course Miss Seymour will speak to you, I'll go and get her at once.'

'Thank you,' said Andrew, experiencing an enormous sense of relief. Perhaps after all things *were* going to be all right! Five minutes later he was hearing Diane's voice.

'Hullo, Diane here,' she said – uneasily. 'Is that Andrew?'

'Yes,' he replied, but before he could go on, she was saying in quick, tense accents:

'Why are you ringing like this – and late too! Are you in Spain?'

'No, I'm home – in Camberford,' he answered, feeling suddenly anxious at the girl's abrupt manner. 'I've just got back. Listen, Diane,' he went on, feeling it was important to present his message at once. 'I've decided at last. I want to marry you, whenever you like ... I love you, Diane, really!'

There was a total silence at Diane's end of the phone, though Andrew was convinced she could hear his heart beating like a sledge hammer. At last she spoke but as she did so, he wondered whether it might have been better had she remained silent.

'It's marvellous to be talking to you, Andrew,' she began with slow care. 'It seems a long time since San José ...'

'Less than a month ...'

'I know, but a lot can happen in a month ...'

'I don't understand.'

'It's just – it's not so easy for me to say, 'Yes' to you now as it would have been then ...'

'But why?' asked Andrew desperately, feeling the ground beneath him beginning to move. 'What's happened? Has something – gone wrong since I last saw you?'

'Not exactly, but yes, I suppose it has. Though it actually happened *before* I saw you in San José.'

'You mean, there's someone else?'

'Yes, Andrew, I'm afraid so! That's why I was a bit annoyed just now, I had to leave him to come to the phone ...'

'Oh! How long have you – known this man?'

'Quite a long time. I wasn't going to say anything to you; I wouldn't have, but it's why I came to San José. To see if you'd changed towards me ...'

'I see,' said Andrew bitterly. 'It was to be my last chance!'

'To put it bluntly, yes! If you'd come back with me, or at least said when you were coming back, I'd have stuck with you, I promise. But you didn't, you still kept me waiting! And there was Helen too ...'

'I told you I didn't love her ...'

'I know but she was there – and you'd known her – how long had you known her?'

'About two years,' said Andrew dully.

'Two years! And you kept her a secret! So what was I supposed to think when I met her for the first time in Spain?'

'I'm sorry,' Andrew sighed. 'I suppose you're right. But it's true what I said, I don't love her, I love only you, that's why I've come back.'

'It's too late now,' said Diane, her tone becoming colder. 'I'm committed to this man, I can't change now.'

'Do you love him?'

'We've been lovers for six months.'

'Lovers?'

'You needn't sound shocked!' said Diane indignantly. 'You've had God knows how many women out there, I've had one man! Andrew, I'm sorry,' she went on more gently. 'You don't know how I hate turning you down – after all we've been to each other. Because I'm sure you always did love me, only you allowed things to get in the way ...'

'Well then...,' Andrew began.

'But you've proved it's not as simple as that! In the end we'd not have made a good team, and you were right to feel that when you did.'

'Perhaps ...'

'So let's not prolong this any longer, I've got to go! You *can* write to me if you like, I still want to be your friend ...'

'I do too, I will write,' said Andrew wretchedly.

'What will you do now? Go back to Spain?'

'No, I can't go back there; Spain's finished for me now.'

'I'm – sorry. Well, goodbye, Andrew, and – thanks for everything. It's a pity it had to end like this. I feel it more than you do – in a way...'

Andrew made no reply; he kept the receiver to his ear until he heard a click, only then did he slowly replace it. He felt completely numb, all he wanted was to retire to some private corner where no one would speak to him. He needed time to adjust, to get things back into perspective.

But as he came out of the drawing room, his mother was waiting for him, all agog for the news.

'Yes, dear?' she breathed, confident it would be what she wanted to hear; then, seeing his miserable expression, she realised her joy was premature. 'What – happened?' she asked nervously. 'She wasn't in?'

'She was in all right,' muttered Andrew bitterly, glad in a way to tell the sad tidings at once and get it over with. 'But she turned me down; she won't marry me!'

'Won't marry you?' Catherine repeated, suddenly very pale. 'I – can't believe it! She loves you, I'm sure she does!' She led Andrew to the kitchen and put the kettle on, hoping mechanical tasks would drive these problems away.

'She may love me, I don't know,' Andrew said, sitting down on one of the kitchen stools with a feeling of absolute fatigue. 'But there's someone else....'

'This is getting worse and worse! Who? Someone you know?'

'She wouldn't say – she's known him for years ...'

'You mean, she was deceiving you all the time?' Catherine was still incredulous.

'No, not really! She just knew him, that's all.' Andrew had no desire to tell his mother the full story as described by Diane.

'I see.' Catherine found herself resorting to the time honoured phrase she used when she was completely stumped; after which she fell into helpless silence.

Not that her mind was inactive, far from it, she was thinking feverishly how this was yet another of Andrew's lost opportunities, another failure, and as she thought these things, two tears ran down her cheeks.

'Oh, Mother!' Andrew exclaimed. 'Don't get upset, I'll be fine, honestly!'

'Of course you will!' said Catherine, pulling herself together. 'I'm sorry, it's just that she seemed so nice, so – right for you ...'

'Maybe I wasn't right for her ...'

'Nonsense!' Catherine was quite annoyed. 'You were perfectly right for her! Have some tea – I'm sure *I* could do with a cup.' She scooped a teaspoonful into the pot and poured in the boiling water. 'I know I'm foolish, going on like this,' she sighed. 'It's not your fault if she changes her mind; and it shows she really wasn't so wonderful...' She seemed about to weep again, and Andrew could hardly believe, as he sat sipping his tea, that his mother could be apparently more disturbed by these events than he himself; as to sensation, he had none, he was in a state of complete deadness.

'I'm tired, Mother,' he said. 'I think I'll take this to bed with me if you don't mind.'

'Not at all, dear,' Catherine answered, more calmly now Andrew was at least doing something. 'You must be exhausted after your journey. Don't worry about Father and Deborah, I won't say anything to them, certainly not now. Bad news can keep ...'

'Thanks. I'll see you in the morning,' said Andrew, with an attempt at a smile. 'Sleep well.'

He hardly slept at all. He tossed and turned continually in his bed, trying to decide if he was really as much to blame for this state of affairs as he feared – and his mother believed. He was sure in the end she was right: he had an ingrained knack of failing where everyone else would have succeeded. Quite a record! he said to himself filled with contempt. In the space of twenty four hours he'd managed to lose two splendid girls; not so many could boast of such an achievement!

Finally he fell asleep; it was 5.30 and light was already filtering into his bedroom, it seemed seconds later that there was a knock at his door.

'What is it?' he mumbled, for he'd only been lightly asleep.

'Someone to see you,' his mother replied.

'Who?'

'Come quickly!'

'Just a moment ...'

It took Andrew two minutes to dress and two and a quarter to go downstairs to the hall where his mother was waiting. She pointed in the direction of the reception room; he went uncertainly in.

'Diane!' he exclaimed as he saw her sitting on the settee, as composed as ever. 'What are you doing here?'

'What do you think, silly?' she smiled. 'I've come for breakfast.'

Epilogue

.

T HEY married – at last; it wasn't till their honeymoon in the south of France that Andrew dared ask Diane what had brought about her complete change of mind.

'Simply this! You told me – right at the end of our phone conversation, you'd finished with Spain, which to me meant Helen ...'

'But why didn't you say something then?' Andrew asked petulantly. 'You just hung up and left me, I didn't sleep a wink that night!'

'So what? You'd kept me waiting two years; I didn't think one night would do you too much harm ...'

'Bitch!' grinned Andrew, giving her a kiss. 'And that fellow, there *was* someone, I take it ...'

'Oh, there was, I wouldn't lie! I had to keep him entertained another couple of hours ...'

'You were making love to him?'

'Of course! And he really was a great lover, you don't quite compare, I'm afraid.'

'But you said I was pretty good in San José ...'

'You were, darling, I'd not have married you if you actually failed that little test! In fact it was partly your performance in your Passworth flat that made me so determined to get you – somehow or other.'

'I love you!' Andrew sighed.

'Good, now you can seduce me again!'

The wedding had taken place, at rather short notice, the first Saturday of Passworth Community College's half term. The previous September, Andrew had found himself reinstated at the school – as a deputy head. It was the perfect post, giving him all the status he needed as one of the hierarchy; and his contact with the kids becoming sporadic, he was easily able to maintain the position he'd enjoyed a year ago. Not to mention the perks that accompany his post, the private phone, the drinks cabinet, and the attractive secretary whose personal services he did *not* employ, Diane made sure of that.

Their marriage was extremely happy as well as fruitful, producing in six years four children, two boys and two girls. You could say Andrew had it made! He never did discover it was Parsons who'd been Diane's lover, though he was rather puzzled – and relieved – when he arrived at the school to find him no longer there. He later discovered he'd been appointed at extremely short notice deputy head at Passworth's rival comprehensive, which just beat the Community College for general awfulness.

In Miramar the two restaurants under Helen continued to thrive, with her mother and young Tom established as co-managers, Rodrigo as head waiter, and Bernardo promoted to second in command. Kristina soon departed, Helen's rigorous demands proving too much for the girl; her relationship with Bernardo and Colin had cooled almost to zero. Bernardo was definitely taken with Helen now, she was by no means unresponsive, and the Hardings' fortunes having reached an unprecedented high, Pilar and Colin had become quite reconciled – at Kristina's expense. She could see no way of wreaking the revenge on Helen she'd dreamed of when given her first dressing down, but gained some consolation by leaving at the restaurant's busiest time one Saturday night.

Andrew and Helen remained friends. He'd telephoned her the news of his engagement to Diane soon after their memorable breakfast, and she insisted that the next opportunity the pair should spend a holiday in Miramar. The spring following their honeymoon, they went over for two weeks, and the three plus Don and Margarita Spencer had a real bonza time.

Don and Margarita – from their villa overlooking Miramar Bay – are still alert for interesting developments; any that materialise will doubtless be recorded.

ESCAPE TO PARADISE

Escape to Paradise is Keith Minton's first novel, although he has had various short stories published, and non-fiction publications in the world of languages.

His enthusiasm for Spain and Spanish stems from his Spanish mother who came to England with the Spanish Basque refugee children in 1936, escaping the Spanish Civil War. She met Keith Minton's father to be in Suffolk where they were both looking after the Basque children.

Keith's parents returned to Spain in 1969 where they lived their remaining years. Though this novel is based on their village, *Agua Amarga,* on the *Costa de Almería,* the story and characters are quite imaginary, and can be taken completely as romantic fiction. However without the village Agua Amarga, this novel could not exist in its present form.

Escape to Paradise is a romantic novel and escapist fantasy, but like all fantasy it has to have its roots in some reality ....

Front painting by Julian Minton

ESCAPE TO PARADISE

As he moved, he saw a shape behind some rocks; a boy and a girl lay close together under their clothes, fast asleep, quite unaware anyone was watching them...

Miramar is the Paradise. Tucked away to the east of the Costa del Sol, south of Mojácar, this dazzling array of white Moorish cottages encircling a perfect boat-specked bay is like honey to refugees Helen and her boyfriend Andrew.

Helen forms the corner of a passionate love triangle with rich Diane at the other, and Andrew at the apex. Which girl will he get – if any? These and other *imbroglios* will keep you tantalised through this romantic adventure set in front of the idyllic back cloth of Miramar, the ex-pat's paradise. You will be kept in suspense as to the outcome – and entranced – until the last page.

ABOUT THIS NOVEL

This novel is based on an actual place, Agua Amarga, on the Costa de Almería near the famous Cabo de Gata. Nowadays it's a lively village with plenty of modern hotels and good restaurants on the sea front, my favourite being La Palmera, thus called because of the palm tree which grows right in the centre of the main court yard. I've had many a delicious meal at La Palmera, my favourite being *emperador* or sword fish. It is thank goodness a far cry from nearby Mojácar, with its ghastly high rise hotels, and is a secret resort for Spaniards who will come from Madrid and from as far afield as Galicia. Connoisseurs from all over Europe will also make their way to Agua Amarga and in the height of summer the bay is thick with boats of every kind, the most popular being yachts and sail boards.

But it wasn't always like this. When my parents, my Welsh father and Spanish mother, arrived at Agua Amarga in 1971, exactly like Don and Margarita Spencer at the beginning of this novel, Agua Amarga was just an obscure little fishing village quite cut off from civilisation as one recognises it. There was no paved road leading to it from the main road to Almería, just a winding dust track fringed with cacti and fig trees. The environment was (and is) bare and isolated, and in fact it is a desert, the only European desert that I know of. Not only were the notorious shaghetti westerns filmed near Almería in the cowboy village of Tabernas, but as Don Spencer mentions at the beginning of the story, the celebrated "Lawrence of Arabia", though they did have to paint the sand yellow to make it look like real desert.

But just as Don and Margarita did, my mother and father also took an enormous chance in staking their all in the barren rocky plot they had just bought for a song. They too lived in Almería, suffered from the noise of midnight revellers, and longed for the peace and quiet that seemed beckoning from that conch-like bay. I know all this because I was there, a callow thirty year old, and I urged them not to take the chance.

'It's madness,' I said. 'Look at it, a barren rocky desert, no facilities such as sanitation, no telephone, and miles from anywhere....'

In spite of me, they went ahead, with miraculous results. For the next twenty years, they enjoyed a heaven on earth in Agua Amarga, and their house was a haven for people wandering through. I remember with nostalgic delight the parties we had, not just in the bungalow itself, but in the houses of the expatriates nearby, who also knew a good thing when they saw it and had settled their roots in Agua Amarga. There really are artists living there, and Iris Murdoch had a house in nearby Carboneras which is called Ferroviaria in this story.

Anyone who wishes to experience the flavour of what the village looked like in the 1950s should read Juan Goytisolo's *Campos de Níjar*, (*Fields of Nijar*) written in 1960 and describing his travels on foot and van through this district. I have to say he was by no means respectful about the region at all, considering it almost prehistoric compared with Barcelona where he came from. But then Juan Goytosolo now living abroad, says very little in favour of Spain at all, so one shouldn't be too surprised. Maybe he was just writing for effect, and if that was he case, who can blame him?

Now of course Agua Amarga is very different from those balmy days, and my mother and father are no longer on this earth, though they share adjacent resting places in the lovely cemetery just above the village that looks onto the idyllic bay. I should like to dedicate this novel to their memories.

A Note About the Author

Writing is my great pleasure and it was my great pleasure to write this novel. You could call it a form of catharsis as it does have quite a few autobiographical elements. I know the village on which Miramar is based, I was and am a teacher as well as a writer, I have a great passion for Spain, and the adventures of the ex-patriates, Spaniards and Brits, are invented but I think could have happened – in fact they may have happened – somewhere.

My experience of this area began in 1959 when I aged 19 first visited Almería staying with my mother's relatives. I was immediately conspic-uous as one of the few English people in the area. There was another, an elderly Yorkshire lady named Nora Bulmer whom I visited one memorable afternoon for tea. I don't know why she was living in Almería, all I can remember was she had been there nearly forty years but spoke hardly a word of Spanish. And no wonder! For her drawing room could have been in an old fashioned English cottage, from the pretty white curtains, to the little tables covered with dainty mats and the English papers and magazines that lay upon them. All so beautifully English!

Each person has at least one Golden Age; this was one of mine! I made many Spanish friends, and we used to go from bar to bar in the carefree manner that only the young can enjoy. I spent three perfect months in Almería, and even played tennis in the only tennis court in the town.

Since then much as happened. I have written a lot, some published, some still to be published. My passions, apart from Spain and languages, are drama and the cinema. To sit in a darkened room and lose myself in someone else's experience is another of my great pleasures. And of course there is writing. I love writing, and if this little volume has provided at least someone with some of my pleasure, I will consider the effort to write it additionally worth while.

— *Keith Minton*

January 2006

£7.99

ISBN 155246698-1

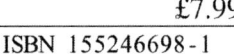